Vivien's
Heavenly
ICE
CREAM
SHOP

Abby Clements worked in book publishing before she started writing. She lives in north London with her fiancé, and loves lazy Sundays, eighties films and sausage dogs. Hers is a waffle cone with a scoop of pistachio and chocolate, with hazelnut sprinkles.

Also by Abby Clements

Meet
me
Under
the
Mistletoe

Vivien's Heavenly ICE CREAM SHOP

Abby Clements

Quercus

First published in Great Britain in 2013 by

Quercus
55 Baker Street
7th Floor, South Block
London W1U 8EW

A CIP catalogue record for this book is available
from the British Library

PB ISBN 978 1 78206 428 2
EBOOK ISBN 978 1 78206 429 9

10 9 8 7 6 5 4

Printed and bound in Great Britain by Clays Ltd, St Ives plc

Typeset by Ellipsis Digital Limited, Glasgow

For James

Vivien

35 Elderberry Avenue, Hove, East Sussex

'What's this one, Anna?' Vivien McAvoy asked, sitting forward in her velvet armchair and looking at the cake in front of her.

'Cherry and almond. Bit of an experiment, but I thought you might like it.'

Anna cut a slice of the home-made cake for her grandmother. She'd spent all morning baking but knew it would be worth it when she saw the look on Vivien's face.

Vivien accepted the plate gratefully and took a bite. 'My, oh my, Anna,' she smiled. 'You've excelled yourself this time.'

'Phew,' Anna said. 'I'm glad. It's a new recipe, as I say, so you're my guinea pig.'

'Always an honour,' Vivien said, taking another forkful. Her silver-grey hair was loosely pinned back and she was wearing a smart burgundy dress with a diamond print on it and a cream cardigan. Sunlight filtered in through the ground-floor bay windows of her house and cast a warm glow over the room.

Anna took a slice of cake for herself and a few crumbs scattered onto the floor. Her grandmother's dachshund, Hepburn, scurried over to the Persian rug.

'Cheapest kind of Hoover, he is,' Vivien laughed. The black-and-tan sausage dog had been a steady fixture by her grandmother's side for over eight years. Vivien had named him after her favourite film star, refusing to be swayed by a little detail like gender.

'You should hire him out,' Anna said.

Movement in Vivien's front garden caught Anna's eye and she turned round to see a large man standing by the hedge, surrounded by daffodils.

'Who's that in your garden?' Anna asked, peering forward to get a better look through the window.

'Oh, that's Tomasz,' Vivien said, barely looking up from her cake.

'Tomasz?'

'He's a friend. He and his wife Rebecca are staying here for a while.'

'You don't stop, do you?' Anna said, shaking her head with a smile.

'What?' Vivien said, looking up, her blue eyes shining. 'Being human?'

Anna laughed. 'Now, don't tell me, they came into the ice cream shop and . . .'

'Lovely couple – never had more than a few coppers they'd collected for tea, but always polite and kind.'

The story was a familiar one to Anna and her family. Vivien was known for collecting waifs and strays, helping local people out, and supporting the community. As if he could hear them through the glass, Tomasz turned and gave Vivien a wave and a smile, which she returned cheerfully. 'A really genuine chap, he is,' she said. 'Anyway, where was I?' she continued. 'One day I was closing up and I saw Tomasz and his wife walking into one of the disused arches further down towards Hove. I asked him about it the next day, and he told me they were sleeping there.'

'That's awful,' Anna said. 'It must be so damp, and those places aren't secure at all.'

'I know. They didn't even have a proper sleeping bag between them. Came to this country ready to work, looking for a better life, and instead . . . well. Anyway, they're staying upstairs and earn their keep better than any paying lodger could.'

'It looks like it,' Anna said, watching Tomasz sawing down a heavy overhanging branch that Vivien had been concerned about for months.

'Rebecca has been helping me with some of the filing upstairs, too. I'll be sorry to see them go. There's too much space here for just me, and you know I'm happier when there are other people around.'

'When are they leaving?'

'Next week. A room's come up with a friend of theirs, and Tomasz has had a lead for a construction job.'

'The revolving doors of Elderberry Avenue,' Anna said. 'I wonder who'll be next.'

'If life's taught me anything,' Vivien laughed, 'it's that you can never guess that. The ice cream shop has always brought me new friends, and surprises.'

'How's it been lately,' Anna asked, 'at the shop?'

'Oh, ticking along. Like always,' Vivien said with a smile.

The seafront ice cream shop, Sunset 99s, was a local landmark: it had been around since the mid-1950s, and Vivien herself was well known across Brighton. At times the shop had thrived, but Anna got the sense that lately business had started to slow, with people as likely to stop by for a chat as buy anything. With organic smoothie shops and upmarket cafés springing up all over town, Anna often thought it was something of a miracle that the shop was still going.

'Actually I'm taking a breather at the moment,' Vivien said. 'A week, perhaps two. Sue, my new assistant, I've left her to keep an eye on the place. She's not had the easiest of times lately, with her son Jamie going into prison, and then her losing her job at the Co-op – she'll look after the place well, I'm sure.'

'Dad will be happy to hear that you're taking a break,' Anna said. 'I suppose there's still no chance of you deciding to retire?'

'Of course not,' Vivien said, shaking her head dismissively. 'Retire and do what? That shop's been my life for so long I wouldn't know what to do with myself. I've got my friends down there, Evie next door, and that nice young man, Finn. A week or two to recharge my batteries, that's all I need. Sue'll keep things shipshape.'

'OK, well, I hope you use the time to rest,' Anna said. She resolved to pop by the shop and introduce herself to Sue as soon as things quietened down at work. It had been a while since she had last visited.

'I will,' Vivien said. 'Although just you try and stop me coming to have a look at your new flat. When are you moving in?'

Anna beamed at the thought. 'I'm picking up the keys next Saturday.'

'That's wonderful. And will Jon be moving in the same day?'

'Yes,' Anna said, 'he'll be there.'

'I look forward to seeing it,' Vivien said, reaching down to stroke Hepburn, who was curled up on the rug by her feet. 'We're pleased that you'll be moving a bit nearer, aren't we, Hepburn?' The dog rolled onto his back, exposing his bare belly and inviting her to tickle him.

'You'll like it. There's a nice window seat,' Anna said, recalling the view from her top-floor flat, taking in the horizon and the bright lights of Brighton Pier. The sound of the wind whistling against it made the flat feel even cosier, protected from the elements.

'Sounds perfect,' Vivien said. 'I already like the place, because you'll be just around the corner.'

'I will. And of your two favourite granddaughters, you may have to make do with just me for a while. Doesn't sound like Imogen's coming home any time soon.'

'She enjoys it, doesn't she?' Vivien said. 'The travelling life. I got a nice postcard from her the other day, with a picture of a golden Buddha on it. Reminds me of your father. Always has. Free spirits, those two.'

'It sounds like she's having a ball, taking loads of photos – she had a hard time looking for a job here after uni, and I think it was what she needed.'

'I do like it when she sends me her photos. I always loved hearing about your father's adventures through India, Asia – it was quite a thing in those days. On that lumbering great motorbike of his,' Vivien said with a smile. 'And now we have Imogen's updates to keep us entertained.'

'How is Dad?' Anna asked. She'd been so busy at her marketing job for Brighton Pavilion, and finalising the flat purchase, that she hadn't called her parents for a couple of weeks.

'Oh, he's well. He rang this morning as a matter of fact. He's finished work on one of his new sculptures – a heron, this one. It's just gone in the kiln. I asked if he could make another one for my garden pond, so that's next on his list.'

'Good,' Anna said. 'That should keep him out of trouble.' Her dad liked nothing better than working away in his garden studio, making clay sculptures of the birds and wildlife he was so fond of. 'I should get going really,' Anna added, checking the time on her phone. 'I've got a lot of packing still to do for the move, and Jon's coming around in an hour.'

'So,' Vivien asked, a mischievous smile on her face. 'Permit your nosy grandma a question. Is he the one – Jon?'

'I think so,' Anna said, feeling suddenly shy. 'It definitely feels like the right thing to be moving in together.'

'I'm glad,' Vivien said. 'Because you deserve a good man. You're a strong woman, always have been, and a talented one. You'll remember that, won't you?'

'Don't go getting soppy on me, Granny,' Anna laughed. 'I'm not going anywhere. I'm getting nearer, not further away.'

'I know that, love,' Vivien said, placing her hand tenderly on Anna's denim-clad leg. 'But there's no harm in reminding you that you're special, is there?'

Imogen

Imogen McAvoy leaned forward slightly in her crouched position to add the final touches to the tattoo. She dipped her fine paintbrush back into the pot of henna, squinted against the sun and outlined the last petal.

'There you go,' she said with satisfaction, sitting back so that her customer could see her handiwork.

'I love it,' the blonde British girl said, tilting her shoulder blade so that her boyfriend could admire it. 'What do you reckon? Wish I could show it to Mum now, pretend it's real – she'd go nuts.' The teenage boy with her, bare-chested and wearing a pair of combat shorts, nodded his approval and took a swig from his bottle of Tiger beer.

'Glad you like it,' Imogen said, taking the 200-baht note from her with a smile, and tucking it under the string of her turquoise bikini top, against her tanned, freckled skin. Retying her elephant-print sarong, she stood up. 'Enjoy your time on Koh Tao.'

As the couple walked away, Imogen counted through the notes she'd been given that day – enough for two nights' rent at her beach hut, plus some Pad Thai noodles and a beer or two that evening. Not bad for a morning's work. She checked the position of the sun in the sky – it must be about midday. She could probably still join Davy on his afternoon scuba-dive if she got down to the beach quickly. She jumped on her beach bike and pedalled towards the shore; the island was so compact that it only took her a few minutes to get there.

'Space for one more?' Imogen asked Davy as he loaded his boat with oxygen canisters, picking them up from a crate on the pristine white sand.

'You're in luck,' he said, turning to face her. 'I've had a guy cancel today, so you can come along with this group if you want.'

'Cool,' Imogen said, tying her wavy, sun-lightened brown hair back with a band, then sifting through the pile of wetsuits to find one in her size. 'Is it a wreck dive you're doing?'

'That was the plan, but I've just heard there might be something more interesting out there today.'

'Not a . . . Don't tease me,' Imogen said.

'I can't promise anything,' he said with a shrug.

She hurriedly pulled on one of the small wetsuits, still a little damp and with sea-salt crusting from its last outing. Lifting her small bag with her waterproof camera inside, she climbed into the boat. 'Let's get out there.'

They'd been out on the sea for about fifteen minutes when Davy settled on a good dive spot. The water was aquamarine and clear, the sun reflecting off it in sparkles. It was an intense beauty that after six months Imogen had almost become immune to, but not quite. Together with the rest of the dive team, she turned her back on the ocean, strapped on her oxygen tank and helped her dive buddy with the regular safety checks.

Taking a seat on the side of the boat, she readied herself, and then tipped backwards into the water with a splash.

In an instant her world was transformed as she was surrounded by a cloud of brightly coloured clown fish, some darting away, others tentatively drawing closer to her, curious about the intrusion into their underwater territory. Imogen released some of the air in her lifejacket and slowly sank deeper, towards the vibrant pink and orange coral on the seabed below. From the corner of her eye she glimpsed Davy motioning to her, waving her over to join the group. And she would, she thought, spotting a tiny reef shark weaving in among the other fish. Just a few photos first. She took out her camera and snapped the wildlife around her, luminous against an even brighter coral backdrop.

Then a dark shadow passed above her, casting the fish and coral in a darker hue. For a moment she was frozen. She looked up and there it was – right above her. The creature she'd been longing to see, from the day she set foot in Thailand – and during the dozens of dives she'd done since.

She saw Davy's group were getting agitated, some moving away and others heading towards the dark creature. Davy motioned to them to stop, to stay still and watch.

The whale shark, languorously slow, glided through the water, as big as a van, yet barely making an impression on the watery environment around it. Pale dots were scattered over its skin and its large round head and barnacles clung to the underside of its body. The name 'shark' was so deceptive, Imogen thought. It was one of the calmest and most peaceful animals she had ever seen. A cluster of small fish hovered underneath its belly, moving in harmony with the gentle creature.

Steadying her breath, Imogen rose up closer to it, brought her camera up towards her goggles and began to take photos.

Back at the dive shop, Imogen handed back the equipment, thanked Davy and hopped on her beach bike, adrenalin coursing through her veins. The rest of the dive group were still chattering away excitedly behind her about what they had seen – a once-in-a-lifetime experience. She cycled down rutted, dusty roads towards the far coast, towards her beach hut – the horizon stretching out before her, uncluttered apart from the odd palm tree. The world above ground always looked different when you had just seen the wonders below.

As she neared the row of simple wooden huts on Koh Tao's most isolated beach and the dust road turned to sand she got off the bike and pulled up outside the place that for half a year she'd called home.

Luca, the American guy she'd been seeing for the past two months, was resting in his striped hammock, a paperback in his hand.

'Hey,' she called out, making her way over, barefoot in the sand.

'Hey, gorgeous,' Luca called out sleepily. 'How are you doing?'

'Good,' Imogen said. She hopped up onto the veranda and sat down in the hammock beside him. 'Really good.' He shuffled over to make room and kissed her hello gently. His deeply tanned skin and hands were warm, just as they had been last night, even after they'd gone skinny dipping at midnight.

'Really good?' he said, intrigued.

'Fantastic dive this afternoon, got some beautiful photos. I think some might even be good enough to exhibit. We saw a whale shark . . . '

'Nice one,' Luca said, with a mischievous smile.

Imogen's sentence tailed off as Luca put down his book, then slowly traced a line up her arm and lingered close to the edges of her bikini top.

'It was incredible,' Imogen said, distracted, but trying to keep in her mind the majestic movement of the shark in the water. She didn't want to forget any of it.

'Sounds it,' Luca said, meeting her eyes with his long-lashed ones. The chemistry between them was even stronger now, in the heat of the early evening. He pulled Imogen towards him gently and kissed her on the lips, running a hand over her hair, salty and sun-bleached.

'So, do you feel like going to the full-moon party tonight? The boat leaves at eight, and I've got some Thai whisky here that we can get an early start on.'

'That would be amazing,' Imogen said.

Waves lapping on the white-sand shore, a night of dancing under a star-filled sky ahead . . . when she'd arrived in Koh Tao last October, Imogen thought, she really had stumbled on paradise.

Anna

The keys Anna McAvoy had been waiting for were finally in her hand.

Right there, with the estate agent's keyring still attached. As she stared at the front door of her new home: Flat 12, 38 Marine Parade, Brighton. The years of working long hours and saving, then the rollercoaster of offering, getting gazumped, contractual toing and froing – it had all been worth it.

She jangled the keys gently, and smiled. At twenty-eight she was officially a home owner, and better still – she glanced back towards the street where her boyfriend's car was parked – Jon was moving in. In the past she'd wondered whether this day would ever arrive. But here they were. Still together, in love, and taking a big stride forward as a couple. When they'd first met, introduced by their mutual friends Jess and Ed, Anna had thought about holding back – Jon was in the throes of a messy divorce, and his son was just over a year old. But they'd taken the leap together, and against the odds it had worked out.

Jon was still on his phone, his son Alfie, three years old

now, asleep in the car seat behind him. Anna walked back to the open car window.

'Jon,' she whispered. 'OK if I go in?' she asked, pointing at the front door.

'Sure, sure,' he said, glancing up at her, his green eyes bright, and covered the mouthpiece of his phone. He winked at her and then showed her his own set of keys. The faint creases on his forehead softened as he focused on her. 'I'll follow you in a minute. Just working out childcare for next week,' he explained. 'Nursery's shut for two days.'

Anna glanced into the back window. Alfie looked so angelic when he was asleep, his cheeks rosy and a blond curl pressed against his temple. Her heart softened at the sight of his chest rising and falling. Beside him were two crates of Jon's things – a tennis racket and some DVDs in one, another full of neatly folded polo shirts and chinos, and then a third with toys and books for Alfie. Jon worked hard as a brand manager and graphic designer, and what spare time he had was precious. Whether it was letting off some steam on the tennis court or taking Alfie to the park, he made sure he took advantage of every moment.

'Watch out for him,' Anna said, pointing to the parking attendant making his way up Marine Parade, stopping and ticketing the cars of everyone who'd stopped to admire the sunny sea view without paying.

'Oh crap,' he said, the phone still at his ear. 'Sorry,' he said hurriedly. 'Not you, Mia. I'm about to get a ticket. I'll call you right back.'

He put the phone down and turned to Anna. 'You go in, hon – I'll see you up there with Alfie once I've found somewhere to park.' With a hasty kiss, Jon restarted the engine of his Audi and pulled away from the kerb.

Anna retraced her steps up the path towards her apartment building, then took out her own mobile and dialled her Grandma Vivien's landline. It was the third time she'd tried that morning, and again it went through to answerphone.

Anna hesitated. She could drop by her grandma's house now, it wasn't far – just up the side streets to the quiet tree-lined road. But – she checked her watch – she and Jon would need to give Alfie his lunch soon. Vivien could always come and see the flat another day: the papers were signed now, and the place wasn't going anywhere.

Anna opened the door and stepped inside the entrance hall of the block, saw the postboxes for each of the flats. She climbed the wide, grandly proportioned stairs that hugged the curves of the Art Deco building. With dark-red carpet on the stairs, and brass fittings, Anna could just picture how it had once been a hotel.

She took the stairs two at a time, striding easily – while it hadn't always helped her when it came to dating, being just under six foot certainly had its advantages. She reached the third floor and opened the door to her flat, number 12. She looked into the hallway with a buzz of anticipation, and laid her handbag down on the floor. The carpet, cleared of furniture now, was a little grubbier than she remembered.

But, she thought, stepping forward into the living room, it was airy, and spacious. And out of the bay windows at the front of the flat – what a view. Waves crashed onto the pebbly beach, dogs ran up and down, and lights shone brightly on Brighton Pier. Vivien was going to love it. And Alfie always got excited about seeing Hepburn.

Working around the clock these past few years had all been worthwhile – because now she had her very own home.

Anna spotted Jon walking up the front path, with Alfie toddling along beside him. She tugged the sash window open, and felt a rush of cold air against her face and ruffling her grey silk blouse. 'Happy new home!' she called out. 'Come up.'

Jon raised a champagne bottle and waved it in celebration. 'Just you try and stop us,' he called, laughing.

Anna closed the window gently. She couldn't wait to toast the new flat – and to show Alfie where he'd be sleeping when he came to stay at the weekends. She crossed the living room and peeked into the small room next to the bathroom. The previous owners had used it as a study and now it stood empty, but Anna knew exactly how it would look once she and Jon had finished decorating it. They'd ordered a lovely wooden bed and a colourful toy chest and wardrobe with animals on them, plus a mobile and some pictures for the walls. It was going to be perfect.

She turned round, and took a look inside the master bedroom opposite. She chewed her lip in excitement – it was even more beautiful than she remembered. The large windows overlooked communal gardens, and flooded the room with light. Carefully restored wooden floorboards and an original 1920s fireplace gave the room character – and once her cream fluffy rug was in there it would be cosy too.

Tomorrow, she and Jon would be waking up in their very own place. It didn't matter who had put down the deposit. Jon's situation was complicated, and Anna understood that. Two years after the divorce, he and Mia were still struggling to find a buyer for their three-bedroom, mid-terrace house, meaning he wasn't able to pay into the new flat. But he and Anna had gone to the viewing together, and both fallen in love with the flat on Marine Parade as soon as they'd stepped inside. This place belonged to both of them: the flat was their new beginning.

Anna caught sight of her reflection in the mirror above the mantelpiece and attempted to tidy the frizzy mess the sea air had made of her usually sleek shoulder-length brown hair. The one and only downside of living in Brighton, she thought.

She heard the thud of Alfie's steps on the main staircase and his excited squeals as he ran. He and Jon must be just a floor or so away now. She couldn't wait for them to arrive.

Her phone buzzed in her pocket. She took it out and checked the screen: Mum.

'Hi, Mum,' she said.

'Hello, love.'

'You'll never guess where I am,' Anna said, unable to keep the excitement from her voice. 'I'm at our new flat.'

At that moment, Jon and Alfie burst in through the front door, wide smiles on both their faces – the family resemblance was unmissable. Alfie dashed from room to room, exploring excitedly, his dad following close behind. Anna walked back into the hallway and smiled to greet them.

'You know I mentioned the damp?' she said, talking into the phone and putting her head around the bathroom door. 'It looks like they've sorted it out. It's much better than when we came for the viewing. I can't see any of the black stuff anyway – you know, the bad mould.'

'That's good,' her mother Jan said, sounding distracted. 'Listen, Anna. I've been trying to get hold of your sister.'

'Imogen?' Anna said. 'Why? What's up? Is she OK?'

Jon must have heard the concern in her voice, as he looked back at her, his worried expression mirroring her own.

'She's fine,' Jan said. 'Or at least I think she is, she's impossible to get hold of.' Anna could hear that her voice was strained.

'Then what is it?'

'I'm afraid we've just had some terrible news. It's about your Granny Vivien.'

PART ONE

The Tide Turns

Chapter One

The 'fasten seatbelts' sign pinged, and Imogen undid the clunky metal clasp that held her to the aeroplane seat. She sat back, reclined the chair and looked out of the narrow window at the puffy white clouds that filled the sky over Bangkok: below them a layer of thick smog hung over the city. In just a few air-conditioned minutes they'd be moving out of Thai airspace and even further away from the island.

It had been thirty-six hours and a long boat and bus ride since Imogen had spoken to her sister Anna. She had hardly slept since then, save a few minutes with her head resting against a rattling bus window, her iPod drowning out the sounds of chickens in the aisles.

Imogen recalled her elder sister's familiar face over the shaky Skype connection in the internet café on the island's main street. 'It's Grandma Vivien,' she'd said, her brown eyes and thick brown hair pixellating as she moved. 'Imo, she's gone.' The words still swam in Imogen's head, unreal.

Knowing the details of her grandmother's death didn't help – a heart attack, existing health issues she'd kept hidden and only spoken to the doctor about. It still didn't make sense. Grandma Vivien wasn't supposed to die, or at least not yet. As soon as she'd finished talking to Anna, Imogen booked her flight home.

The stewardess approached with the bar trolley, and Imogen stopped her.

'Could I have a vodka tonic, please?'

She thought about what she was going back to. Home – to England, in March. But a different kind of home, without her grandma, one of the people she cared about most. She hadn't even had a chance to say goodbye.

'Actually,' she said to the stewardess, 'can you make that a double?'

Imogen took the drink and sipped at it. Slowly, the alcohol lulled her into something approaching sleep. She lost focus on the movie she was watching, and her eyelids drooped shut.

In her dream they were in her grandmother's back garden, she and Anna playing on the swing-ball set with Vivien keeping score, the sisters battling to hit the ball the hardest. Vivien stood cheering on the sidelines, next to a table laden with home-made lemonade and flapjacks, in a full-skirted flowery dress, a straw hat and those elegant high-heeled sandals she used to wear. As if she was awaiting a call that would sweep her away to a more glamorous party. Sparkling blue eyes, lined with liquid eyeliner. She had always looked, to Imogen, like a 1940s film star.

When Imogen awoke with a start, she could still smell

her grandmother's distinctive scent – almond and honey from the bath oil she used, then a layer beneath that, homier – the trace scents of cooking that clung to her clothes.

Imogen switched off the screen, and tried to focus on the magazine she'd picked up at the airport. But the images of red-carpet dresses blended into one.

She wanted something, anything, to block out the hurt of knowing her grandmother was gone. On the island the news had seemed like a strange dream, but now, on the way home to England, it was becoming painfully real. The last thing she wanted to do was cry here on the plane, in front of everyone, yet the tears felt dangerously close to the surface. To distract herself, she shut her eyes and cast her mind back to the night she'd left the island.

'You'll come back, won't you?' Luca had said, bringing her towards him in the dark water. Bright fire-fly-like scatterings of phosphorescence glittered in the sea around them, and Luca's face, with tanned skin, dark, wet hair and stubbled jaw, was partially lit by moonlight. They'd spent the evening in Komodo, a beach bar with live music, and then, after Imogen had explained that she'd have to leave, they'd separated off from their group, and she'd come down to the beach with Luca, just the two of them.

'Of course I'll be back,' Imogen said, laughing and kissing him again. This was a necessary trip, not a holiday. Thailand was her home now, and she was only halfway through compiling the underwater photographs for her project. Plus – palm trees swaying, days on the beach and nights with Luca, versus drizzly days and fish fingers in Britain? There was no contest.

'Promise me,' Luca said, a wry smile on his lips. 'You'll be one of those girls, won't you? Who gets an offer she can't refuse when she's back home, leaves a beach bum like me over here alone, pining and broken-hearted. I've seen it before. I just hope I'm not dumb enough to fall for it myself . . . ' He looked at her, a shyness and uncertainty in his eyes that was unfamiliar.

'Oh, you've got nothing to worry about,' Imogen said. 'It's only a fortnight. I need to be there for the funeral and to spend some time with Dad and my family. Then I'll be straight back on the plane to Bangkok. Wild horses couldn't keep me away.' She leaned towards him and into a salty kiss.

'Take this,' Luca said, as he pulled away from her. He took off the shark's-tooth necklace he wore around his neck. 'Put it on,' he said, sweeping her wavy, shoulder-length hair to one side and slipping the leather thong over her head. 'Then bring it back to me.'

Imogen smiled. Her hand went to the smooth pendant. 'You've got a deal.'

She touched the leather band around her neck now, and thought of Luca. Missed the feeling of his warm skin against hers. Two weeks apart seemed like an eternity.

It would be good to see Anna again, and her parents – well, her dad at least – but still, the thought of going home made Imogen's heart sink. The last time she'd been there, she'd just graduated from Bournemouth with a photography degree. After sending out eighty job applications, she'd failed to get a single interview, and at twenty-two, living at home with her parents, with her mum constantly checking up on her progress, she'd realised she needed to get away.

After two months, she'd got a bar job, and put away a little each month, dreaming of a way to get out of Lewes and away from her mum's demands and questions. When she and her friend Lucy had saved enough money for a flight to Asia, they were out of there – and while Lucy had returned six months ago, Imogen hadn't looked back. She had quickly made friends on the island, including Santiana, a Colombian girl as passionate about diving as she was.

Asia felt a world away from where she was heading back to, the small town of Lewes where she'd grown up.

'Chicken or pasta?' the stewardess asked gruffly, rifling through her metal trolley.

Imogen thought of the fragrant Thai green curry and rice she'd eaten just before she left the island. The delicious coconut lassi she'd sipped at a roadside stall while the bus refuelled.

She lowered her tray table. 'Pasta, please,' she said, and took the foil tray.

Imogen opened her rucksack in the spare room of her parents' house, and a little sand fell out onto the hand-made quilt. She brushed it off, then felt a tug at her heart as her hands touched the lovingly created squares. She looked up and her eyes met her sister's. Anna broke the melancholy silence. 'There are reminders everywhere you look, aren't there?'

'It still doesn't feel real,' Imogen said. 'To think that when we go to Brighton she won't be there. The ice cream shop, without her . . .'

Anna passed Imogen a mug of tea from the oak side table, and put a hand on her arm, sympathetically. Her own eyes were puffy and red, and the tip of her nose pink from blowing it.

'I feel awful. A whole year I haven't seen her, Anna.'

Outside seagulls cawed, the unmissable reminder that they were back near the south coast in Lewes, in their parents' two-storey eighteenth-century cottage.

'Don't beat yourself up about it,' Anna said. 'She loved your phone calls and the postcards – it brightened her days hearing what you were up to out there.'

Imogen fought the lump rising in her throat.

'You must be exhausted,' Anna said.

'It was a long journey, but my mind's sort of buzzy,' Imogen replied, taking a comforting sip of the hot drink. 'How did Granny seem, the last time you saw her?'

Anna perched on the edge of the bed and placed a cushion on her lap. 'I was round at her house just over a week ago,' she said. 'And she seemed fine, good even. She didn't want to go out to lunch, said she'd rather stay in, but that didn't seem too unusual. I should have sensed, though, that something was up.'

'She always seemed so young,' Imogen said. 'You know,

compared to other people's grandmas. I was sure we'd have a few more years with her.'

'Me too,' Anna said. 'It doesn't seem fair. Dad's crushed, as you'd expect.'

'Poor Dad,' Imogen said, biting her lip. They'd hugged hello downstairs, and while they'd barely spoken, she'd seen the grief etched into his face.

'The cremation's on Thursday, Mum told you that, right?'

Imogen nodded. 'Yes. You'll lend me something to wear, won't you?' she said. 'I haven't been to one before but I'm guessing the clothes I've got in my rucksack aren't going to be right.'

'Of course,' Anna said, smiling warmly and getting to her feet. 'Listen, Mum said dinner would be ready in about twenty minutes. Jump in the shower and we'll see you down there.'

'Sure,' Imogen said, taking a neatly folded towel from the end of her bed. The room, once her teenage bedroom, felt alien to her. Now it was like a well-kept B&B, her music posters replaced with framed flower prints.

'It's nice to have you back,' Anna said, giving her sister a gentle hug. 'I wish you were here for other reasons, but in any case, it's lovely to see you.'

'You too,' Imogen said, appreciating the familiar warmth of her sister's arms.

Imogen showered, wrapped her hair in a towel, and threw on the first clean clothes she could find. Downstairs, through the kitchen doorway, she could see Anna chatting and preparing dinner alongside their mum. She walked past quietly and went through into the dining room.

It looked exactly as Imogen remembered it – with photos on the mantelpiece and fresh flowers on the table. This room was the smart dining area, the one usually reserved for when guests were over.

Her dad, Tom, was sitting in a chair at the table, his head in his hands. His hands – large and strong. They'd held Imogen and Anna as children, lifted the girls up onto swings, onto his broad shoulders. Now her father looked fragile, as if the slightest breeze would break him. Imogen approached him and put a hand on his arm.

'You OK, Dad?' she asked, softly.

'Oh yes, sweetheart,' he said, weakly. 'And you –' his pale blue eyes implored her to take over the talking – 'you enjoying your travels still?'

'Yes,' Imogen said. 'It's beautiful out there.'

'I remember how it was,' her dad said, slowly. But the usual gusto with which he told the stories of his hippy days was missing from his voice. 'In the sixties, with nothing but my motorbike and the wind in my hair . . . of course that was when I still had some. Travelling through Vietnam and Laos. It was all different in those days . . . '

His words tailed away and his gaze dropped to the white tablecloth.

'Dad,' Imogen said gently. 'It's OK to be upset, you know. We all are.'

'The thing is,' he said, without looking up, 'you know it's

coming. One day. Of course you do – and with Dad, somehow it wasn't such a shock, he'd had more than his fair share of health problems. But I didn't think it would happen so soon with Mum. It's awful.'

It pained Imogen to hear the hurt in her father's voice. Any other day, he'd be cracking open a bottle of wine and enthusiastically telling her and Anna about the latest sculpture he'd made out in his garden studio. But today, he was ashen-faced, a ghostly version of himself.

'She was an amazing woman,' Imogen said, squeezing her dad's arm. 'We're all going to miss her.'

'It's the little things I'll miss,' Tom said. 'Even the same things that once drove me mad about her. The way she'd call me up when we were having dinner, excited about something that had happened in her drama serial.'

'Or the way she'd filter out all of the purple Quality Streets at Christmas and pretend there never were any?' Imogen said.

'That's right,' Tom laughed. 'And then of course, she'd always bring someone along on Christmas Day, wouldn't she? Some waif or stray we'd never met, but who'd had nowhere to go.'

'Without fail,' Imogen said. 'Poor Mum never knew how many people she'd be buying the turkey for.'

'It was her way,' Tom said. 'Even when Dad was around. But he didn't mind, they'd grown so used to one another, and he always said he'd never have set up the shop with her if they hadn't enjoyed being around people.'

Imogen smiled in understanding.

'She wasn't perfect,' Tom continued. 'But you know what, she was all the better for that.'

'Imogen, you're here,' Jan said, interrupting them. 'I didn't hear you come down.' Imogen was suddenly aware of her mum's disapproving gaze at her towel turban, loose, hand-dyed trousers and baggy T-shirt. 'Are you not going to dry your hair, love?'

Imogen shrugged, feeling a bit of her teenage self creep back.

'I thought we could eat in here today,' Jan said, passing Imogen some mats to lay out on the table. 'It being a bit special with the whole family back at home. I've cooked a nice beef casserole with sage dumplings, and your sister's made some crème caramel.'

'You didn't need to go to any trouble,' Imogen said, glancing back at her dad, whose eyes had glazed over.

'I think we all need a good meal inside us,' Jan said. Imogen bit her tongue. Food was her mother's solution to everything. As Jan went back to the kitchen, Imogen took her father's hand under the table, and he squeezed it back, very gently.

A moment later Jan reappeared in the doorway holding a pile of plates between tea-towels, Anna following behind carrying the casserole dish in oven-gloved hands.

'Watch out, plates are hot!' Jan said with a smile, putting them down on the wicker mats, leaving one free for the casserole.

Anna and her mother took their seats at the table. 'Tuck in,' Jan urged them cheerfully, 'or it will get cold.'

As the family started to eat, the room fell quiet.

'So, can we tempt you to stay this time, Imogen?' her mum said. 'Business is picking up a little round here, they say – some green shoots. I could ask around, or I'm sure we could find some admin work for you at the agency.'

Imogen picked at her food with a fork, breaking one of the dumplings in half. She pictured working with her mum, at the PR agency she'd founded once her daughters were at school. It was hard to imagine a more agonising way to spend her days. 'I'm just here for the funeral, Mum. I'll be flying back to Thailand in two weeks.'

Jan sighed. Then, after a moment, changed the direction of her questioning.

'Someone special, is there?' she asked, raising her eyebrows hopefully.

'Mum . . . ' Anna said, attempting to defend her sister from the regular inquisition. 'Do you have to . . . '

'I'm only asking,' Jan countered defensively.

'No, it's OK,' Imogen said. Anna looked surprised at her response. It was a new tactic, but this time Imogen reasoned that honesty might be the best way to silence her mum's enquiries. 'I've met someone on the island, but it's very early days still. Let's see what happens when I get back.'

Jan raised her eyebrows and gave a nod at her husband, who was focusing on his food, chewing it slowly, his expression distant. 'Hear that, Tom?' she said. 'Imogen's found someone special out there.'

'It's not serious,' Imogen said, starting to regret her previous openness.

'Oh, but you never know,' Jan said. 'That's what I thought about your father when he first strolled into the bakery.'

The sisters exchanged a knowing look at the familiar story.

'I was only eighteen, in my first job here in Lewes – and I'd never even met a man who rode a motorbike before. But your dad was there, tanned and handsome, just back from one of his trips – and I couldn't resist.'

'Never mind driving those rough roads out in Asia,' Tom said, joining in. 'It was getting up the guts to ask your mother out that was the hardest.'

'Saying yes was the best thing I ever did,' Jan said with a wistful smile. ' I wouldn't have you two otherwise. So, Imogen, why don't you persuade this boy to come over here?'

'Neither of us wants to live in the UK at the moment.' Imogen braced herself for her mother's wounded look, which was immediate.

'I mean, for now I'm in the middle of a photography project. It's taking shape really nicely and I just want to focus on that.'

'Your father's daughter, through and through,' Jan continued. 'These creative dreams – admirable, of course. But be careful, Imogen, you'll end up with a studio full of unsold sculptures just gathering dust.' She gave a hollow laugh, and the sadness in Tom's eyes seemed to deepen.

'But seriously, it's important to think about your future. Now more than ever. If it wasn't for the agency, girls, I don't think we'd have two pennies to rub together.'

'Do we need to talk about this now, Mum?' Anna asked, softly. 'With Grandma's funeral coming up I think we all have other things on our minds.'

'Well, yes,' Jan said, speaking more quietly now, and returning to her meal. 'And of course with your Uncle Martin and Aunt Françoise arriving tomorrow there's a lot to organise.'

'We can help make their bedroom up,' Anna offered, 'if that's what you're worried about.'

'Oh it's not just that,' Jan fussed. 'I'll have to get a lot of food in. Not just for the wake, but for the whole of the stay. You know what your aunt's like, very sophisticated tastes, she has.'

'There's no need, Jan,' Tom said. 'Really.'

'It's nice to make an effort. And your brother – well, he hasn't been to stay for years, has he?'

'No, but Martin . . . It doesn't matter, does it, with brothers? We may not see each other all the time, but we'll always be close.'

Chapter Two

'The last will and testament of Mrs Vivien McAvoy,' the lawyer read out.

The office was completely still and quiet, and the air was thick with tension. The lawyer, a middle-aged man in a charcoal suit sitting behind an aged oak desk, held Anna and Imogen's grandmother's final wishes in his hands.

Over the last two days their family had barely been apart, and yet here, in a cramped room up on the second floor of the lawyer's office in Brighton, there was a distance between them.

The funeral, held the day before, had passed calmly. The crematorium had been so full of Vivien's friends and past customers there to pay their respects that they'd had to turn some people away. At the end of the service, a little boy had placed a sympathy card into Tom's hand, with a hand-drawn ice cream on the front, covered in glitter. 'She was a nice lady,' he'd said, before walking back to his own mother.

Afterwards, the family and a handful of friends had travelled back to Tom and Jan's cottage in Lewes for sandwiches and drinks. Listening to people exchange stories and memories of her grandmother had brought Anna a kind of closure – but she was conscious that her father hadn't been part of any of it, that he had stepped away from the crowd and gone out to his studio halfway through the afternoon.

Anna had dressed for today's will-reading in a black blazer and fitted trousers, with bronze jewellery, her long dark hair wound back in a French pleat. She looked capable and composed, even if she didn't feel it. Pushing aside her sadness, she got out her notepad and pen ready to take notes.

Her dad, in the wire-framed glasses he rarely wore, was staring straight forward, his expression blank and numb, and their mother was searching for something in her leather handbag. Imogen was looking absently at the bookshelf, fiddling with a strand of her hair. Also in the room were her Uncle Martin, and his wife Françoise, whose posture was upright and rigid.

'*Oh honestly, you lot. Lighten up, would you?*' Anna smiled as she imagined what her grandma would say if she could see them now.

What was done was done, and nothing could change it, Anna told herself. Certainly not getting stressed out about dividing up some property. It was just part of the process. That morning, her father had insisted that he didn't want to come, that he didn't care about his mother's things, it was her company he missed, but Anna finally persuaded him that it was important he be there.

'Mrs McAvoy has given prominence to one matter in

particular,' the lawyer read, shuffling the papers to show that his client's wishes had gone beyond one sheet of A4. Françoise sat forward in her seat, listening more intently.

'And that is, ahem . . . the care of her dog, Hepburn.'

Anna suppressed a laugh of surprise, calling to mind her grandmother's beloved sausage dog. She should have known – it was typical that Vivien would put Hepburn top of her list – they had been inseparable. Apparently he'd stayed faithfully by Vivien's side to the very end; the ambulance men said it was his barking that had alerted the neighbours. He was currently dozing away, oblivious, on the sofa at her parents' cottage.

The lawyer continued. 'Mrs McAvoy has asked that Hepburn go into the care of her granddaughter Anna, so that –' and he glanced at the paper again – 'he can still stroll along his favourite parts of the beach, and have his bacon treats from Dogs 'N' Co in Hove.'

Anna nodded her agreement, outwardly calm, but inwardly panicking about how she was going to fit a dog into her life. Would her boss allow him into the office? Did Jon even like dogs?

At least Alfie would be happy, she thought, recalling how he'd thrown his chubby toddler arms around the sausage dog the first time they'd met. So Hepburn would be a sure-fire hit on that front.

'Now, on to property,' the lawyer continued, looking relieved to be moving on to weightier matters. 'Mrs McAvoy's residence in Hove, a five-bedroom house.'

The whole family knew the house well, particularly Tom and Martin, who had grown up there. A Victorian terrace on a quiet residential road with spacious, high-ceilinged rooms and a large garden with a pond, it held memories for all of them. It was a house that had always been filled with noise and life.

Vivien had been talking for years about downsizing and finding somewhere more practical. But Anna had sensed that it was hard for her to leave the home she'd shared with her husband Stanley for so many years.

'Equal shares go to her two children, Tom and Martin.'

The brothers exchanged an amicable nod.

The lawyer moved his reading glasses a fraction up his nose and returned to the papers. 'Now on to another key asset . . . '

They all knew what was coming next. Françoise's manicured hands rose to her necklace, twiddling the delicate cream beads.

Anna bit her lip. As the lawyer shuffled through his papers, she thought back to the conversation the family had had that morning over breakfast at her parents' house.

'Well, the location of the shop isn't too bad,' Françoise had said, pouring a cup of strong coffee from the cafetière. The food in front of her remained untouched. 'There is potential, I think. Hopefully Vivien will have thought carefully about who is best placed to realise that.' The ambition in her voice was impossible to miss.

'Yes,' Tom had said, a little dreamily. 'Well, I'm not sure

what I'd do with the shop,' he added, dipping a soldier into his soft-boiled egg, and then holding it still in mid-air. 'Hardly a business mind, me, and I have my hands full with making the sculptures these days. And Mum knows how busy Jan is with the agency.' He rested the egg-covered slice of toast on the side of his plate as if his hunger had deserted him. 'Mum *knew*, I mean.'

'And of course we're over in Paris . . . ' Martin said, buttering his toast.

'But that doesn't need to be a problem,' Françoise said, bringing the coffee up to her red-lipsticked mouth. 'Martin, you know I have been looking for a little, how do you say . . . a little "project". Perhaps this could be it? I mean, of course, we must wait and see what Vivien's decision was . . . but hopefully she has been more businesslike in that than she was when she was running the shop.'

Françoise looked out of the kitchen window of Anna's parents' cosy, traditional English kitchen. 'I've long thought, from our visits here, that the south coast – it could do with some more sophistication. A restaurant, a touch of French elegance. Perhaps I could set one up.'

Imogen had looked at Anna and raised an eyebrow discreetly. Their grandmother – elegant in her own way, but a lifelong devotee of home-cooked meals and fish and chips for a weekend treat – had never so much as stepped foot inside a fancy restaurant.

Now, in the lawyer's office, Imogen was looking over at her sister again, as they anxiously awaited the news.

'So,' the lawyer continued. 'To Mrs McAvoy's shop, commercial premises in the Granville Arches in Hove, currently used for the sale of ice cream and drinks.'

Anna tried not to take the detached, cold description to heart, the lawyer was only doing his job. But Sunset 99s, her grandmother Vivien's shop by the sea, was more than just a premises 'used for the sale of ice cream'. So much more than that. Since the 1950s, when Tom and Martin were just little boys, the shop had been Vivien's dream, her livelihood – a business she set up with her husband, Stanley, and kept running long after his death.

But now, in what felt to Anna like an impossibly long silence in the lawyer's office, they were about to find out which way things would go.

'Mrs McAvoy has requested that the ice cream shop premises go to . . . '

Silence fell. Anna willed the lawyer to carry on talking. This suspense – it was worse than *Deal or No Deal*.

' . . . her granddaughters, Anna and Imogen McAvoy, to be shared equally between the two. There's also a sum of money here that's been allocated to cover any start-up costs.'

'Christ,' Imogen said, sitting bolt upright, her bright eyes flicking wide open. 'I mean,' she brought her hand up to her mouth and shook her head slightly, 'sorry, but, Christ, seriously, Anna,' Imogen said, turning to her elder sister, 'what the heck does she think we're going to do with a shop?'

Anna was still slowly digesting the information. She had

been so sure that the options were limited, that the shop would go either to her father or her uncle. She hadn't foreseen this at all. Looking after Hepburn was one thing – but taking control of Vivien's business? That was quite another.

'She's put a note here for you . . . ' the lawyer said, turning back to an additional pink sheet that was stapled to the front. Then he cleared his throat and spoke 'She's written here: "I know I didn't keep up with the times, but you two are just the ladies to give the shop a modern spin. So here it is – for you. Our family business. Do me proud."'

'She's also left this photograph album for you,' the lawyer said, passing a heavy, gilt-embossed black book over to Anna. 'In terms of the shop, we'll need to arrange a time for you two to come in, sign the deeds and pick up the keys.'

Anna took the album numbly, then felt a surge of panic rising in her. Judging from the expression in Imogen's eyes, she wasn't the only one.

After the meeting, they went back to Vivien's house and settled in her front room. Anna looked around at the grand-father clock, the Persian rug, the black-and-white framed photos – it was the same place she'd been with her grand-mother a week and a half ago, but this time Vivien was only a whispered presence.

Jan dutifully poured out tea from Vivien's treasured but-tercup teapot, and Anna passed around the steaming cups, one of her home-made stem-ginger cookies balanced on each saucer.

'That was a bit of a surprise,' Tom said, sitting back in his mother's dark-green armchair next to the fireplace.

'It is not going to be easy, girls,' Françoise said, looking over at her nieces. She was standing by the bay window, holding her teacup and saucer aloft, her mouth tightly pursed. 'You'd be better off selling the place, really.'

Uncle Martin tilted his head, then enquired kindly, 'Unless you'd be keen to run it yourselves, of course. Imogen?'

'Don't look at me,' Imogen said, through a mouthful of biscuit, shaking her head with conviction. 'In ten days' time I'm going to be back on the beach.'

'What about you, Anna?' Martin asked. 'I suppose one thing to consider is the flat you've just bought. Right now you have a regular income, but if you were to take on the shop, it wouldn't be the same.'

Anna stirred a spoonful of sugar into her tea and nodded politely. Newly promoted to Marketing Director at Brighton Pavilion events, she finally had a decent, stable salary. She was well aware that with the arts sector feeling the pinch, she was one of very few lucky ones.

And yet, after seven years in events and with an increasing amount of her time spent in meetings and answering emails . . . perhaps it *was* time for a change. She hardly dared think it, but hadn't it always been her dream to work with food, something she'd been passionate about since she was a little girl?

'Martin's right, of course,' Jan said, looking over at Anna and bringing her back to the moment. 'I mean there's not much security in it, is there, darling? Running a shop. Especially not at the moment.' Tom was sitting by her side, drinking his tea slowly and silently. 'And I think we all know it's been a long time since your grandma did anything more than break even on that place.'

Anna remembered the last time she'd visited Sunset 99s – her mum was right. It wasn't the adorable cake shop she'd often dreamed of running . . . it was shabby and run-down, not to mention critically short on customers. Without a day's experience, it would be too much for her to take on alone.

'Just going to get a glass of water,' Anna said, getting up and slipping out to the kitchen. Imogen followed her into the room and caught her sister by the elbow.

'Hey,' Imogen said. 'Not surprised you wanted to escape. Don't let them boss you around, sis. What do you think about all this, really?'

'I don't know, to be honest,' Anna said, leaning up against the kitchen counter.

'Well, I, for one, need a proper drink right now,' Imogen said, rifling through their grandmother's drinks cabinet. 'You were saying?'

'I need some space to think. I mean I'm touched, of course, that Granny V would do this. But the responsibility . . . what do either of us know about running a shop, Imo?'

'Absolutely zero,' Imogen said, locating an old bottle of cherry brandy and pouring herself a glass. She raised a questioning eyebrow at her sister, but Anna shook her head. 'No thanks, that doesn't look like it's been opened for a decade.'

Imogen took a glug and made a face that confirmed her sister's suspicions. 'Which is why I'm saying now, from the start, that this is not for me. And you shouldn't feel pressured either: just because she left Sunset 99s to us doesn't mean we have to take it. You've got your swanky new job to think about.'

Anna gave Imogen a playful jab in the ribs. 'It's not swanky,' she said. 'I still have to make my own tea, you know.'

'You know I'm just jealous,' Imogen said. 'That, the flat. You've hit the big time, sis. And you don't want to throw all that away.'

Here, in Vivien's house, with her favourite recipes still up on the fridge and her trinkets lined up on the windowsill, it was difficult for Anna to overcome the feeling that Vivien could still, somehow, hear what they were saying.

'She's getting worse, isn't she?' Imogen said, with a nod towards the living room.

'Who, Mum?'

Imogen laughed. 'No, not Mum,' she said. 'I'm pretty used to her getting at me by now. No, I was talking about *Madame* out there –' she lowered her voice to a stage whisper, which, in effect, wasn't a lowering at all – '*Françoise.*'

'Hmm,' Anna said. 'Yes, I can see what you mean. She really wanted the shop, didn't she?'

'She's made that pretty clear,' Imogen said, taking a sip of her cherry brandy. 'And her eyes lit up when she was talking about her French restaurant idea. She was talking as if it were already hers.'

'I suppose,' Anna whispered back. 'But you know as well as I do how Granny V would feel about that – definitely not her cup of tea. Anyway, you'd think that what with the villa in the Dordogne and the flat in Paris Françoise and Martin must be pretty settled in France.'

'Maybe she's got itchy feet,' Imogen said. 'But anyway, why don't we go down and have a look at the shop together? That's if you don't mind me crashing at yours for a couple of nights while we work out our next move. I'm curious to see the place again, have a fresh look at the gem Granny V's left us.'

'Of course, come and stay, you can see the flat, see Jon again and meet Alfie properly. But if you're expecting the shop to be a gem . . . Well, let's just say that it's one that needs a whole lot of polishing.'

Chapter Three

Imogen fiddled with the car radio and eventually found a station she was happy with, then turned the volume to maximum. Bob Marley's 'Stir it Up' blasted out of the car's speakers on the crisp Saturday afternoon, as the sisters headed down the A-Road back to Brighton.

Anna gripped the steering wheel tighter. 'Do we need to have it on that loud, Imo? It's a bit hard to concentrate. And I'm not sure Hepburn likes it either.'

'Little darllllllllllling,' Imogen sang, pressing the button to open the car window and giving the dog a rough stroke. For a moment, with the wind catching her hair, she was on the island again – the reggae track taking her back to her last night with Luca. Less than a week ago, and yet already it felt like forever. She couldn't wait to get back online and talk to him.

She glanced behind her and saw a red sports car nearing them, with a horsebox close behind it. 'Anna, speed up a bit. There are a couple of horses back there that want to overtake.'

Anna reluctantly pressed her foot on the accelerator so that the speedometer crept up beyond sixty.

'At last,' Imogen said. '*And* a bit more – would be good to get to Brighton some time before supper.'

Imogen stood awkwardly on the landing outside Anna's flat, still wearing her rucksack and holding Hepburn's lead. With her prompting, they'd made it to Brighton in a record thirty-five minutes.

'I missed you,' Jon said, bringing Anna into his arms in a warm hug, his eyes closed.

Imogen kept quiet, not wanting to interrupt the emotional homecoming, but the silence was shattered by a piercing bark from Hepburn.

Jon pulled back, catching sight of Imogen and the dog. 'Imogen,' he said, stepping away from his girlfriend. 'I didn't see you there. Hi.' He came forward to give her a kiss on the cheek.

'Hi, Jon,' Imogen said with a smile. 'It's been a while.'

'Imogen's coming to stay for a few days,' Anna explained. 'Hope that's OK. And as for the dog, well, there are a few things I'm going to need to explain.'

'Right . . . ' Jon said, his brow furrowing a little as he looked back at Hepburn, who was now circling Imogen's legs, his lead getting tangled between them.

Jon's brown hair was cut shorter than before, Imogen noticed, with sideburns blending into light stubble. He looked more relaxed, but then that wasn't exactly surprising – when she'd last seen him, just before she left for Asia, she knew from Anna that the final stages of his divorce had been going through.

'Alfie and I are making pizza,' he said, motioning for them to come through into the kitchen. 'We've got plenty of dough left. We'll whip you up another one.'

'That sounds perfect,' Anna said, stepping into the hallway and dumping her bags. Alfie dashed towards her and she swept him up into a hug. 'Hello, sweetie. It's good to see you.'

'Pizza!' Alfie said excitedly. 'Me and daddy, making pizza.'

'That's great, darling,' Anna said, taking his hand and walking through to the kitchen.

'So there were a few surprises in Granny V's will,' Anna explained. 'Not least Imogen and me getting Sunset 99s.'

'So, let me get this straight,' Jon said, cutting the freshly cooked pizza into equal pieces. 'You've inherited an ice cream shop?'

'That's right,' Anna said, sitting back in her chair. 'And, yes, as you've seen – a dog.'

'Heh-urn!' Alfie said, sitting up straight in his high chair. 'Doggy! Ice cream!'

'Oh God, both the magic words at once,' Jon said, smiling and feigning weariness. 'Yes, we have a doggy now. But no ice cream, Alfie. Sorry. But there's some delicious pizza for you to eat.'

'Alfie likes pizza,' he said, taking a bite of the slice Imogen was offering up to him, and seeming to forget about ice cream altogether.

'Anyway, the shop, yes – she wanted Imogen and me to take it over. She and Grandpa Stanley started it up, and she wants to keep it in the family.'

Jon listened patiently. 'I'm still reeling from the dog part,' he said. 'But carry on.'

'Sorry,' Anna said quietly, when Alfie was distracted, 'that we didn't get to talk about Hepburn first. Granny V was just so keen that he stay in Brighton.'

'And in terms of the shop, there's nothing to worry about,' Imogen said. 'I'm going back to Thailand, and Anna's going to stay at her job.'

'That's the long and the short of it.' Anna said. 'But we're going to have a look at the shop tomorrow all the same – Imogen wants to see what kind of state it's in.'

'It was pretty run-down the last time we went,' Jon said, tilting his head. 'Could do with a bit of TLC before you sell it on. I'm assuming that's what you're planning to do?'

'Yes,' Imogen said, nodding.

Anna hesitated. Should they really throw in the towel before they'd even thought the idea through properly? 'Actually,' she said, 'we haven't decided for sure what we're doing yet.'

Early the next morning, a Sunday, Imogen and Anna strolled down to the seafront. The sky was streaked with orange, and small sailing boats had been laid to rest in a row upside down on the pebbles. A humming and tinkling, like tiny bells, rang out as the rigging on the small vessels knocked against the masts. Further up the beach, a few men lined the shore, holding their fishing rods in peaceful companion-ship, looking out on the dawn waves. To their right, a weary landmark next to this stretch of the beach, were the black-ened, burnt-out ruins of West Pier.

Sunset 99s was located under the Granville Arches, just past a row of brightly coloured beach huts – a bold wooden sign in sunset colours and a picture of an ice cream hung above the graffitied metal shutter. The Granville Arches weren't buzzing like the area closer to Brighton, Imogen noted. Here, there were none of the tourists who flocked to the Brighton Pier and the doughnut and fish-and-chip shops around it. Instead, there were a few local boys practising their skateboard tricks, wheels rattling against the flagstones, and a solitary dog-walker. Imogen cast a glance over the other businesses on the parade – a souvenir shop with some inflatables and postcards out the front, a newsagent, and a smaller doorway with surfboards propped up against the wall, with a yellow sign advertising surfing lessons.

Anna turned the key in the padlock that bolted down the shutter on Vivien's shop and then lifted it up slowly. Imogen bent down to help her.

'God, this is heavy. How did Granny manage this on her own?' Imogen said.

'She wasn't completely alone,' Anna said. 'She had that assistant, Sue, and I think her friend Evie would sometimes help out.' Anna pointed over at the souvenir shop. 'Do you remember Granny left Evie some of her jewellery, in the will, that ruby and gold locket she always wore? They were very close, those two.'

Imogen peeked underneath the shutter and caught sight of the grubby black-and-white chequered floor, almost covered with dozens of unread letters, leaflets and lolly wrappers. 'Yikes, it's a right mess in here.'

Anna bent down to look at what her sister had seen. 'Oh dear,' she said.

The metal shutter rattled noisily as they wound it right up to the top. Anna opened the glass door with another key and they stepped tentatively inside.

The marble counters were littered with menus and papers with orders on them – it looked as if a storm had blown through the old ice cream shop. The mirrors on the walls, which Imogen remembered being sparkling and bright – that had once reflected images of her and Anna as children, tucking into Coke floats – were now dark, tarnished and flecked with black.

'Didn't you say that the shop was only closed for a fortnight?' Imogen said, opening up one of the freezer cabinets to inspect it and then gripping her nose tightly at the thick smell of sour milk and damp. 'Yuck,' she exclaimed, taking a closer look. 'That smells rank. There's loads of mould at the bottom.'

'Sue was looking after it on her own for a while before that so Granny could have a break. Looks like she wasn't doing a great job,' Anna said, with a stab of guilt. She should have realised that things had got so bad. Maybe there was something she could have done to help.

Imogen spotted the Mr Whippy machine at the counter. 'Remember this?' she said. 'Our treat in the summer holidays when we'd come down and visit.'

Anna walked over to join her sister, running a hand affectionately over the sign on the machine. 'Looks like it's seen better days,' she said. She tried the tap that used to release curls of soft-serve ice cream. A trickle of dirty water came out instead. The sisters looked at each other with the same mournful expression.

'I haven't been down here for a while,' Anna said. 'But Granny would never have let the place get like this. I guess that when Sue started helping out she must have stepped away from the day-to-day running of things. Maybe she was starting to feel unwell even then.'

'Didn't she talk about it – how the shop was doing?' Imogen asked, flicking through an accounts book that was lying out by the till.

'Not much, she always preferred to hear about how we were getting on. She did mention the other shop-owners – Evie, and a younger guy, Finn, who used to pop in and check up on her sometimes. But the business side of it – not much. Left to her, it would never be in this state, though. You know how houseproud she was. Shop-proud.' Anna forced a smile.

'Shop-proud,' Imogen said quietly, running a finger over

the filthy countertop. It came away black. 'Poor Granny V. It's not quite how I remember it from the old days.'

'I agree it needs work,' Anna said, her expression relaxed, but a shade of worry in her eyes. 'Although all the original fifties features are still here.' She pointed at the wall lamps and the stools lined up at the counter. 'We could spruce it up, couldn't we? Keep the retro style, but give it a modern twist?'

Anna went behind the counter. 'I'm sure there are loads of interesting nick-nacks hidden away too . . . ' She ducked down to open one of the cupboards. Imogen could hear plates clattering out onto the floor.

' . . . It would entail a bit of vision, of course.' Anna's muffled voice came from below as she tidied the crockery back into the cupboard. She got to her feet. Above her, there was a heavy chalkboard hanging on the wall. Anna read the pastel-coloured writing out loud,

"Vivien's Specials"
Pancakes and vanilla ice cream with chocolate sauce

She paused. 'Imagine it, Imo – we could make warm crêpes with hazelnuts and chocolate ice cream, sundaes brimming over with freshly scooped sorbet and fruit sauces—'

'That chalkboard looks like a hazard,' Imogen interrupted.

'Really?' Anna held the edge, but the heavy board swung perilously on its hook now, threatening to fall. She steadied it and moved away. 'Maybe you're right.'

'Look, sis. I like that you're trying to put a positive spin on all this, but let's be honest. This place is shabby, full of junk – and it hasn't been profitable for goodness knows how long.'

'I know,' Anna said, feeling defeated. 'But –' she placed a steady hand on the counter where the two sisters had once sat as little girls – 'I feel something, being here. Don't you?'

'I think you're being sentimental,' Imogen said. It had started to drizzle outside now, and some of the rain was drifting in through the open glass door. She got to her Converse-clad feet and went over to shut it tight. 'Don't get me wrong, Anna. I have happy memories here – and I know this place meant a lot to Granny, and still does to Dad. But some things are just better left in the past. I've got other plans right now. And with the best will in the world we'd need more than Mary Portas to turn this place around.'

Anna tucked her loose chestnut hair behind her ear, and started straightening some of the leaflets and scribbled orders into a neat pile. Silently, she ordered the stray pens and notebooks alongside them, perfectly in line with the edge of the counter.

'Don't go all OCD on me, Anna. I know it's upsetting for you, but the simple truth is I don't want to manage a run-down ice cream shop in drizzly Brighton. I mean, seriously,' Imogen said, her voice softening a little. She cast her gaze down to the floor, and motioned to it, littered with empty Tangle-Twister wrappers.

'Do you? Is this your big dream? Have you worked in marketing since uni to end up cleaning floors here?'

'I guess not,' Anna said, biting her lip. 'And I certainly couldn't do it on my own. But what are our options? Sell it to a complete stranger and ignore what Granny V really wanted?

'It doesn't have to be a complete stranger,' Imogen said, with a shrug.

Anna's forehead furrowed. 'You don't seriously mean . . . '

'Aunt Françoise, yes,' Imogen said, matter-of-factly. 'I'm just trying to be realistic, Anna. Isn't it worth thinking about?'

It wasn't like Imogen didn't feel anything. Of course she did, but she just pushed those feelings to one side. She was too young to be tied down.

'Guess what?' Imogen said to Luca later that afternoon, bending close in to the laptop so he could hear her from the busy seafront café.

'What?' he asked, smiling and taking a long drag of his hand-rolled cigarette. He let the smoke out slowly. Imogen took in the image and tried to keep it in her mind: Luca, with his top off, tanned skin, two-day stubble, dark hair. She missed him, but with nearly half her trip behind her now, the longing was almost sweet. With the goal of returning to the island in sight, she felt excited and energised – like herself again.

'Just over a week now until I'm back,' Imogen said, enthusiasm bubbling up in her voice.

'Really?' he said, grinning widely. 'That's fantastic. It's gone really slowly. I can't wait to see you again, baby.'

'Well, you're not going to have to. Or not for long, at least. I'm flying back the Tuesday after next.'

'That's great,' Luca said, with a winning, lazy grin. Imogen bit her lip – he was so damn sexy. She could handle the wind and rain-lashed seafront, knowing that soon she'd be basking in the warmth of a Thai beach, with Luca rubbing suntan lotion onto her back.

'I fly into Bangkok and then I'll be coming down by bus and boat, so I'll be with you on Thursday. Tell everyone to get ready.'

'I will,' Luca promised, a warm smile still on his lips. 'Just leave the welcoming committee to me.'

'Brilliant,' Imogen said, feeling a piece of her regular life fall back into place. Staying on in Brighton out of guilt, or some sense of obligation to her grandmother, would have been wrong. She could see that clearly now. 'So, what are you up to tonight?' she asked.

'There's a beach party on, a few of us are going to that,' he said. Imogen tried to ignore her envy: she'd be back there soon enough. 'You?' he asked.

'Our for a drink with Anna and her friend Jess,' she said. 'Her wedding's next weekend and they're sorting out some last-minute details. I know Jess from school days too, so I'm just going along for the fun of it, some wine.'

'Well, enjoy. And I'll get your homecoming sorted,' he said.

'Thanks. I can't wait. Bye, Luca.' She blew a kiss at the screen.

Reluctantly, she logged off Skype, wishing she could keep his face in her mind all of the time.

She opened Facebook and posted an update:

One more week in the rainy UK and then I'm back on the beach! Save me a place under those palm trees . . .

'Can we have another of these?' Imogen said, a couple of hours later, holding up the empty bottle of white wine with a smile and waving it towards the barman. Jess, Imogen and Anna were tucked into a quiet candlelit corner at Smokey Joe's, a bar in the Lanes with friendly staff, an extra-long happy hour and a legendary jukebox. Even on Sunday night, it was packed inside.

'You look amazing, Imogen,' Jess said. 'The only woman in Brighton with a tan right now, that's for sure. You still enjoying Thailand?'

Imogen still found it difficult to reconcile Jess, the gothy teenager glued at the hip with Anna, and the Jess she saw now, a successful human rights lawyer, elegant in a red shift dress. Of course the biggest difference of all was that now Jess and Anna were older, Imogen was actually allowed to hang out with them.

'Oh yes,' she said. 'I mean it's been nice to see Anna and all that, but . . . '

'Not sure we'll ever get her back,' Anna said, with a playful sigh.

'Listen, sorry,' Jess said awkwardly, as the barman filled their glasses from a chilled bottle. 'If I'd known you were going to be here, I'd have sent you an invite to the wedding . . . '

'Oh God, don't worry,' Imogen said, batting away Jess's concern. 'Even I didn't know I was coming back until last week.'

'Come to the evening do, though?' Jess said. 'Anna's got all the details. Ed and I would love to have you there.'

'Sounds good to me,' Imogen said, grateful for something to look forward to. Her plans for the coming week consisted mainly of helping her dad and Uncle Martin sort through Vivien's belongings and get some of the furniture ready to go to auction. It was a big task, and she could tell that her dad needed some moral support.

'So . . . ' Jess said, running a pencil over her list, most of the entries now crossed through with a single line. 'You're still OK to do the cupcakes, aren't you, Anna?'

'Now about those . . . ' Anna said.

A flush of panic passed over Jess's face. She had one of those English rose complexions that the slightest hint of stress washed a rosy colour over.

'But you promised . . . ' Jess said, desperation in her voice. 'Don't mess with me, Anna.'

'Don't worry,' Anna said, placing her hand reassuringly on her friend's arm. 'I just wanted to make one hundred per cent sure that you were set on cupcakes. Because I was thinking . . . Cupcakes are a little been there, done that, don't you think? I once made these tiny ice cream cones.' She held two fingers up, close together to indicate the miniature size. 'They were delicious. Inside, it's not really ice cream, more like a chocolate mousse, but absolutely mouth-watering, I promise you. And it will fit right in with the summery theme.'

'I like it,' Jess said, her relief visible. 'Love it, in fact. Phew. Sorry for freaking out. It's just been one of those weeks.'

'Trust me,' Anna said. 'I won't let you down. Fancy helping me out, Imo?'

'Sure,' Imogen said. 'That would be fun. It's on Saturday, right, your wedding?'

'Yes,' Jess said, biting her lip exaggeratedly and then laughing. 'Only three more days. I'm torn between excitement and blind terror. But thankfully I've had no doubts about marrying Ed. I'm pretty sure about that part.'

'So what was it that happened this week?' Imogen asked.

'The travel company we've used for our honeymoon to Antigua. We saw on the news that they are having financial problems, and they haven't answered any of my emails or calls.'

'Oh dear,' Anna said. 'Are you insured?'

'I don't even know,' Jess said. 'Ed was in charge of that, and I haven't asked him. There's been so much to think about with the wedding. For now we're just keeping our fingers crossed it'll all work out.'

'Sure it will,' Imogen said. 'There's always a last-moment hiccup or two, isn't there?'

'I hope you're right,' Jess said. 'Ed and I have been looking forward to this holiday since last year. And to be honest, after the stress of organising the wedding I think we're really going to need it. ' Jess took a swig of wine from her glass. 'Anna, I've been meaning to ask you. You're OK, aren't you, with the whole Mia thing? I know it isn't ideal, but we couldn't not ask her.'

Mia . . . Imogen tried to remember where she'd heard that name before.

'I mean she and Ed are still good friends,' Jess went on. 'We know what she did wasn't right, cheating on Jon, and especially when Alfie was so young – but Ed didn't want to take sides. Jon seemed OK with the idea of her being there.'

'Of course,' Anna said, calmly. 'I see her quite often when we pick Alfie up and she's always nice enough. It's your and Ed's day, and you should invite who you want to.'

'Fine, good . . . ' Jess said. 'You're all being very grown-up, I must say.'

'With Alfie in the middle, it's the only way to be,' Anna said. 'We all want the best for him. I knew from the start that going out with Jon wasn't going to be entirely straight-forward, but he's the man I fell in love with. I feel lucky I found him.'

'You're right,' Jess said. 'Jon's a keeper, and anyway, who

hasn't got a bit of baggage? I still can't believe you two are actually living together. It's brilliant. Before he met you, he was adamant he was steering clear of women and commitment. In fact I really wasn't sure about introducing you two. But you changed his mind, and you both seem really happy.'

'We are,' Anna said. 'You and Ed have definitely earned your matchmaking points. But back to your wedding. What else is on the list, Jess?'

'You may regret asking that,' Jess said, laughing and picking up her thick notepad.

Chapter Four

'I got up early to do the mousse, so that's all ready,' Anna said to Imogen, on the morning of Jess's wedding, pointing to a giant bowl of creamy, light milk chocolate on the kitchen counter. 'So now we need to roll the waffle for the mini cones.'

'MOOOSE,' Alfie said from his high chair, chocolate smeared across his face. 'MORE MOOOOSE.'

'I think you may have had enough,' Imogen said to him. She put on an apron, tying it at the back, and peered into the oven where the sections of waffle were cooking.

'Yep,' Anna said, wiping his face with a cloth. 'Any more and your dad'll kill me when he gets home.'

'Tasty,' Alfie said. 'Alfie likes the mooose.'

'There's our seal of approval,' Anna laughed. 'Now we just have to hope that the wedding guests are as easy to please.'

Anna had woken at six to get started, relishing the time on her own, preparing food for Jess's friends and family to enjoy. When she had a wooden spoon in her hand, she instantly forgot about the working week, the subtle flavours and aromas in her kitchen whisking her away to a sweeter place.

This week was one she was only too happy to forget – with back-to-back meetings and a new budgeting crisis at the Brighton Pavilion, she'd hardly had a moment to manage her team, let alone work on her own projects – she was still checking her emails at midnight, in bed. The new promotion she'd been so excited about a month ago was starting to look worryingly like two jobs in one.

'I promised Jess a hundred,' Anna said. 'The thing with the waffle is we need to roll it while it's still warm. It should be ready by now, I think.'

Imogen took the tray of waffle sections out of the oven and laid them gently on a rack to cool. After a moment she took one off and rolled it on a wooden board into a loose cone shape. 'Like this?' she asked.

'Messy!' Alfie called out from his high chair.

'He might, erm, have a point,' Anna said, tilting her head as she examined Imogen's handiwork. 'Maybe stick to the picture a bit more?'

'Fine,' Imogen huffed, looking back at the photo on the recipe.

'Like this,' Anna said, as she deftly rolled three and placed them in one of the dozen circular stands Jess had dropped off for them to use, ready for the scoops of chocolate mousse to be added.

Imogen sighed, tried again and produced two neater cones.

'That's more like it,' her sister said approvingly. 'Now we just need another ninety,' she smiled. 'With enough time left over for me to get ready for the wedding. Not sure Jess would think much of me turning up like this.'

'Oh, I don't know. The apron kind of suits you,' Imogen said, 'and the chocolate on your jeans gives them a fancy touch.'

Anna gave her sister a playful swipe with a clean spatula. 'Well, that's eighty quid I've wasted at Karen Millen then,' she said, thinking of the coral silk dress she hadn't been able to resist, now hanging up on her wardrobe door.

'But seriously, Anna. You've always looked at home in the kitchen, you're such a natural at this stuff. Everyone says so. Why don't you do something with it?'

'You mean as a job?' Anna said. 'I always thought of it as a hobby, something I do to unwind. I never considered it something I could do for money. But lately, I suppose, I have started to wonder . . . '

'I saw your face in the shop,' Imogen said. 'I know that Granny V's not the only reason you don't want to sell that place.'

'To the bride and groom,' Anna said, chinking her champagne glass with Jess's Uncle Gareth in the marquee at Jess and Ed's wedding.

'These ice cream things are incredible,' Gareth said, cracking one of the cones with his teeth. 'Jess tells me we've got you to thank.'

'Yes, me and my sister made them,' Anna said, glowing at the compliment. 'I'm glad you like them.'

Anna glanced over at Jess, who was seated at the top table. In an ivory satin 1940s-style pencil dress with lace sleeves, and high T-bar heels, she looked more beautiful than ever. Her black curls were loose, adding a natural, unfussy touch to her stunning outfit, and a simple bouquet of pink roses set off her complexion. She was one of those brides who still looked like themselves – just a particularly stunning version. She caught Anna's eye and smiled.

'Hey, sweetheart,' Jon said, taking his place next to Anna and putting his arm around her waist. He lowered his voice to a whisper. 'Do I need to watch out for this guy?' he said, nodding at the man in his sixties Anna had been talking to, who was currently reaching for his second miniature ice cream.

'I think he's more interested in the cones than me. You're safe,' Anna said, kissing Jon gently on the mouth. 'Where did you disappear to anyway?' she asked. 'You missed Jess's dad's speech.'

'Ed's mum was feeling faint, and he asked if I could go out with her for some air.'

'Is she OK now?' Anna asked, concerned.

'Oh yes, she's fine. Got a bit carried away with the fizz and she's not meant to drink on her medication. She's back to her brightest. Now, let me try one of these famous ice creams,' Jon said, reaching towards the stand. 'These ones are dairy-free, right?'

'Yes,' Anna said. 'You got your own personal batch. So you can go for your life.'

He ate one in a single bite. 'Delicious,' he said, squeezing her hand.

As Jess and Ed's first dance came to an end, the bride desperately encouraged her guests onto the fairy-lit marquee's dancefloor.

Jon took Anna's hand. 'Shall we put them out of their misery?' Anna nodded her agreement.

'I thought no one else was ever going to come up,' Jess said, laughing. 'We look like a right pair of prats up here on our own. You know what a terrible dancer I am, last thing I need is a spotlight.'

'The two of you look gorgeous up there,' Anna said. 'So happy.'

Anna and Jon started to dance together, and she nestled into his shoulder. *Maybe we're getting there too*, she thought to herself. After two years of ups and downs, with Jon adjusting to his new life, and both of them trying to balance Alfie's at the same time, things finally seemed to be on an even keel. And that was more than enough. Perhaps one day it would be the two of them getting married, but for now, being held by Jon, feeling secure and going home to the flat they both loved – it all felt just right.

'It's been a perfect day,' Jon said, whispering into Anna's ear. 'And I don't think I've told you yet, but you look beautiful in that dress.'

Anna smiled and lifted her face to meet Jon's in a kiss. In that moment, the music from the live band washed away the sadness and stresses of the previous couple of weeks, leaving only lightness.

That is, until she felt a shoe land squarely on her toe. 'Ouch,' she yelped, lifting it up instinctively.

'So sorry.' She turned to see the awkward perpetrator, a young man in a navy suit, handsome in a way he seemed unaware of. 'Two left feet, me,' he said. 'God, I feel terrible.'

'You'll probably want to put some ice on that,' said his partner, as Anna bent down to remove her shoe and inspect the damage. 'When Ian gets me I usually need to.'

'Right, yes.' Anna said. Her little toe was throbbing fiercely, but at least it wasn't bleeding. She put her shoe back on and looked up to see the woman she was talking to. In a green 1950s-cut dress, her dark-red hair styled into a sleek chin-length bob, she was composed and elegant.

'Oh, Mia,' Anna said, attempting to stand up straighter. 'Hi. I didn't realise it was you.'

'Hi,' Jon said, giving his ex-wife a kiss on the cheek hello and shaking Ian's hand.

'Hi,' Mia said. 'Sorry about this, Anna. What a way to start the evening's dancing. Let me get you some ice from the bar.'

'Booze is still free, then?' Imogen said, when she arrived twenty minutes later. She picked up two glasses of champagne from a table and passed one to Anna.

'Yes, all night.' Anna said, taking a sip of the drink grate-fully: it numbed the pain in her foot a little. She'd only been able to tolerate holding the ice on it for a short while.

'I'm glad you're here,' Anna smiled, 'even if you have nicked one of my favourite dresses.'

Imogen had arrived for the evening party in a one-shouldered silver dress that fell to just below her knees. She'd pinned her hair up loosely, with sun-kissed strands spilling out onto her tanned, lightly freckled shoulders. It was such a glamorous look you could almost miss that she'd teamed it with black flip-flops.

'I knew you wouldn't mind,' Imogen said with a wink.

'I don't,' Anna said. 'But honestly, Imo, you could have at least stolen some decent shoes to match it,' she shook her head in disapproval.

'So which one is she?' Imogen put down her drink and scanned the room, without attempting to hide her intention. 'Not the one talking to Jon at the moment, surely?'

'That's her,' Anna said, taking another sip.

'Hmmm,' Imogen said, then let out a whistle. 'She's pretty hot.'

'Thanks. Yes, I'm aware of that.'

'She's also a heinous, unfeeling cheat who doesn't know a good thing, of course.'

'Also true. Although I don't think I'll ever know the full story on that.'

'What full story?' Imogen said. 'She had a young kid, then shagged the neighbour. End of.'

'I think Jon still blames himself a bit for leaving her on her own with Alfie. He'd just started his new job and was travelling for work a lot.'

'Oh come off it. Other women manage not to sleep with their neighbours,' Imogen said, rolling her eyes.

'Shhh, will you?' Anna said, conscious that other guests might know who they were talking about. 'Anyway, Mia's a wonderful mother, and she's always been open to including me in Alfie's life.'

'You're so darned *reasonable*, Anna,' Imogen said. 'Is there nothing that fazes you?

'It's none of my business what happened back then.'

'I guess,' Imogen said, accepting her sister's point. 'Anyway, it's plain to see Jon's smitten with you, which is what matters. It's revolting really.'

As the band struck up a new song, Imogen tugged on her sister's arm. 'Finish up your fizz. I know you're the walking wounded, but I love this one.' She took off her flip-flops. 'Put these on, give me yours and let's join Jess for a dance.'

Chapter Five

Imogen had the flat to herself on Monday morning, and now that her champagne-head had cleared, she felt energised and ready for some detoxing.

She whipped herself up a mango-and-passionfruit smoothie in the kitchen and rolled out her yoga mat. She was going to start the day just the way she did back on the island, with a series of sun salutations, facing out towards the sea. Yes, it was a grey, murky kind of sea, but it was the sea all the same. She let her breath carry her fluidly from one pose to the next, each one stretching her muscles and relaxing her.

There, in Downward Dog, as she tried to declutter her mind, there was one thought she couldn't shift: tomorrow she would be on a flight back to Koh Tao. Soon she'd be in Luca's arms, on the beach, taking photos underwater again – enjoying star-filled nights and golden days. Imogen smiled to herself, and focused on pushing her bum up as far towards the ceiling as it would go, ignoring her complaining hamstrings.

The ring of her mobile cut into the silence. Reluctantly

getting to her feet, she strode over to the coffee table, ready to silence the phone. She read the name on the screen with a sigh: Mum. Any chance of relaxing was already shot; just the thought of her mother made the muscles in her shoulders tense up.

She pressed the green button. 'Hi, Mum,' she said, attempting to retain some of her yogic serenity.

'Imogen, you're there. Good. Have you got a moment?'

'Sure,' Imogen said, sitting down on the sofa and bringing her legs up underneath her. 'What's up?'

'It's your dad, Imogen. I'm afraid he's in a bit of a state. He's locked himself in his studio and he's refusing to come out.'

As soon as she'd hung up the phone, Imogen left the house and went straight to the station, boarding the first train to Lewes. On the journey she thought back over the past week, the long evenings sorting through her Grandma Vivien's things – old photos and ornaments and toys from his childhood. It was Martin who'd done most of the talking, with her father conscientiously sorting and filing his mother's belongings. The emotion of being in his childhood home, surrounded by memories, must have taken its toll.

Once she reached the small town, she walked the familiar route to her parents' cottage, and up the front path. She lifted the knocker on the front door and let it fall. Her mum was there to answer it in just a few seconds.

'Thanks for coming, darling,' Jan said, ushering her in

and pulling out a chair for her at the kitchen table. 'I have to say I didn't know what else to do.'

'How long's he been in there?' Imogen asked, looking out of the window towards her father's shed in the garden.

'Since yesterday morning. He slept in there last night, and for hours now he's just been sitting on the floor. I can see him through the window, but I couldn't persuade him to come out.'

'Has he been eating anything?'

'I've been putting sandwiches through the gap under the door, but I've no idea if he's touched them.'

'Do you think it was last week that brought it on?' Imogen said. 'It can't have been easy going through all of his mother's stuff . . . but I didn't think, I mean . . . Mum,' she said, looking at her mother directly, noticing the strain in her forehead and new wrinkles around her eyes. 'Dad doesn't get like this,' she said, searching to make some kind of sense of the situation. 'He doesn't get depressed.'

'Martin and your dad were discussing what to do with Granny Vivien's house,' Jan said, in a measured tone. 'It seems Martin wants to sell it as soon as possible, and has already got an offer from a developer. He's told Dad he wants them to accept and draw a line under it all. Tom isn't against selling as such, but the developers plan to knock Vivien's house down and build a block of flats.'

'That's awful,' Imogen said. 'I mean, the two of them had to decide something, of course – but so soon after Granny's death? How could Martin agree to that?'

'Well, exactly. And it's not hard to guess who has put Martin up to it. But you know your dad and his brother – I don't think they've had an argument since they were teenagers. He's barely said a word since he spoke to Martin apart from to tell me what happened, but it's clear it's tearing him up.'

'He doesn't have to give in,' Imogen said. 'The split is fifty-fifty. Martin can't go ahead without his agreement.'

'You know your dad,' Jan said, her voice softer than usual. 'Once a hippy, always a hippy. He'll give in, to keep the peace.'

As Imogen got up from the table she noticed something she'd never seen before. Her mum looked as if she was about to cry.

'I'm going out there,' Imogen said, with determination.

'You do that, love,' her mum said. 'I'm hoping you might have more luck than me. You two have always shared something special. You're the apple of his eye, you know.'

Imogen left her mum and went out into the garden, walking towards her father's studio.

'Dad, I know you're in there,' Imogen said, through the studio wall. She waited for a moment, but there was only the sound of a distant woodpecker.

'Listen, I'm leaving the country tomorrow, so I hope you're going to talk to me.'

Imogen waited a few minutes for a reply, and when none came, she sat down with her back to the door, rays of gentle midday sun warming her face on the early April day.

In front of her, in the sprawling garden her mother

despaired of ever beating into submission, was a broad oak tree. Up in the top branches she could see the slats of wood, nailed together, and a sheet of corrugated metal for a makeshift roof. Over fifteen years ago, her dad had made that treehouse, a den that she and Anna had played games and whispered secrets in. He still hadn't taken it down.

After ten minutes of silence, Imogen reluctantly got to her feet and walked back to the kitchen, where her mum was anxiously looking on through the window. 'Do you have any Bakewell tarts, Mum?' Imogen asked. 'You know what he's like with them.'

'Good idea,' Jan said, opening the cupboard and taking out a packet. 'He'd normally have demolished these by now. But he's barely eaten a thing since the funeral.'

She passed Imogen the packet. 'Can't really put them on a plate or they won't fit under the door.'

'Thanks, Mum,' Imogen said.

Imogen walked back out into the garden with a fresh wave of optimism. Her words might not be enough to lure her dad out, but she'd never seen him resist Mr Kipling's finest.

As she approached the studio, she saw a movement, like a shadow passing. Pressing close to the murky window, she tried to make out where her dad was, somewhere hidden from view. As her eyes adjusted to the gloom, though, it wasn't her father's figure that she saw. It was the dozens of sculptures, on the workbench, on the floor. His delicate birds smashed into pieces.

*

'Anna,' Imogen said. 'Can you come and meet me? I'm round at Granny V's house.'

'You are?' she replied, sounding puzzled. 'What are you doing there? I thought you'd be at the flat, packing up your stuff.'

'I don't know,' Imogen answered honestly. How could she explain that when she got off the train from Lewes, she'd simply found herself walking here, dazed? 'Looking for some answers, I suppose . . . Just say you'll come? It's important.'

'OK,' Anna said. 'I'm just finishing up, give me ten.'

Imogen looked down at the coffee table. The photo album that Vivien had left them in her will lay open in front of her.

On the first page was a dedication, handwritten in black ink:

To my beautiful granddaughters, Imogen and Anna. A little history for you, of this very special business. May you enjoy the ice cream shop as much as I have, all these years.
Your loving Granny V x

Imogen turned the page slowly. There, tacked in with photo corners, was a black-and-white image of the shop, with a note next to it – '24 July 1953. Opening Day!'

In front of the shiny shop, Vivien and her husband Stanley were standing proudly. Vivien was wearing a full-skirted dress with poodles printed on it, her hair styled in loose, wide curls that fell to her shoulders. Stanley had his arm around her, his hair brown rather than the grey that Imogen remembered, and he had on dark-framed glasses. Stanley's other arm was draped affectionately around his youngest son Martin's shoulders, as Vivien's was around Tom's. The two young boys, in shorts and smart shoes, looked excited and eager.

Dad already risks losing one childhood home, Imogen thought to herself. *Could they really take Sunset 99s from him too?*

She continued to look through the history of her grandmother's shop. At the back of the album was a much newer photo, printed out in colour and almost filling the page. Vivien was at the centre of it, smiling, her hair pinned up, wearing a navy dress with cream detailing. Surrounding her were her family: her two sons, Jan, and Imogen and Anna. It was before Martin met Françoise, and back when they'd all thought of him as the eternal bachelor. Imogen peered at the image more closely judging by her heavy eye make-up and faded band T-shirt, she must have been about sixteen when it was taken.

Her dad looked so different in the photo, heading up his family – the strongest of all of them. Imogen was pretty sure that was the summer that her English teacher, Miss Carter, had finally diagnosed her dyslexia, after Imogen unexpectedly came bottom of the class in her mocks. Years of difficulty keeping up in English and writing essays started to make sense to Imogen and her family at last. But her dad had been there all along – each time she'd come home in tears after being made to feel stupid, or lazy, by her teachers. He knew, like her, that it would take more than a diagnosis to undo all of that damage. Tom had gone straight into school, thanked Miss Carter personally, and then demanded to see the headmaster to find out what had gone wrong, and to demand better special-needs provision in the future. Imogen had been outwardly embarrassed, but was secretly proud that her dad would do that for her.

Imogen thought back to the broken sculptures she'd seen in her father's studio that afternoon. It was hard to connect the father who'd hidden, holding back from talking to her, with the open, dignified man she was looking at now. When she flew back to Thailand tomorrow, what would be the next thing she'd hear? Maybe her dad would be back to his usual self in a couple of days, but what if . . . ? She couldn't bear the idea of hearing he had got worse when she was so far away.

Her mind had been fixed on the island – on the sun, yes, and Luca – but above all, on getting back to the photography project she was putting together. She wanted it to be good, she wanted to exhibit it, and the one person, above everyone else, who she wanted to see it, was her dad. He'd nurtured her ambition from the start, bought her her first camera, helped her set up a darkroom. She wanted him to see that his efforts hadn't gone to waste, for him to be proud of her.

But being on the other side of the world wasn't going to help him now, she realised, with a stab of guilt. What he needed was support from those who loved him in order to get better. To see that his family were there for him and that they'd all work together to keep Vivien's memory alive.

Imogen thought of the promises she'd made to Luca. Everything was set for her to leave England the next day, if she wanted.

But her dad had put her and Anna first since the day they were born. How could she leave now, when he needed her?

The doorbell rang, breaking into her thoughts. She saw Anna's tall frame through the stained-glass window and opened the door. 'Come in,' she said, leading her into the living room.

'What's with all the urgency?' Anna asked, settling into the armchair.

'I can't do it,' Imogen announced.

'Do what?' Anna said, putting her bag down on the floor and rubbing her temples. 'Today's been a nightmare at work, Imo. I can't process riddles.'

'I can't go back to Thailand right now, and we can't sell the shop,' Imogen said, still standing, energised by her decision. 'Definitely not to Françoise. But perhaps not to anyone.'

'Right,' Anna said slowly. 'Are you OK, Imo? You seem a bit wound up.'

'How could we break Dad's heart all over again?' Imogen said, starting to pace up and down the dark wooden floorboards. 'He needs us.'

'Dad's heart . . . ' Anna put a hand to her brow. 'What are

you talking about? And do you think you could sit down while we talk about this? You're making me feel dizzy.'

'Sorry,' Imogen said, and took a seat on the sofa, perched on the edge. 'It's just . . . I saw Dad today, Anna. Well, I didn't exactly see him. He's a mess. He wouldn't talk to me, and I saw in his studio that he'd smashed up some of his sculptures.'

'God, really?' Anna said, sitting up, her eyes wide. 'That's not like Dad at all. What on earth's going on?'

'It sounds like Françoise is pressuring Martin to sell this place,' Imogen said, gesturing to the walls of the house that had been their father's childhood home. 'Which is understandable, of course, with the inheritance tax and everything – but they want it to go to developers who are going to knock it down, and they've barely waited a week to tell Dad that.'

'That woman . . . ' Anna said, shaking her head. 'I know she's supposed to be family, but she's never really acted like it. Martin would never be doing this if he was single.'

'Well, we can't change any of that. But what we can change is *this*.' She picked the photo album up off the coffee table and turned back to the photo of Sunset 99s on opening day.

'Look at this, Anna,' Imogen said. 'It's Sunset 99s through the ages. Here's a photo from the sixties, that's Dad's motorbike parked up outside – check out his hair! And that sign they had was cool, wasn't it, with the orange and pink lettering?'

Anna smiled. 'This is lovely. But I don't get how—'

'The shop was his second home, back then,' Imogen

explained. 'You know how he's always talked about it. We can't let the final piece of Granny V's legacy disappear. Not without even trying.'

'Are you thinking what I think you are?' Anna said, hesitantly.

'Imagine if we could bring it back to the glory days,' Imogen said, brightening. 'For Dad. For Granny V.'

Anna paused for a moment. 'I don't know,' she said. 'This is all quite sudden. It's a lot to take on.'

'What was that quote Granny would always come out with?' Imogen said. 'From *Alice in Wonderland*. "Why, sometimes I've believed as many as six impossible things before breakfast." Anna, I've changed my mind, it's time for us to believe some impossible things. I think we should give it a shot.'

'After the day I've had, this all sounds very appealing,' Anna said, starting to smile. 'I suppose we really could do it, couldn't we?'

Imogen nodded. 'Why not?'

They sat there in silence for a minute as the decision they'd just made together began to sink in.

'But . . . ' Anna started, 'I thought you wanted to go back to the island?'

'I do,' Imogen said. 'I really do. But it doesn't feel right to go back now, when Dad's like this. I could stay long enough to help you get the place set up, and for us to pick a good assistant to replace me.'

'And then you'd go back?'

'Yes. My flight's valid for another six months, I just have to pay a bit to change the date.'

'And what about that guy you met, Luca?'

Imogen touched the shark's-tooth necklace around her neck, remembering him.

'I'll tell him,' she said. 'I don't know how he'll react. But I feel like I need to put our family first right now.'

Imogen called Luca's mobile and heard the foreign dialling tone. Her heart beat hard in her chest as she waited for him to pick up.

'Imo,' he answered, sounding drowsy.

She checked the time on Vivien's grandfather clock. Damn, it must be the middle of the night over there, she'd completely forgotten about the time difference.

'Hi, Luca,' she said.

'You're nearly home,' he murmured sleepily.

The words she wanted to say caught in her throat.

'Everything's ready – the guys at Komodo have reserved an area for us on Thursday night for the party, and I've invited Santiana, Davy and all of your dive friends along.'

'Thank you,' Imogen said, the guilt of what she had to say weighing heavily on her. 'But actually that's the reason I was ringing. I know I was going to be flying home tomorrow, but it turns out I can't come back right now.'

'You're kidding,' Luca said, suddenly alert.

'I need to sort some family stuff out. It's important.'

'And I'm . . . I'm what, Imogen? God, I knew you'd do something like this. How long are we talking?'

'I don't expect you to wait . . . '

'How long?'

'Four months, maybe five,' she said. 'I'd be back by September, definitely.'

'September. Are you serious?'

'You could always . . . come here and visit. If you wanted,' Imogen said, realising as she spoke how unlikely it was.

'Right,' Luca said, and Imogen heard the hurt in his voice. 'Listen, I need to think about all this. I don't know what to believe from you right now.'

Chapter Six

'Here you go,' Jon said the following Friday, passing Anna some tea in her favourite Orla Kiely-print mug. She pulled her duvet-covered legs up towards her and cradled it in her hands, taking a sip.

'Thank you,' she said. 'I need a bit of perking up to be ready for today.'

Jon sat down next to her on the bed, doing up the buttons on his white shirt.

'You're really serious about this, aren't you?' he said, his green eyes meeting hers. 'It's all happened so quickly. Monday night is the first I hear of it, and I've barely seen you since then, with you and Imogen beavering away on that business plan every evening.'

'Tell me about it,' Anna said. 'I'm not sure if the whole thing is a crazy pipe dream or a real-life possibility for us to run our own business. All I know is we need to find out.'

Her head still felt fuzzy from the late night; she and Imogen had been up until three a.m. finalising details.

'Today should give us more of an idea,' she said. 'The small business advisor was really helpful when we saw her on Wednesday, and now that we've got more to show her, she should be able to help us firm things up.'

'Well, good luck with it,' Jon said, kissing her on the nose. 'It's nice to see you so passionate about something, even if I can't quite understand why you'd give up the security you have in your job. But it sounds like you have to see this through.'

'There's no risk – at least not yet,' Anna reassured him. 'If the figures don't add up, then I still have my job to go back to. I haven't said a word to anyone in the office yet – I told my boss I was taking today off to do some DIY.'

'That's good. Leaves your options open. What do your parents think about it all?'

'They're excited. Apparently it's making a difference to Dad. Mum said it was the news about us looking into running the place that got him to open the door to her.'

'You don't think maybe he's getting his hopes up for nothing?' Jon said, fiddling with the knot in his tie. 'I don't mean to be negative, but it sounds like he's quite fragile at the moment.'

'He knows it's only early days. But the main thing is, Dad's showing some signs of improvement, even if he's refusing to see the GP. It's still a real worry though. He's never been like this before, and as much as Mum loves him, she isn't always the most approachable about emotional stuff.'

'It must be really hard,' Jon said, 'whatever age you are. I can't imagine losing a parent you're so close to.'

'I know,' Anna said. 'Imogen and I do our fair share of moaning about Mum, but we'd be lost without her. She's always been there in our lives, a steady presence. Maddening sometimes, but steady.'

'That's important,' Jon said. Anna sensed he was distracted, and, looking at her alarm clock, saw that it was time for him to leave for work. He picked up his briefcase. 'Hope it goes really well today,' he said, leaning in to kiss her. 'Let me know.'

'Thanks, I will.' Anna smiled, got up and pulled on her dressing gown. 'Now I need to wake up my potential business partner.'

As Jon left the flat, she rapped on the spare-room door.

'Imo,' Anna said, opening the door gently and peering in. 'We need to leave in half an hour.'

Imogen groaned gently and then opened her eyes. 'Is it morning already? I swear we only just went to bed.'

'Afraid so. It's eight,' Anna said. 'And we're meeting the small business advisor at nine, so you need to get your skates on. You can wear something of mine, if you like,' she went on. 'I'm planning on wearing that trouser suit – the black one. We should probably be smart to make a good impression.'

Imogen wrinkled her nose.

'Come on,' Anna said. 'It's only one meeting – and just imagine, if we get this off the ground you'll be able to wear jeans to work every day.'

Imogen pulled back the duvet. 'OK, I'm sold. And the business plan?'

'It's on my iPad, but I also printed it out so we can leave a copy with her.'

'I feel a bit nervous,' Imogen said, perched on the edge of the bed in her pyjamas.

'Me too,' Anna said. Her stomach was so fluttery she'd barely been able to drink her tea. 'But maybe that's a good thing.'

After the meeting at the building society, Anna and Imogen stepped out into the street, blinking as their eyes readjusted to the morning sunshine.

'Coffee?' Anna said.

'Definitely,' Imogen said, pointing to a nearby café. 'I need a minute to digest it all.'

'She seemed positive, didn't she?'

'I thought so,' Imogen said, pushing open the café door.

'We did make it sound pretty amazing. "A gourmet ice cream shop, with delectable flavours and retro styling."'

'We let our imaginations run quite wild in that pitch, didn't we?'

'A little,' Anna replied, looking up at the menu board over the counter. 'But from what she said, we can make it all happen. It sounds as if the money from Granny V should be enough to help us set up and run the shop for the next three months, at least. So we've got a while to hone our skills, build a customer base, and get the hygiene and health and safety stuff sorted. That seems doable, doesn't it?'

'Yes, I think. I need some caffeine first.'

'What are you having?'

'A cappuccino for me, please.'

'One cappuccino and one iced coffee, please,' Anna ordered from the guy at the counter. 'Shall we take these up to the roof terrace, Imo? The weather's beautiful today. Feels like spring's finally arriving.'

'Yes, let's.'

They climbed the stairs with coffees in hand and stepped out onto the decked terrace. There was a view out over the whole of Brighton from the Pavilion to the pier, rows of white Georgian houses forming a maze of streets between the two.

'Sometimes I think there's no better place to live,' Anna said, looking out. 'And imagine, we could be getting up each morning with our very own ice cream shop to run.'

'Sounds pretty good, when you put it that way.'

'I know,' Anna said. 'I can't remember the last time I felt this excited about anything. I'm going to do it. I'm going to hand my notice in on Monday.'

'Really?'

'Yes. There's no time like the present, is there? Maybe this is an insane idea, but I want to give it a chance – and to be honest, I can't face another seven years working in that office.'

'How do you think your boss will take it?'

Anna mulled it over. 'I don't know. A colleague of mine left recently and they let him off most of his notice period. I'm hoping they'll do the same with me – there are so many unemployed graduates here it wouldn't take them long to find someone to fill my shoes. Anyway, that's their problem.'

'I'm proud of you,' Imogen said.

'I think I'm a bit proud of me too,' Anna laughed. 'I never do things like this.'

'So where do we start?'

'I know it's not exactly what we put in our business plan, but how about a soft launch while we train up?' Anna said. 'At the start, for the first few weeks, we could run the shop as a kind of retro ice cream shack, with ready-made products. So people get to know the place, and us, and we can slowly introduce our gelati range.'

'Retro ice creams,' Imogen said. 'Like Fab lollies?'

'Exactly. And those giant pink feet, Screwballs – do you remember the ones that had chewing gum in the bottom? Students would be into all that, and well, everyone loves a nostalgia fix. Parents would be able to share the ice creams they loved with their own kids.'

Imogen mulled it over. 'I like it,' she said with a smile. 'Giving people an edible snapshot of their childhood.'

'Great. We can look into suppliers this evening, I'm sure someone must still be making those things, and we could get them cheap if we bought in bulk.'

'It'll be a nice simple way to draw attention to the shop and get things started,' Imogen said, nodding. 'And it'll give us a bit of time to focus on making the place over. Talking of that, before we do anything else, there's one thing we still need to discuss. One very important thing.'

'Oh yes?' Anna replied.

'I think we need a new name, for this new era, don't you?'

'I guess so. But we don't want to erase Sunset 99s completely, do we? Granny V will always be part of the shop.'

'Exactly. So why don't we name the shop after her?'

'Vivien's?' Anna said, sounding it out. 'I like it. But will people know what to expect?'

'Vivien's Ice Cream Shop?' Imogen said. 'No, something's missing.' She glanced around the terrace for inspiration, then looked up at the expanse of blue sky above them. 'Without wanting to sound mega-Godly, don't you sometimes feel like Granny V's looking over us?'

'Yes,' Anna said. 'That's partly why I'm so nervous about messing this up,' she laughed.

'Well, how about "Vivien's *Heavenly* Ice Cream Shop?"'

'I love it,' Anna said. 'Just perfect.'

Just over a week later, on a Saturday, Anna and Imogen got prepared to make over the shop, with Hepburn in tow. Laden down with tins of white, pink and pistachio paint from the local hardware shop, they walked down to Vivien's, ready for a day of interior decorating. Anna's boss had taken the news that Monday surprisingly well, and had agreed to reduce her notice period on the condition that she finish some of her projects for them as a freelancer. So, for now, she was free to focus on the ice cream shop.

Motown hits blasted out of the small radio as Anna scrubbed

the kitchen area of the shop clean, dressed in overalls and rubber gloves.

'Love don't come easy . . . it's a game of give and take . . .' Vivien's radio was still tuned into a local station, Golden Oldies FM, playing hits from the 1960s and 1970s on loop. They'd decided not to change it. Hearing the tunes brought back a little flash of their grandma, cheerfully humming girl-group hits to herself. Hepburn looked on from the comfort of one of the booths.

Imogen had brought Vivien's photo album down and she held it up to show her sister. 'For inspiration,' she said. 'These photos from when Granny V and Grandpa Stanley launched the shop in the fifties are perfect. We can use the original fittings we already have – and the rest we should be able to replicate easily enough.'

Anna got to her feet, sponge in hand. 'She was always so glamorous, wasn't she?' she said, looking at a photo of Vivien standing behind the counter at Sunset 99s. 'Her hair styled so beautifully, those handsewn dresses.'

'I can barely be bothered to blow-dry my hair most days,' Imogen said. 'But she made it look effortless.'

'Day after day, even though she was working here six days a week.'

'Amazing,' Imogen said. 'I hope that between us we can manage it as well as she did alone. She had real dedication.'

'When Grandpa Stanley died, she opened the shop the next day. Do you remember? We were only kids but I still recall Dad talking to her about it, trying to persuade her to take some time off. But she insisted that running the shop was the only thing that would keep her going.'

The glass front door creaked open, interrupting them.

They turned to see a woman in her late forties wearing a duffel coat, greying hair held in a tight, high ponytail. Anna recognised her face, but couldn't place her.

'Hello,' the woman said. 'Hope you don't mind me dropping by, but I saw the two of you working in here. You must be Vivien's granddaughters. I heard a rumour you might be taking this place over.'

She came further into the shop and held out her hand to shake Anna's. 'I'm Sue,' she said. Anna held up her yellow-rubber gloved hand and smiled apologetically. 'Hi, Sue. I'm Anna, and this is my sister Imogen.'

'Hi,' Imogen said, her tone a little cooler. 'We're giving this place a spring clean. Turned out it really needed it.'

Sue frowned, and as Anna detected the change in atmosphere she tried to lighten it. 'Our grandma told me about you, said she was grateful you were helping out. Do you live locally?'

'Just up in Hove, not far from your grandmother's house. Been coming here since I was a nipper, so it was a dream come true when Vivien offered me the job. She needed the help, she said. It was getting too much for her.'

Anna nodded. 'I only wish she'd realised that a bit earlier.'

'Yes. We were really sad to hear the news,' she said. They all fell quiet for a moment.

'I expect you two will need a hand?' Sue said. 'I could show you how your grandmother and I used to run things.'

Anna hesitated. 'Well, yes, we might. Thanks for coming by Sue. Do you want to leave your number and we'll get in touch once we're a bit closer to opening?'

'Number's in the address book,' Sue said with a smile, pointing to the black book on the counter. 'But I walk past here most days, so I'll come by again, see how you're doing.'

'We'll be in touch,' Imogen said.

Sue turned and left the shop.

'Anna,' Imogen said, rolling her eyes, 'you're too nice. You'll never make a decent businesswoman at this rate.'

'Granny V said Sue had had a tough time of things lately,' Anna said.

'Sorry to hear that, but we're not a charity, Anna. We've got the chance of a new start here. And if we re-employ that woman, I can tell you now that we'll blow it.'

'Granny must have had some reason for hiring her,' Anna said, trying to give Sue the benefit of the doubt.

'Yes, she was an endless supporter of the underdog. We all know that. Anyway,' Imogen said, changing the subject. 'This doesn't look so bad up close,' she continued, pointing to the chequerboard tile floor. 'It should scrub up quite nicely.'

'I agree,' Anna said. 'It looks original, and I'm not sure we'd be able to afford new flooring anyway, not with all the paint we've just bought. I'll get the mop out.'

She filled a bucket with hot water and poured in some floor soap. Hepburn darted around her feet and she bent down to tickle him behind the ear. 'I'm getting quite fond of him, you know.'

'He's not so bad,' Imogen conceded. 'For a dog.'

Anna dipped a mop in the soapy water and got to work cleaning the floor. Hepburn jumped on the mop and chased her, barking, as she swirled it around on the tiles, the bright white underneath the grime beginning to shine through. 'I think he belongs here. He makes it feel like home.'

'Well, all the same, I think we'd be better off keeping him out of the kitchen when we have the hygiene inspectors in.'

'What do you think?' Imogen called out from the rickety wooden ladder she was standing on. They'd been working for three hours, and she was painting a band of pistachio trim around the top of the white walls. 'I saw it on one of those home decorating programmes.'

'I like it,' Anna said, putting an old lightbulb down on the counter. With the new, brighter lights she'd installed, the place was starting to look a lot more cheerful. 'Time for a tea break?'

Imogen nodded. Anna brought out a packet of custard creams from her bag and put the kettle on.

'I ordered three ice cream makers online this morning,' she said. 'They're fairly basic, but should be good enough for us to get started with.'

'Great,' Imogen said, rummaging through one of the

cupboards until she located a box of tea bags. 'No clue what we're going to do with them, but that's part of the fun, right?'

'Exactly. They're being delivered early next week, so it won't be long before we can get started experimenting.'

Anna got some mugs out of the cupboard, then paused. 'Do you think we should ask one of the neighbours to join us? I've met Evie before, and she's really nice.'

'Sure, why not?'

'OK, I'll be back in a minute.'

Anna left Vivien's and walked out into the fresh air and around to Evie's souvenir shop.

She stepped inside and and spotted her grandmother's friend beyond the shelves full of buckets, spades and inflatables. 'Hello,' she called out. Evie was about the same age as Vivien, in her seventies, but in place of Vivien's full-skirted dresses and trademark apron, she had on a pair of jeans and a fitted gingham shirt, her candyfloss-pink hair up in a loose bun. She didn't seem to register who Anna was.

'It's Evie, isn't it?' Anna said, venturing past the inflatable fish and walking towards the counter. 'I'm Anna, Vivien's granddaughter. My sister and I have just taken over the ice cream shop.'

'Anna. Oh, of course. Hello,' Evie said with a smile. 'I remember you now. Vivien told me she'd always hoped you two would be able to take over from her one day. Although we all wish it hadn't been so soon.'

'Yes,' Anna said softly.

'Would have come to the funeral, only . . . ' she drifted off for a moment. 'Well, there's an awful lot to think about, with the shop.'

'Do you have time for a cuppa?' Anna said. 'We've got biscuits.'

Evie smiled. 'You read my mind. I'll put the sign up, but when I'm not here most of my customers know that the ice cream shop's where they'll find me.'

Anna smiled. 'Great. You can meet my sister too.'

The two of them walked back to the shop together, and Anna opened the door to let Evie through first.

'Well,' Evie exclaimed as she looked around the shop. 'This is looking a good deal better, isn't it?'

'It was a total mess when we arrived,' Imogen said, stepping out from behind the counter. 'Sorry – hi, I'm Imogen, by the way.'

'Evie,' she said, shaking Imogen's hand. 'Pleasure to meet you. I have to say I did wonder if your grandmother made the right decision employing Sue, but you know how she liked to see the best in people. I barely saw Sue do a stroke of work when she was here.'

'That's the impression we got,' Imogen said, giving her sister an *I told you so* look.

'You know how your grandma was; she never stopped. But since Sue took over from her, nothing seemed to get done – she was busy all right, but with the crossword, Sudoku, on the phone . . .'

'Milk and sugar?' Anna asked.

'Both, please,' Evie said. 'Oh, custard creams,' she said, reaching for one. 'My favourite.'

'Evie,' Imogen said, looking at her inquisitively. 'Funny question, I know, but were you ever in a three-legged race?'

Evie smiled. 'Yes, I was once. Why do you ask?'

Imogen got Vivien's photo album from the counter, and brought it over. 'I found this newspaper cutting in the album Granny left us.' She searched through and opened it at the right page. 'It's from 1989. "Charity Event – Local Business Owners Win Three-legged Beach Race",' she read.

'That was a hoot,' Evie said, glancing over to look at the picture of her and Vivien smiling, arms round each other, proudly displaying their medals. 'We had some fun, me and your grandmother. It's terribly quiet without her. We used to go swimming every morning, before opening up. Did she ever tell you that?'

'Oh yes,' Anna said. 'She loved that. No idea how you did it – it must be freezing out there.'

'Tough old birds,' Evie said. 'I still go out there on my own.'

'Well, I'm impressed,' Anna said.

'It's good to have some neighbours again,' Evie said. 'I look forward to seeing this place get back to how it was.'

'We're going to do our very best,' Imogen assured her.

That evening, Anna emerged from her shower all cleaned up after the day's work. It had taken ages to wash the grime from the shop off her arms and face, and out from under her fingernails.

'Come here,' Imogen said. 'You've still got flecks of paint in your hair.' She yanked at a paint-covered strand and Anna gave a yelp of protest.

'Leave it,' Anna said, 'and get some wine out for us instead. I think we've earned it.'

'I couldn't agree more,' Imogen said, choosing a bottle of Anna's finest Malbec from the wine rack and opening it.

If there was ever a night to open an expensive bottle, Anna thought, it was now, after their first full day of work getting the shop ready. Imogen poured them generous glasses and passed one to Anna.

'I know we've only just got started, but when do you think we'll be ready to launch?' Imogen asked.

Anna glanced over at the calendar. 'How about the first Saturday in May? That would give us nearly three weeks. We could get Mum and Dad down, show the place off.'

'Great,' Imogen said. 'I'm so excited that Dad's going to see it.'

'Have you heard anything more?' Anna said.

'Up and down, Mum says. He's very withdrawn still, and doesn't want to talk about Granny at all.'

'What about his friends? Has anyone else been round to see him?'

'He doesn't want visitors, apparently. But I'm sure a trip down here would do him good. Mum says he's been enjoying hearing our updates.'

'Great. I think our launch will be just the thing to pull him out of this slump.'

On Monday morning Anna jumped at the sound of Jon's alarm clock, mentally preparing herself to get up for work as usual. Then a wave of relief and excitement washed over her. *She didn't have to go to the office!*

'Your new life starts today,' Jon said, giving her a gentle kiss on her bare shoulder.

'I never thought I'd say this about work,' Anna said, rubbing the sleep from her eyes. 'But you know what? I can't wait to get started.'

Jon smiled and slowly got to his feet. 'Good luck, sweetheart,' he said, grabbing a towel.

She heard the hot water go on and got up, walking into the kitchen and making coffee for herself and Imogen. She opened the spare-room door, and passed a dozy Imogen a large turquoise mug . 'Here you go. Are you ready to get started?'

'I was diving again,' Imogen said contentedly, rubbing her eyes. 'With clown fish and manta rays. All these colours.'

'OK, dreamer,' Anna said, 'no time for that today. There's still more clearing up to do at the shop.'

Imogen slowly sat up in bed, and Anna showed her the To Do list she'd drafted.

'Oh, and I did some online research after you went to bed,' she continued. 'I found us some good suppliers for the retro lollies, and another one for soft drinks. With any luck we should have enough stock to open at the start of May, like we agreed, provided we have the décor all done by then.'

'God, there's a lot to do, isn't there?' Imogen said, casting an eye over the list.

'We did say we were up for a challenge.'

'I know, I know,' Imogen said. 'Ah. You forgot one thing. We're going to have to call Sue and tell her we're letting her go.'

'Ouch,' Anna said. 'You're right. I'm really not looking forward to that.'

'I know, me neither. But by all accounts she's a liability – and we can't afford staff anyway. We'll just be honest with her,' Imogen said, wrinkling her nose. 'It'll be fine.'

By midday, the freezers and cupboards were clean and clear and the sisters agreed that the shop was looking much fresher.

Anna and Imogen looked back at their To Do list, where 'Call Sue' was the next unchecked item.

'Toss a coin for it?' Anna said, with a feeling of dread.

'I think it might be a bit late for that,' Imogen said, nodding over at the door, which Sue was pushing open.

'Sue,' Anna said, letting her breath out slowly. 'Hi. Kind of you to drop by again.'

'Well, I hadn't heard from you, so I thought I should,' she said, sounding a little irritated.

'The thing is . . . ' Anna said. Her courage ebbed away.

'I'm sorry, Sue,' Imogen said, more confidently. 'But I'm afraid we're not going to be able to re-employ you. I know you were a big help to our grandma, but there are two of us now so we're planning on running the shop ourselves.'

'You're sacking me?' Sue choked out, shocked.

'Well, not exactly,' Anna said. 'But we won't be able to offer you a job at Vivien's under our management, I'm afraid. We'll ensure you get a month of paid leave in lieu of notice, of course.'

'Your grandma would be horrified,' Sue said.

Anna struggled to find words to reply.

'Well, good luck to you,' Sue said. 'You're going to need it.' With that, she turned on her heel and left the shop.

As the door slammed shut, Anna turned to her sister, holding in nervous laughter. 'Wow, that went well.'

Imogen started to laugh, and Anna caught the giggles from her.

'Oh dear,' Anna said, steadying herself on the counter. 'That was awful.'

'*She* was awful,' Imogen said. 'Better that we did it now rather than later.'

'I suppose so,' Anna conceded.

'A fresh start,' Imogen said.

'I still feel bad.'

'Don't. And I'm officially changing the subject. I've found this fantastic local sign makers who do fifties custom lettering that is just right for our new sign. Look, I'll show you.' She went over to the netbook and showed her sister the company's webpage.

Anna looked at the beautiful vintage lettering and in an

instant knew that it was perfect for the shop. 'It's stunning,' she said, clicking through the image gallery and onto the prices page. 'Not cheap though, are they?' she said more cautiously.

She glanced over at the accounts book, but decided not to open it. They had the money from their grandma to get started with, and an eye-catching sign was essential if they were going to rebrand effectively. 'Let's order it.'

'And here's for stage two of the McAvoy Sisters' Grand Ice Cream Project,' Imogen said later that week, back at Anna's flat in the afternoon.

'Equipment, READY,' Anna said, getting the ice cream makers out of their boxes, and then pulling out a thermometer.

Imogen looked at it suspiciously. 'What on earth is that thing for?' she asked.

'I read something about how it's safer to use them,' Anna said, holding it up to the light. 'So I bought one along with the makers.'

'Do you think we might need more than one session to master all of this?'

'We'll be fine,' Anna said confidently, excited about the cooking ahead. 'You'll see.'

They worked together through the afternoon and evening, mixing, heating and stirring, losing all track of time as they focused on their ice cream creations. They'd just finished a batch of blueberry when they heard Jon's key in the front door.

'Wow,' Jon said, as he walked into the kitchen and saw the mess that Anna and Imogen had made in the kitchen. Mixing bowls covered every surface, and there were ice cream splatters on the wall from where they'd overfilled the maker on their first try. 'What on earth . . . ?'

'We've been experimenting,' Imo piped up, offering him a bowl of one of their finished creations. 'This one is blueberry.'

'Very nice,' Jon said, with a nod, then turned to flick the kettle on and get his regular mug out of the cupboard. 'Anyone want a cuppa?' he asked.

'We just had one, thanks. But seriously, Jon, try some,' Imogen said, passing him a silver spoon with blueberry ice on it.

Anna shook her head, and motioned for Imogen to put the spoon back. 'He's not our ideal ice cream tester.'

'Afraid I'm lactose intolerant,' Jon said, adding a dash of soy milk to his mug of PG Tips. 'And even if I wasn't, I'm trying to stay healthy. Sorry. It looks delicious though.'

'Fair enough,' Imogen said. She turned to Anna with a smile. 'More for us, then.'

Jon took his tea through into the front room, and Imogen decanted the first of their ice cream creations – a rich vanilla – into a Tupperware freezable tub. 'Not bad, for a first attempt.'

'I think we achieved a lot today,' Anna replied. She ran the hot tap until the sink was full of warm water and washing-up bubbles.

As she rinsed the whisk under the tap, it really started to sink in. They were doing, or at least were going to be doing, the thing she had always dreamed of – making a living through selling culinary creations, making money, yes, but hopefully making people happy along the way too.

'Is Jon OK?' Imogen whispered to her sister, once he'd left the room.

'Oh, he's fine,' Anna said. 'He likes a bit of space sometimes, that's all.'

'It's me, isn't it? I said I was only going to stay a couple of nights and I'm still here cramping your style two and a half weeks later. Well, don't you worry,' Imogen said. 'I've got the keys to Granny V's house. Mum suggested I move in there for a while actually, keep an eye on the place. She thinks she's managed to stall Françoise and Martin on selling it to the developers, but she's still not sure what they're capable of.'

'Are you sure? You're welcome to stay here, you know. Don't mind Jon, really. You're family.'

'It's fine,' Imogen said. 'Honestly. You've been so generous already, and the house is only round the corner. I'll move next weekend.'

'Alfie,' Anna said. A week had passed, and the sisters were at Anna's flat on the night before their shop launch. 'Can you come and help us with something? Me and Imogen are doing some colouring.'

Alfie scooted out of his bedroom and followed Anna into

the living room of her flat. The floor was covered with newspaper and laid out in the middle was a large banner that Imogen had just finished the lettering on. It read: OPENING DAY!

'Let's get you an apron,' Anna said, returning in a moment with a child-sized one. 'We've got paints and crayons. Do you think you can help us?'

'Yes!' Alfie said, excitedly kneeling down and choosing a bright red crayon as Imogen did up his apron straps. 'Alfie's making letter A red.' He scribbled over the outline, pressing hard with the crayon.

'Bagsy blue,' Imogen said, picking up another crayon and joining him on her hands and knees colouring in another letter.

'Is this for Ice Cream?' Alfie asked Anna, tilting his head towards her as she crouched down.

'It's for the shop, yes,' Anna said, with a smile in Imogen's direction. 'We open tomorrow.'

Jon came in through the door, attracted by the noise. 'What's going on in here, and can I join in?'

'Here, Daddy,' Alfie said, passing him a paintbrush.

'More the merrier,' Anna smiled. 'This banner's going to go out the front,' she said. 'Pretty hard to miss, don't you think?'

'It looks terrific,' Jon said. 'Very striking. And you got all the flyers handed out OK?'

'Yes,' Imogen said. 'We've been doing an hour here and there all week, so we should have a good turnout.'

'I'm sorry Alfie and I will miss it,' Jon said, looking disappointed. 'But we've had this date booked in with Mum and Dad for weeks.'

'Don't worry, I totally understand,' Anna said. 'And to be honest we'll probably be rushed off our feet.' She turned to Alfie. 'You're going to the safari park tomorrow with Grandma and Grandpa, aren't you?'

He stood up to his full height and roared. 'Liyons,' he said triumphantly.

'Sounds like we've all got an exciting weekend ahead,' Imogen said, moving on to a new letter. 'I can't wait to see everyone's faces when they see the shop.'

'We're really doing it, aren't we?' Anna smiled at her sister.

'Oh yes,' Imogen said, laughing. 'Nothing's going to stop us now.'

Chapter Seven

The first weekend in May had come at last, and everything was set for the launch. Everything, that is, Imogen thought to herself, as she stared through her sister's rain-lashed window, loud thunderclaps ringing out in the sky overhead – except the weather.

'Oh God, Anna,' Imogen said, nose almost pressed to the glass. 'How are we meant to sell ice creams in this?'

She checked the Met Office website on her phone. They were predicting some of the most powerful thunderstorms ever to hit the south coast, and from the look of things the storms had already arrived.

Imogen had heard the rain during the night, and it had got steadily heavier through the early hours. Unable to sleep, she'd tossed and turned, praying that their launch day wouldn't turn into a washout.

'Get your boots on, Imogen,' Anna said, 'because there's no way we're backing out now. We've publicised the launch everywhere and we can't change our minds just because of a bit of rain out there.'

'A bit of rain?' Imogen countered. 'It's hardly that, sis. It looks like a typhoon. Noah's probably herding the animals on as we speak.'

'You've been out of Britain far too long, Imogen,' Anna said. 'What you need is a good dose of Blitz spirit. It'll all be over in an hour or so. Grab some of my wellies from the hall cupboard and let's get going.'

They made their way down to the seafront, dressed in bright yellow macs, trying desperately to keep hold of their umbrellas. They hurriedly hung the handmade banner up, knowing that it would be a soggy mess in minutes. Windblown wet flyers were stuck to the ground. Once inside the shop, they put the shop lights on, turned up the radiators, and walked back to the shop's glass front to look out.

'Are you sure this rain is going to stop?' Imogen said mournfully. The sheets of rain were almost horizontal, deterring all but the hardiest stroller from the beach and seafront.

The phone rang and they both jumped in surprise. 'I'll get it,' Anna said.

'Oh, OK, Mum. See you in half an hour.' She put the phone back in the cradle. 'Mum's on her way. Dad's not feeling up to the trip.'

Imogen felt a stab of disappointment. But, she thought, maybe it was better that their dad didn't see the place empty like this. It was increasingly apparent that the only people who had ventured down to the seashore – in waterproof trousers and anoraks, dutifully taking their dogs for walks – weren't in the market for Fab ice lollies.

'Do you think we should just close up?' Imogen said, glancing at the stacks of Calippos in their freezers.

'Of course not,' Anna said. 'It's early still, and I'm sure I saw a patch of blue sky out there. You'd be surprised how quickly the weather can turn around on a day like this.'

'You promise?' Imogen said, squinting into the distance, and trying to fight her doubts. The clouds were heavy and grey, and a bolt of lightning briefly lit up the sky.

'Oh, girls,' Jan said, coming through the door to the café and turning to shake off her sodden umbrella outside, before she put it down. 'Awful luck you've had with the weather.'

Imogen looked at her sister. 'Really?' she whispered sarcastically. 'We'd hardly noticed.'

Anna hastily mouthed a warning: 'Be nice.'

'Thanks for coming down, Mum,' Anna said, walking over and taking Jan's wet coat from her. 'I'll hang this on the radiator. Imogen, can you put the kettle on?'

'Hi, Mum,' Imogen said dutifully, getting some mugs out. 'So what do you think?' she said, putting her arms out to show off the new shop décor.

'Very nice,' Jan said, giving her daughter a hug. 'You've done a lovely little job. Given the time and money you had, I mean.'

Anna reappeared. 'Let's sit down,' she said. 'It's not like we're exactly overwhelmed with customers, as you can see.'

'Such a shame,' Jan said. 'I mean, you should have let me know. We could have done something at the agency, put a

... what do you say –' she glanced up and to the left, searching her mind for the words – 'We could have put a shout out on Twitter for it,' she said. 'We've got an account now. "At" something, it's called. That's our handle. The work-experience girl set it up.' Jan smiled proudly.

'We did some publicity,' Imogen said, thinking back to the hours she and Anna had spent both online and standing in the street chatting to shoppers and promoting the shop.

'Well,' Jan said, 'that's good. But there's no harm in asking the professionals, that's all I'm saying. Especially when they're family – bargain rates!' Imogen glared at her. 'I'm not trying to take over, sweetheart. Just saying we could have got a few Lewes locals down here. Sad to see the place empty like this. Not everyone's scared off by a bit of rain.'

'Maybe next time,' Anna said diplomatically. As the kettle clicked she jumped up at the excuse to escape.

'So Dad couldn't make it,' Imogen said. 'Probably for the best, though. All things considered.'

'He wanted to come, sweetheart,' Jan said. 'He was talking about it just the other day. But then this morning ... Well, never mind,' Jan said, shaking her head. 'Your mum's here now – is that not worth something?' She put on a smile, but her expression was strained and sad.

'You don't need to pretend, Mum. If something's wrong, we all need to know about it,' Imogen said. Anna returned to the table and put down the three mugs.

'There's no need to be dismal though, is there?' Jan said.

'No use both of us walking round with big black clouds over our heads.'

'Is there anything we can do, Mum?' Anna asked. 'Maybe one of us could talk to him?'

'You can try,' Jan said with a shrug, her frustration starting to show. 'But he's . . . ' Her words fell away.

'Are you OK?' Anna said, touching her mum's arm.

'No, Anna,' Jan snapped. 'No, actually, I'm not.' Her eyes welled up with unshed tears. 'It's been bloody awful.' The words burst out, as if she couldn't hold them in any longer.

Anna and Imogen sat in stunned silence.

'I'm sorry,' she said. 'Now look what I've done. I don't mean to take it out on you.' Her tears started to fall. 'But it's horrible, seeing him like this. Wouldn't even get out of bed today, and won't say a word to me. One day I think he's better and that we stand a chance of getting back to normal again, and then the next we're back where we started. Our anniversary this week, that's been and gone without a whisper, obviously. Not that either of us would have wanted to do anything.'

'I'm sure with time . . . ' Anna said. 'It's not been long.'

'That might be so,' Jan said. 'But I guarantee you wouldn't be saying that if you were living at the cottage, day in day out. I know it's not his fault, I know that. And I want to support him. But I *can't*. He's the strong one – Tom's my rock. Always has been. I don't know how to be his.'

Jan stayed another hour, and then made an excuse to leave, her eyes still red with tears. Shortly afterwards, a man in his late twenties, his dark-blond hair rain-drenched, put his head around the door of the shop.

'Hi,' he said, with a warm smile. 'How are you doing?'

Imogen's heart lifted. Could this be their very first customer?

'I'm Finn,' he said, stepping inside the shop. Raindrops hung from the end of his eyelashes and the tips of his hair, dripping onto his hooded sweatshirt. He was holding two cardboard cups. 'I run the surf shop two arches down.'

'Oh, hi,' Anna said. 'Our grandma mentioned you.'

'I saw you were opening today. Worse luck with the weather, eh?' he said sympathetically.

'I know,' Anna said, with a smile. 'We haven't exactly had a run on the ice creams yet.'

'I thought maybe you could do with some hot chocolates. Me and Andy were just making some for our clients, seeing as we've had to cancel the classes today.'

He passed them a cardboard cup of steaming chocolate each.

'Thank you,' Imogen said, as she took a sip of the rich, creamy liquid. 'It's good,' she said, wiping away a chocolate moustache that she realised had formed on her upper lip.

He glanced around the empty shop. 'I'm sure you'll be flooded with customers,' he said, his eyes full of encouragement, 'when people see that you're open again.'

'Thanks,' Anna said earnestly. 'We hope so. I mean our grandma ran this place for decades – we want to do just as good a job, hopefully better. But I guess it takes time,' she said, with a shrug.

'That's right,' Finn said. 'And a good dose of sunshine never hurts.'

Anna smiled. 'Today's been a bit of a disaster really,' she said sheepishly.

'A hiccup,' Finn said, with a smile. 'This place will be busy before you know it. Your Grandma Vivien always made it feel like home. She really was a wonderful woman. I was there at the funeral but I didn't see you two – not that I'm surprised, the whole of Brighton was in there. We all miss her, Evie especially, of course. And our customers loved her – they'd often pop in for an ice cream when the surf was flat.'

'Talking of ice cream,' Anna said, 'where are our manners? Can I tempt you to a Funny Feet?' She took one of the giant pink foot-shaped ice creams out of the freezer and offered it to him.

'I'm good for now,' he said. 'Just about managing to stay warm. But those are brilliant – haven't seen once since I was a kid.

'Well,' he added, 'I'm sure we'll be seeing a fair bit of each other over the coming months. In the meantime, good luck.'

Later that evening, after they'd shut the shop, Imogen lugged her bags out of Jon's car and in through the front door of her grandmother's house.

She stepped into the hallway, which was cold and silent, and then went through to the living room. She, her dad and

Martin had boxed up some of her grandma's valuables, but most of her furniture remained; the armchair, the sofa, the heavy gilt mirror over the mantelpiece. Imogen would have her own space for the first time in three weeks. She placed her camera and other equipment carefully on one of the living-room shelves.

She checked her phone again. Luca hadn't replied to any of her text messages asking if they could talk. She should probably give up. But there was still a chance he might change his mind and agree to wait – she clung onto that hope.

Imogen walked up the stairs of Vivien's spacious Victorian house. On the first floor were three bedrooms and a bathroom, with a wooden staircase leading up to a third floor where there were another two small rooms. For a moment the first floor was alive with laughter as she recalled how she and Anna used to play there – darting up and down the stairs, hiding in blanket cupboards and under beds. Used to the small proportions of their family's cottage, this place had felt like a castle to them. Vivien had known they liked the two top rooms the best, with the small doorway linking them, so she would always make those up especially.

She went through into her grandmother's bedroom. This room she, Tom and Martin had barely touched, so most of Vivien's possessions were still just where she'd left them. On the mantelpiece was a wedding photo of her and Stanley, taken in the early 1950s. Vivien must have been around twenty, with Stanley a year or so older. Imogen picked it up, and looked at their smiling faces. It was strange to think that she was already older than Vivien had been then, settling down with the man she'd spend most of her life with. It was romantic and lovely, but nothing Imogen would ever want for herself. Her own spirit was restless, perhaps it always would be. She missed Luca, sure, but the thought of staying in any one place – even on the island – with one person, leaving so much unexplored, made her feel claustrophobic.

She walked over to the dressing table. The costume brooches Vivien used to wear were still lying there, and brightly coloured strings of glass beads were draped over her mirror. Her hairbrush, inlaid with mother-of-pearl, looked as if it were waiting to be picked up.

Imogen gave another glance around the room, the biggest in the house. She couldn't sleep in there, or even in either of the adjoining rooms – ones that had so often been filled with friends and visitors. She made her way up the second flight of stairs, to the attic rooms which she and Anna had thought of as their own. They looked just the same, and while Anna's head would be touching the ceiling now, Imogen, who hadn't inherited their mother's height, fitted snugly. She sat down on the single bed and took off her shoes, tired after the long, disappointing day at the shop. This bedroom was where she'd sleep tonight.

Chapter Eight

'Imogen didn't need to move out, you know,' Jon said, sorting through his DVD collection and putting aside some older ones for charity. He was in jeans and a grey T-shirt, freshly shaved.

'Oh, it's OK,' Anna said, sitting down on the sofa. 'She didn't mind. It doesn't make any sense Grandma's house sitting empty. And now that we're working together all day, it's probably a good thing if we give each other a bit of space.'

Anna thought back over their first week of trading at the shop. She and Imogen had done their best to keep each other's spirits up as the bad weather continued. Their most regular visitors were Evie, during her tea breaks, and an elderly couple who popped in to say hello to Hepburn. In a week, they'd had just three paying customers.

'You know what you need?' Jon said, coming over to the sofa where Anna was and sitting beside her, then gently stroking her hair.

'No idea,' she said, turning slightly to face him, with a

hopeful smile on her face. Maybe Jon would come up with an ingenious solution – a way to draw customers out of their warm, dry houses and down to the quiet end of the beach for ice cream. They might not be able to fix the weather, but perhaps there was a publicity trick they'd missed?

'A break,' Jon said, landing a gentle kiss on her neck. 'Let's get away somewhere this weekend.'

'Are you sure?' she replied. Normally she'd have jumped at the chance of spending some time alone with Jon. But not now, when there was so much at stake with the new business. 'But the shop . . . ' she started. 'And what about Alfie?'

'Mia's parents are over this weekend and she's asked if he can stay with her to see them. So the weekend's free. Imogen can watch the shop, can't she? You said there are hardly any customers at the moment, didn't you?'

It was true – yet Jon's frank words still stung a little. 'I don't know . . . ' Anna said.

'Come away with me this weekend, Anna. I'll book us somewhere. We'll head off on the Friday evening and have the whole weekend to ourselves. No ice cream shop, no tod-dlers . . . just us. How does that sound?'

'It sounds pretty good,' she said, snuggling into his embrace. As much as she enjoyed spending time with Alfie, the idea of spending a weekend with Jon on his own had definite appeal. 'Where do you want to go?'

'Let me surprise you,' Jon replied with a smile. 'Just pack a weekend bag, and be ready.'

*

On Friday evening, Jon and Anna were cruising down the coastal road, rain pattering on the roof of Jon's car. Storm clouds had been hanging over them all for more than a week now and the sun seemed no closer to breaking through, but as Anna stretched out her legs she began to feel something she hadn't felt for months – a little bit relaxed.

The cluttered townscape of Brighton and Hove gave way to Sussex's rolling hills, lush and green, and the stresses of the past two weeks of slow business started to fade.

'Hey, dreamer,' Jon said, glancing over at her, his hands on the steering wheel.

'Winding down,' Anna said, with a contented smile. 'Slowly. There's been so much to think about lately. What with Granny's funeral, then the shop . . . and you busy at work. We've hardly had any time just to *be*.'

'My thoughts exactly,' Jon said. 'But now we'll have some uninterrupted time together. So get ready for a whole lot more of just *being*,' he laughed.

Around twenty minutes later they came to the outskirts of a small village, and Jon turned right up a narrow dirt track. In front of them was an avenue of oak trees, and at the end of it stood a grand hotel, in a picturesque Edwardian building.

Anna was transfixed. 'This place is gorgeous,' she said, as the car's tyres crunched against the gravel of the pathway.

Jon smiled. 'You deserve something special,' he said, giving her a kiss. 'Now let's get our things and go inside.'

They went in through the main entrance, and the receptionist gave them their keys. Their room was at the top of a steep wooden staircase, and Anna's excitement built with every step. Jon pushed open the heavy wooden door to their room, to reveal a four-poster bed and a huge sofa, a door to the left leading to a luxurious en-suite bathroom.

Anna went straight over to the bed and gently bounced up and down. 'This is great,' she said. 'Come and try it out.'

Jon put down their suitcases, then settled down beside her. 'Nice,' he said. 'Now, did you remember your bikini? Because there's a pool and spa downstairs with our names on it.'

'I don't need asking twice,' Anna said. She got up and unzipped her suitcase, getting her swimming things out. Downstairs, they found they had the pool area entirely to themselves.

'Jacuzzi?' Anna suggested.

They climbed in and let the water bubble up around them until Anna could barely see Jon through the steam. He reached through the foam and ran a hand up her leg, sending a tingle through her.

'I could get used to this,' Anna said, slipping in deeper so that the water warmed the back of her neck.

'Me too,' Jon said, with a smile.

'Reminds me of how it was when we first got together. The blind date, staying out until dawn, nothing to think about but enjoying each other's company.'

'You were every bit as lovely as Ed and Jess told me you'd be. I couldn't believe my luck.'

'Ah, you charmer,' Anna laughed. 'Although to be honest I felt pretty lucky too. It wasn't a bad result for my first ever blind date.'

'And there was I,' Jon said, 'worried that me being the separated dad of a baby would scare you off. Little did I know you'd be far more smitten with Alfie than me.'

'You had nothing to worry about. Who wouldn't fall in love with Alfie?' Anna said, running a finger through the bubbles on the surface of the water.

'I'm glad you did,' Jon said.

'I love this – being with you,' Anna said. 'I wouldn't change a single thing.'

'It'll be up in half an hour,' Jon said, putting the phone down after ordering room service, and leaning back on the bed. Wind and rain lashed against the hotel-room window, but inside they were warm and cosy. 'They said they'd leave it outside.'

Anna went to join him, her fluffy white robe wrapped around her. A three-course meal cooked by a Michelin-star chef and they didn't even have to get dressed to eat it. It was a whole new level of luxury.

Jon gave Anna a kiss, then got up and walked over to the mini-bar. He opened it and pulled out a bottle of champagne. 'I think it's time for some fizz,' he said, getting out two glasses and popping the cork. He passed one to Anna.

'Wow,' she smiled, taking it. 'What's this in aid of?'

'Some time alone with my girlfriend,' he said. He reached

towards her for a kiss, drawing her close. 'Do I need any other excuse?'

After their kiss, Anna took a sip of champagne, and relished the feeling of the bubbles on her tongue.

'Ah,' Jon said. 'Just realised I've forgotten something. Give me a minute.' He got out of bed and pulled on his trousers and a sweater. 'Just nipping down to the car.'

'OK,' Anna said, a little confused. Didn't they have everything they needed, right there?

With a wink Jon closed the hotel room door behind him. Anna leaned back against the cushions in bed. Unless it was . . . ?

Anna looked from the glass of champagne in her hand to the extravagant room they were in – and recalled the romantic moment they'd shared dancing together on Jess and Ed's big day. Her heartbeat quickened and she took another sip of her drink. He wasn't going to . . . was he?

Jon's mobile rang from the side table, interrupting her thoughts. She peeked out of the window and saw him out in the car park by his car, holding his jacket over his head to shield it from the rain.

Anna looked over at the phone. Mia's name flashed up. She hesitated. She wouldn't normally answer it – but what if it was something important?

'Hello?' Anna said, picking up.

'Oh Anna, hi,' Mia said. 'That is Anna, isn't it?'

'Yes, it's me,' Anna said. 'Jon's just had to pop out, I'm afraid. Can I pass on a message to him?'

'Yes, please,' Mia said, sounding stressed. 'Look, I'm really sorry about this, I know you two are away this weekend. But it's Alfie. We were out all day with my parents and now he's got a raging temperature. He keeps calling for his dad. Could you ask Jon to give me a ring when he gets back?'

'Poor Alfie,' Anna said. 'Of course. I'll get Jon to call you back right away.'

Chapter Nine

Perched up on a vintage stool at the ice cream bar, Imogen opened her netbook. She resisted the urge to check Facebook – with the weather still grey and drizzly, seeing her friends on Thai beaches was the last thing she needed. She still couldn't help wondering what Luca was up to. Over a month now, and not one word.

She refused to dwell on it, though. Today, her search was for *inspiration*. It was time for her and Anna to up their game. It was clear enough from the account books that what they were offering at the shop wasn't enough to draw the locals away from their regular stops, let alone attract Londoners or other south-coast tourists. It was time to move Vivien's to the next stage.

She opened Ben and Jerry's site, and read the story of how they went from small business to global ice cream empire – setting up their first store in a disused petrol station, serving free ice creams to friends and employing a piano player to entertain customers in the long queue for scoops. Now, that was more like it, she thought with a smile. She glanced around, wondering where they might fit in a baby grand. Perhaps not.

She clicked on a new site – a man who'd set up the world's first mobile liquid-nitrogen truck, creating flavours from port to Stilton, and experimenting with jellyfish to make glow-in-the-dark ices. It looked like he had customers flocking to him. But instinct told her that quirky innovations and piano-players weren't going to work for Vivien's. If the busiest cafés in the Lanes were anything to go by, it was quality food and seasonal ingredients that local people really cared about.

Imogen saw it now – with the right approach, they could make the arches, this remote part of the seafront – a destination venue for gourmet ices. But an afternoon or two in Anna's kitchen with recipes printed out from the internet definitely wasn't going to do the trick. Vivien's needed to offer something special – something that would give it the edge that would put it firmly on the south-coast foodie map. It was time for them to train up.

She browsed through high-end gelateria workshops and courses online and then saw the accompanying price tags. OK, this was going to cost serious money – but they could still afford for one of them to attend. Anna had always been a natural foodie, and her passion could end up being their biggest asset. With some investment, a few days learning the craft, surely Anna would be able to produce quality ice cream with the best of them? Then she could teach Imogen, and they'd both be trained. How hard could it be?

Imogen's excitement started to build as she scanned details

of a London cookery school – 'We'll teach you how to make sorbets, custard-based ices . . . ' But where were the creamy, delicious-looking ice creams, the real gelato?

Of course, Imogen thought, tapping her head and laughing out loud at her own ignorance. Italy!

As she typed in the new search terms, a message popped up on her instant messenger. **From:** Santiana.

She brightened instantly. It had been over a fortnight since she'd heard from her best friend on the island and just seeing her name was a ray of sunshine.

Imogen, hi.

Hello! Imogen typed back quickly. **How are things? Miss me?**

Yes, of course. Different here without you.

Different? Imogen thought, furrowing her brow. Strange way of putting it. She typed back a reply.

Different how? Boring? she tapped out. **Lost without your drinking partner and dive buddy?**

She stared at the blank screen.

Imo, came Santiana's response after a moment, **there's something I need to explain.**

The serious tone of Santiana's message came as a surprise. Their friendship was simple: they ate together, they swam together, they laughed together. They didn't have heavy conversations. New lines of text appeared with a ping.

Before you see anything on Facebook
really sorry
Luca and me

Imogen felt like she'd been punched in the stomach.

She opened Facebook in a separate window and clicked through to Luca's page. She saw the photo on his wall immediately – him and Santiana with their arms round each other, kissing – in the Komodo bar where Luca had once planned to welcome her home.

Luca had said that he'd need time to think – but how did getting off with her supposed best friend come into it?

A new message from Santiana:

Sorry.

Hope we can still be friends when you come back.

Imogen's hands froze on the keyboard, as she struggled to take in what was happening. This wasn't how things were supposed to turn out.

She heard the shop door swing open and a male voice cut into her thoughts. 'You on your own today?'

She looked up, and clocked Finn standing in the doorway. 'Yes, hi, Finn.'

Her fingers hovered over the keyboard. What could she possibly say to Santiana? How could she put the way she was feeling right now into words?

'I just wondered if you wanted help with anything,' Finn offered. 'We've had no one sign up for classes today, so I have a bit of time on my hands for once.'

'We're fine,' Imogen said, turning back to her netbook, where **Are you OK?** had just popped up on the screen. 'But thanks. It's quiet today, but that won't last,' she said, forcing a smile. 'I'm working on some business development ideas.'

'Sounds interesting.'

'Yes, yes, it is,' Imogen said, impatient to end the conversation and get back to the computer.

He smiled apologetically. 'I get the sense I'm interrupting something.'

'You're not,' Imogen said, but her eyes drifted away from his and back to the screen.

'OK. Well, in any case, I'll leave you to it,' Finn said, turning away and walking back out of the door.

'You're back early,' Imogen said, staring at Anna, who was standing on the doorstep of their grandmother's house, sheltering under an umbrella.

'I know,' Anna said, a downcast expression on her face.

'It's just . . . I wasn't expecting you back so soon. I thought you two were away all weekend?'

'So did I,' Anna said, stepping inside and putting her umbrella down.

'I'll get some tea on.'

Anna followed Imogen through to the kitchen, Hepburn trotting closely behind them. Imogen put the kettle on to boil. 'We've had some bonding time while you've been away,' Imogen said, nodding in the dog's direction. 'I'm kind of getting used to him. Anyway, what happened?'

'Alfie's sick,' Anna said. 'Poor little mite. Jon and I were at this lovely hotel – spa, incredible food, total bliss – but then we got the phone call and came back up here. I dropped Jon off at Mia's house and now here I am.'

'It is serious?' Imogen asked, concerned.

'I don't think so, thankfully,' Anna said. 'Jon texted me to let me know he was reading Alfie a story and that he seemed calm and happy. His temperature had dropped by the time we arrived.'

'Shame you couldn't even stay the night, but sounds like you did the right thing,' Imogen said. 'Better to be sure.'

'Oh, of course,' Anna agreed. 'And we wouldn't have been able to relax and enjoy ourselves, knowing that Alfie was unwell. It's just . . . '

'Yes?'

'This is going to sound stupid. But we were in this romantic setting and at one point Jon went downstairs to get something. I thought, for a moment, that he might be going to get a ring.'

'Ohhh,' Imogen replied. 'Understandable. Although of course it ignores the more likely scenario.'

'And what's that?'

'Condoms,' Imogen said, with a shrug.

'Oh,' Anna replied, flushing. 'God, you're right. That must have been it. I feel like a right idiot.'

'Don't. It was a pretty fair assessment, given the spontaneous break and posh hotel. And who knows, you may have been right. Here,' Imogen said, passing her a mug of tea. 'Let's go and sit in the front room.'

'How's it been at the shop?' Anna said, a little dazed, settling down on the Chesterfield sofa. 'Still quiet?'

'Yes, no change there. Nothing to report, apart from Luca and I have now officially broken up.'

'Really?' Anna said.

'Yep. Santiana told me earlier today that the two of them are now together. With photos to prove it, as it turns out. She said she hoped we could still be friends.'

'What a cheek,' Anna said, annoyed on her sister's behalf. 'Mind you, I suppose when you look at it from Luca's point of view . . . '

'I know,' Imogen said. 'I realise I didn't give him much of an alternative. It would be easier if he'd chosen someone else to move on with, but ultimately I can't really blame him.'

'I'm really sorry to hear it, anyway.'

'I feel a bit rubbish, but I guess I made my choice, and perhaps this means that we just weren't meant to be together.'

'Maybe,' Anna said. 'So you're not regretting staying here?'

'No,' Imogen said, 'of course not.'

Anna raised a questioning eyebrow.

'OK, hardly at all. But listen. Things are going to get better, I know it. And I know how we're going to make that happen.'

'You do?' Anna said. 'I should go away more often.'

'Funny you should say that. How would you feel about a trip to Italy? Because something tells me it might be just the thing to turn our business around.'

PART TWO

Don't Give Up, Train Up

Chapter Ten

Anna waited for her luggage to appear on the carousel in Pisa's tiny, bustling airport. Stepping out onto the runway a few minutes earlier she'd felt the heat immediately, and inside the arrivals hall she was beginning to feel decidedly sticky.

A succession of black and grey bags went past for the third time, followed by a hard-shelled pink suitcase adorned with One Direction and heart stickers. Anna looked out for her familiar red suitcase. What if it never arrived? She bit her lip, thinking of the various outfits she'd packed, and beginning to feel nervous about the whole trip. Had Jon been right when he said the trip seemed like a rush decision?

Here she was in Italy – at the start of June, two weeks after Imogen had first suggested it. Did it really make any sense, going to another country, hundreds of miles away from the man she loved?

Aha! Anna spotted her suitcase and politely wove her way through a young Italian family to swoop on it.

It wasn't that she wasn't excited about being in Italy. As

she wheeled her suitcase over in the direction of the train station, she thought about what lay ahead. While she'd never been the boldest of travellers, she knew she was lucky to be going to Florence, one of the world's most beautiful cities, known for its delicious gelato. And on Monday she'd be learning how to make it with Bianca Romeo, a living culinary legend and one of Italy's top ice cream chefs, at the internationally renowned Accademia di Gelateria. The opportunity of a lifetime. So of course she was excited, but she was well and truly outside her comfort zone.

It did seem that Imogen might be on to something, though. For all her hare-brained schemes, Imogen remained an expert at dreaming big – and with their empty, loss-making ice cream shop staring back at them each day, Anna knew they needed that vision more than ever. If they could offer customers something special – and high quality – then people would go the extra mile to visit. Everyone loved a culinary adventure, didn't they? And they were prepared to travel for it, too. For Rick Stein's fish and chips they'd go to isolated fishing villages, and for the mouth-watering, authentically Italian gelato on offer at Vivien's they'd stroll down the beach, or drive to the Granville Arches.

Now, my job, Anna thought as she strolled towards platform 3, *is to make sure that when they arrive, they get something dazzling enough to justify their journey*. She checked the destination on the front of the train – *Firenze* – and got on board.

The train pulled out of Pisa Station, and in just a few minutes Anna was immersed in the landscape outside her window: sun-drenched vineyards, hillsides scattered with golden-yellow houses with terracotta roofs, and cypress trees punctuating the Tuscan landscape, upright and elegant. Anna sat back in her seat and took in her new surroundings. She hadn't been abroad for years: with Alfie visiting most weekends her and Jon's priorities were different from those of other new couples. But the colours of the fields and the striking blue of the sky overhead lifted her spirits and her nerves about travelling drifted away.

She found the brown envelope in her handbag and opened it, reading over the details of where she'd be staying in Florence. The *penzione*, the boarding house she'd booked into, looked like it was only a short walk from the school, the Accademia di Gelateria, where she'd be starting her course on Monday.

Imogen and Anna had looked into every ice cream school and university from Sicily to Venice, checking food blogs and reviews, until they settled on the Accademia – a practical course in gelato-making, with additional evening classes in sorbets and granitas. As she flicked through the course material, her mouth watered at the thought of the creations to come. And as the train neared the city of Florence, vineyards making way for green-shuttered buildings, with balconies where washing was hung up – she couldn't wait to get started.

Anna took a cab from the taxi rank outside the station and showed the moustached driver the address of where she was going. He nodded and took her bag from her, slinging it into the back of the cab. She was aware of his eyes devouring the cleavage that was visible in her black vest. Flushing, she pulled her top up and got inside. Without air conditioning and on a warm summer's day, Anna was sweltering hot and sweat trickled down the back of her neck, gluing strands of her hair to it. She wound down the taxi window, hoping for a cool breeze – but the air was as still and warm outside as in.

They careered down narrow streets, horns beeping and tooting from every side, and the driver let loose a tirade of what must have been swear words. Anna kept one hand on the door handle next to her – with the cab driver's temper rising, she considered whether walking would be preferable to being trapped inside the cab with a lunatic. If Jon were here he'd be horrified – the car's brakes screeched as they avoided an old lady with a shopping trolley. She looked up – and in just a couple of minutes, the scenery had changed completely. As the traffic cleared, Anna saw that they were in the midst of the most breathtaking architecture – a church with an ornate façade, pretty townhouses with frescoes on the outside and a bustling piazza.

'Via Fortiori, eh,' said the driver. 'Penzione Giovanna.'

'Si,' she said.

He pointed at a tall apartment building, indicating that they had arrived. It was a four-storey townhouse with decorative wrought-iron balconies that looked as if they might crumble at a touch.

Anna looked up, and then around the square. Restaurant

tables spilled out onto the cobblestones, late afternoon crowds filling the tables, and shops and boutiques offered sparkling high heels, wedding dresses and fresh vegetables. Anna was consumed by the smells, the sights, the sounds. The piazza was intoxicatingly alive.

'OK,' the driver announced, jumping out and taking her luggage out of the car boot. Not understanding the figure he asked for, Anna handed him a twenty-euro note and hoped that would be enough.

With one parting, lustful glance at her breasts, the driver got back in his cab and stepped on the gas, heading off into the chaos of Florence's city streets. With a little shudder of distaste, Anna made her way over to the building he'd pointed out. One letter on the neon *penzione* sign was still aglow; the others looked like they'd been dark for some time.

Anna checked the number on the door, then rapped the lion's-head knocker sharply. The sound was lost in the bustle of the square and she wondered if it would be heard at all. A moment later, a stout, grey-haired woman in her fifties opened the door.

'Signora McAvoy!' she said warmly.

Anna smiled in response and said, 'Anna, please.'

The woman pointed to her own generous chest, with a smile. 'Giovanna. Welcome,' she said, in heavily accented English. 'Come in.'

A wave of relief passed over Anna at the sight of a friendly face. Giovanna led her up narrow stone steps until they reached a small room. The modest lodgings, with a single, iron-framed bed next to the window, also contained a chest of drawers, wardrobe and small basin. '*E piccolo*,' Giovanna said with a shrug. 'And you are *alta*,' she laughed, pointing to Anna.

Anna put her suitcase down and smiled politely, used to the comments on her height. The room was a little smaller than it had looked on the website, but it had character – and there was a lovely shuttered window looking out onto the square. With a smile, Giovanna took her by the hand to show her the bathroom, bright and sunny with antique gold mirrors and a large freestanding, claw-footed tub. Anna could already imagine soothing her weary feet in a bubble bath there later that evening. '*Bello*,' she said appreciatively, grateful that she'd scanned her phrase book on the plane.

Next door was an even smaller, empty room with the bed made up, as if Giovanna was expecting another guest to arrive.

She gave a little stretch to loosen up her shoulders after the travelling.

'*Stanca?*' Giovanna asked, giving a yawning gesture. Anna thought of all the sights in her city guide, and wished she wasn't so tired.

'Tonight, rest.' Giovanna smiled. 'Then tomorrow, Sunday – *godere*! Enjoy!'

Chapter Eleven

Imogen poured strawberries into the blender and switched it on. She was up at midnight, in the kitchen of her grandmother's house, preparing home-made ice cream.

Yes, she and Anna had said they'd wait another month, when Anna was fully trained up and could run Imogen through the basics, ready for the launch of the new home-made range – but Imogen needed something. If she didn't keep busy, her mind would drift back to Luca, and the pangs of regret would start to take hold.

So she'd decided to try out two flavours now, keeping things simple – chocolate and a fresh strawberry, with some fruit she'd found discounted at the end of the day at the local greengrocer's. Imogen licked the spoon and let the mixture dissolve on her tongue: the strawberry was absolutely delicious. The chocolate wasn't bad either – but you couldn't really go far wrong with chocolate, could you? She hadn't used all the bits and pieces that Anna had shown her but she'd got the job done with what was in Vivien's kitchen. Imogen smiled with satisfaction – it felt good to do something creative rather than simply feeling sad about what could have been.

She put the tubs in the freezer so that they'd be ready for her to take to the shop bright and early the next day. Tired but satisfied, she climbed into bed, pulled the feather duvet up around her and fell into a deep, relaxed sleep.

On Sunday morning, Imogen took out the standing chalkboard sign she'd found in the shop storage cupboard, and chalked up a message, using the shop's trademark pistachio and pastel pink shades:

HOME-MADE ICE CREAM AVAILABLE HERE TODAY

She smiled as she placed it outside, excited about the day ahead.

The morning sun was quickly drying the rain-drenched concrete in front of their shop, and it looked like for once the weather might actually be cooperating with her plan. Rollerbladers skated up and down, swirling in loops around cones, and even the gulls seemed to be singing out a happy song as they dived down into the seafront bins to find breakfast.

From his regular spot at the front of the shop, Hepburn barked at the birds. Imogen pulled her cardigan around her and looked out for any likely customers. She was startled by a blur of fur as a golden retriever dashed past her, heading straight for Hepburn.

'So sorry,' a woman with a dark bob said, catching up with the dog and grabbing hold of his lead again.

A man in a trench coat caught up with them and came to a breathless stop. 'You got him, Jill. Well done.'

'Harry has a bit of a thing for dachshunds,' the woman said apologetically. 'That's Harry,' she said, pointing at her golden retriever, 'Not him,' she laughed, taking her partner's hand.

'Ah, the old ice cream shop. We've been meaning to stop here, as it happens,' the man said. 'We heard this place was under new ownership. Jeffrey and Jill, pleased to meet you.'

Imogen smiled and shook their hands. 'Imogen. Likewise. And yes, we're the new owners. Still in the family, though – "Vivien's and Granddaughters", it should be called, really. It's me and my sister Anna who've taken it over.'

'It looks tremendous,' the woman said, taking in the new paint job and the retro fittings. They'd made a light out of ice cream scoops, with lightbulbs dangling down into them, a fitting centrepiece. 'Our grandsons would love this, wouldn't they, Jeffrey?'

'Yes, I'm sure they would. Let's bring them next time. We'll have two, please,' Jeffrey said. 'It's just chocolate and straw-berry you've got, isn't it?' Imogen nodded. 'I'll take a chocolate, and a strawberry cone for my wife.'

Imogen scooped out the cones, being careful not to break the delicate waffle. She'd sourced the cones especially – they were a step up from the usual kind.

'Looks delicious,' Jill said, paying Imogen. They headed towards the exit, Harry on a slightly shorter lead this time. Hepburn poked his head out cautiously from the back room, his big brown eyes questioning her.

'It's safe to come out now, Hepburn,' Imogen whispered. 'We've just said goodbye to our very first home-made ice cream customers.'

He gave a gruff bark of approval.

'Do you think our neighbours would like to try some?' Imogen asked him.

He barked again and wagged his tail. Imogen took that as a yes. She walked out of the shop and down the seafront towards Evie's souvenir shop. The bell tinkled as she entered.

'Evie, hi,' Imogen called out when she saw her. 'Can I tempt you to some home-made ice cream?'

'Oh, sweetheart, I'd love some,' Evie said, from behind her shop counter. 'Kind of you to offer. But the doctor would kill me. Says I've got to watch my cholesterol.'

'Oh, I see,' Imogen said. 'Well I'd hate to get you in trouble. We'll just have to come up with some healthier options for you.'

A little boy with freckles pushed his way past Imogen, holding up his large shark inflatable. 'It's got a puncture!' he whined.

'Duty calls,' Evie said, with a smile. 'But why don't you ask Finn? I bet he'd be delighted to take you up on the offer.'

'Yes,' Imogen said. 'I'll do that.'

She walked down the stretch of arches towards Finn's school. Outside, there was a group of surfers preparing to set out and she saw Finn standing in the doorway.

'Enjoy your surf,' Imogen announced to the group. 'Afterwards, there's a fifty per cent discount on the homemade ice cream cones at Vivien's just over there.' She pointed at the shop.

'Sounds good,' one of the wetsuited women said. 'But I expect we'll be freezing.'

'Science is on the side of ice cream,' Imogen said, thinking on her feet. 'The colder your internal temperature, the warmer you'll feel.' She'd read that somewhere. She wasn't entirely sure it was true, but it definitely sounded good.

One of the men in the group, tall and dark, with short black hair, gave Imogen a wink as he finished zipping up his wetsuit. She couldn't help noticing that the rubber clung to him in all the right places.

'We'll be there,' he said.

That afternoon, Imogen looked out with pride at the full ice cream shop. The requests from Finn's surf class had come in so thick and fast, she'd struggled at first to write down all of their orders. It seemed they'd bought her internal/external temperature line, and after a long morning session in the sea were ordering the ice creams by the bucketload to fight off their post-surf shivers.

'Incredible stuff, this,' the guy with the dark hair called out to her.

'Here, try some of the strawberry,' another young man said, passing his over.

A glow of pride built up inside her as Imogen saw them take greedy spoonfuls.

Chapter Twelve

Anna stepped out of Giovanna's house and into the Santa Maria de Novella Piazza, bustling with crowds coming out of the Sunday service. She put on her sunglasses. The night's sleep had left her refreshed and ready to start exploring the city, and with just one day left before the ice cream course started, she was looking forward to making the most of it.

The sun was high, and in her floaty turquoise dress and gold sandals she relished the way it warmed her skin. After the UK's rainiest May on record, she soaked up the much-needed vitamin D booster. The only decision she had to make today, she thought with pleasure, was what to go and see first. She took another look at her guidebook and opted for the river, criss-crossed with historic bridges, that divided the compact city. Walking down the cobbled street, she could make out the glistening of sunshine on water at the end of the path. She instinctively picked up her pace, walking until she saw the Ponte Vecchio appear in front of her: the distinctive landmark she'd seen so many times on postcards and in books, a bridge with little houses like children's toys built onto it, overlooking the water. The backdrop that opened up behind it was lush Tuscan countryside peppered with tall cypress trees. She took a deep breath of fresh air; it even smelled different here – a trace of Italian coffee from a nearby restaurant, with the faint smell of a passing woman's perfume.

'Signora,' said a young man with a bright smile, offering her a fake Gucci handbag.

Anna shook her head politely, and stepped up onto the bridge.

'Will you take our photo?' a Japanese couple with excitable children asked her politely.

'Of course,' she said, taking the camera. As she stepped back, through the lens she saw that the little houses she'd been looking at were actually jewellery shops. Light glinted off the windows, which housed diamond rings and delicate gold necklaces.

'Thank you,' the woman said, taking the camera back. 'This is a special city, isn't it?' she said slowly. 'Very romantic.'

'I've just arrived,' Anna said, with a smile. 'But I'm starting to see that.'

She crossed the bridge, and settled for lunch in a shady, peaceful square in San Spirito, on the other side of the river. Away from the more touristy areas, the scene in front of her was peopled only with locals, children playing in the fountain and a grandma looking out from her shuttered window. She ordered tagliatelle with mussels and garlic, and a glass of white wine.

Anna smiled as the waiter brought over a steaming hot plate of pasta and her drink. She sipped the wine and enjoyed the view out over the square. Once it had cooled a little, she twirled the tagliatelle around her fork and took a bite – fresh with the perfect balance of flavours. It tasted like a dream.

After lunch, pleasantly woozy from the midday wine, she continued her walk, wandering past elegant art galleries and museums, teenagers posing for photos with the statue of David. As the sun lowered in the sky, and the hot day softened to a balmy evening, she realised she'd left her most important stop till last. It was time to try some local ice cream. Giovanna had recommended a gelateria over breakfast that morning, and Anna found the name she'd written down in her notebook: Vivoli.

The shop was tucked away in a neighbourhood called Santa Croce, ten minutes' walk away. When Anna located it, she found a long queue spiralling out and up the narrow street. The Italians in the line in front of her chattered excitedly, and she caught the occasional words, rich with flavour and promise: '*Cioccolato . . . stracciatella . . . frutti di bosco*'. While her everyday Italian might be limited, Anna's knowledge of ice cream flavours was anything but. Her heart raced as the queue went down and she got near enough to see the enticing piles of pastel-coloured gelato on offer in large glass cabinets. The nerves she'd felt yesterday, arriving in a new city, had vanished. Here – with an array of ice cream and sorbets in front of her – she felt right at home.

When she reached the front of the queue, she pointed with an enthusiastic smile to the double cone trimmed with chocolate and hazelnut, and gesticulated towards the dark-chocolate ice cream, hoping the young man serving her would understand. '*Cioccolato*?' she attempted shyly.

'And in the other one?' the young man replied flawlessly, with a smile.

'You speak English,' she said, relieved. 'The raspberry sorbet, please.'

'I used to live in London,' he said. 'I loved it, but there was just *one thing* missing.' He nodded down to the ice cream and added a generous scoop of deep-pink sorbet to her cone.

Anna thanked him and walked away with the ice cream. As the dark chocolate met her lips, she was transported: the gelato was mind-meltingly creamy. She weaved her way back towards Giovanna's under a star-studded sky, interspersing the chocolate with mouthfuls of raspberry – fresh, tangy and laden with fruit. Now this, she thought to herself, is something I could get used to.

Florence is beautiful, Anna texted her sister on the walk home to Giovanna's, and the ice cream is out of this world. How are you? xx

The phone beeped as Imogen's reply came in an instant.

Hey, sis. Green with envy. But talking of ice cream, I made and sold my first batch today! I know we said we'd wait . . . But it went down a storm ☺ x

Anna smiled as she read it – so she wasn't the only person who'd been feeling inspired today. Imogen was blossoming at the shop without her, spreading her culinary wings. Just one night's sleep, and she'd be doing the same.

Chapter Thirteen

'Imogen,' Finn said, a steely look in his hazel eyes, 'what on earth have you done?'

He was standing in front of his shop as she went to open Vivien's on Monday morning, and by the look of things, he wasn't happy. Hepburn barked a cheery greeting, and Imogen bent down to quieten him.

'What do you mean?' Imogen said, trying to push away the uncomfortable doubts that were creeping up. She racked her brains . . . last night she'd closed the shop, then gone home and had a quiet night watching a DVD. Had she done something before she left – put out the bins in Finn's spot? He seemed like the kind of person who might get uptight about something like that.

He shook his head wearily. 'The afternoon session with my surf class yesterday was an absolute disaster. Apart from one guy, Paul – who joined us after lunch – the rest of the class were throwing their guts up.'

Oh no, Imogen thought, as the reality of the situation struck her between the eyes.

Oh NO.

'Yep, that's right,' Finn continued, running a hand raggedly over dark-blond wavy hair, his forehead furrowed. 'And as bad as you imagine it was, believe me, it was worse. Pebbly beach, no toilet for miles around – and ten students with acute food poisoning. It would almost be funny if it wasn't such a frigging disaster.'

Imogen cringed as she took in the full horror of it all.

'And you're sure it was the ice cream?' she asked, aware she was clutching at straws.

'I'm pretty sure it was the only thing that all of them ate. I'd say ask them yourself,' he said, his voice heavily laced with annoyance, 'but they're all at home still spewing their guts out.'

'That's terrible,' Imogen said.

'I don't understand it. Were you using a recipe?'

'Yes,' Imogen said, hearing the defensive tone her voice had taken on. 'I thought it looked OK.' Looking back, she had skipped some sections that might have been important. But the letters moved around sometimes when she read. They always had.

She knew what she should say, those two small words: *I'm sorry*. But she couldn't bring herself to say them – to admit she could have made such a stupid mistake.

'I don't know if these students will be well enough to continue the course tomorrow, and given that I recommended your place to them, I don't think it's right to take their money, do you? But you can't carry on like this, or you'll ruin the

Arches' reputation . . . Have you looked into getting a hygiene certificate yet?'

'No,' Imogen said. It was on the list Anna had left her, the boring thing at the end that she'd been putting off.

'That might be a start,' Finn said, shaking his head.

Imogen closed the door to the shop and locked it behind her. A few minutes of peace and quiet, that was all she needed. She sat down in a booth with her back to the door and dropped her head into her hands. Two days Anna had been away and she'd managed to mess things up monumentally already. She took a deep breath, and then another. Perhaps Finn was wrong, she told herself. Perhaps something else had triggered the group's sickness – norovirus, maybe? She'd heard everyone was getting that. She wouldn't let him make her feel bad about something that was unproven.

Drawing on her inner strength, she got to her feet and went over to the front door to open it again. There, standing in front of her, were the couple who'd visited yesterday, Jeffrey, his wife Jill and their golden retriever. Their faces were ashen.

'Good morning,' Jill said politely. 'Sorry to bother you, but we wanted to ask if maybe there might have been something wrong with that batch of ice cream yesterday. It's just . . . '

'We started to feel unwell,' Jeffrey continued. 'When the vomiting started yesterday we called NHS Direct. We weren't sure, you see, if we should go into A&E.'

'Oh God,' Imogen said, biting her lip. 'You'd better come

in.' She motioned for the two of them to take a seat. Their postures were slightly hunched – it was as if they'd gained ten years overnight, and they seemed relieved to sit down. The fine lines on their faces had deepened.

'I have a horrible feeling this is my fault,' Imogen said. 'I'm so sorry.'

'These things happen,' Jill said kindly. 'And we feel a little better today, don't we, Jeffrey?' Her voice sounded strained and weak.

'I managed to eat a cracker this morning,' Jeffrey said, the tiniest hint of a smile appearing at his mouth. 'And Jill kept her cup of tea down.' He reached over to stroke their retriever. Even he seemed less lively that morning, barely reacting to Hepburn, who was skulking around in the kitchen, keeping a low profile.

'Oh dear,' Imogen said, guilt twisting her stomach into knots. 'I'm afraid you're not the only ones who seem to have been affected.'

'Is that so?' Jill asked.

'Yes, I managed to poison one of the surf classes too,' Imogen said, feeling mortified. 'How I can possibly make it up to you?' she said. 'Can I offer you some compensation?'

'Don't worry,' Jill said, putting her hand on Imogen's reassuringly. 'Everyone makes mistakes, dear. And we know you're just starting out.'

'But you've been stuck at home, being sick . . . ' Imogen said. 'I feel dreadful about this.'

'We're always at home,' Jeffrey smiled. 'No difference there.

And while it hasn't been the most pleasant twenty-four hours, we're relieved that it's nothing serious, aren't we, Jill?'

'That's right,' she said. 'We're almost back to our brightest now.'

'Well, I still wouldn't blame you if you wanted to see us shut down,' Imogen said.

'We know you and your sister are new to this. And we had our share of bad luck, back in the day.'

'You thinking of that barbecue?' Jeffrey laughed.

'Can hardly bear to remember it,' his wife said, shaking her head. 'Half our friends were off work after eating some chicken we hadn't cooked through. We shouldn't laugh. But you learn from these things, don't you? To be more careful next time?'

'Believe me,' Imogen said, 'I've learned my lesson. I won't be selling any more.'

'Well, we'll be off then. But we thought it was best to check and let you know.'

'Thank you,' Imogen said. 'Thank you so much. And I hope you feel much better soon.'

The couple left the shop, and walked out into the sullen grey morning, weary shadows, but still joking gently with one another.

Imogen slowly let out the breath she'd been holding. Some people had so much kindness in them, she thought, with intense gratitude and relief. She longed for Anna to come home and restore some order. How had she ever thought she'd be able to run the shop on her own? A week was a very long time, it turned out, when things weren't going well.

The following morning, Imogen forced herself to get up and dress, and poured coffee into a thermos flask for her walk down to the shop. If she wasn't about to get sued, then it was back to business as usual. Albeit with no more home-made ice cream.

'You're not a quitter,' she told herself, as she strode along the seafront towards Vivien's. 'Today is a whole new day.' By the time she arrived at the door of the shop, she was feeling ready to open up. Today could be the day that things got better.

There was a pile of post on the doormat, and she bent down to pick it up, putting the bundle of leaflets and a local paper on the counter. She turned on the stereo and propped the front door open to make the place look more inviting.

She sorted through the letters, filing an electricity bill and throwing away a couple of takeaway leaflets. With no customers in sight, she opened the local newspaper and looked at the headlines – pictures of homes damaged by the recent floodwaters, with mournful-looking residents outside. They'd been lucky that Vivien's hadn't been affected, Imogen thought.

She flicked to page three, and almost missed it at first. But then her eyes came to rest on the story:

SEAFRONT BUSINESS POISONS
A DOZEN BRIGHTON RESIDENTS

Imogen gasped as she read over the feature – Vivien's was named, and the story of Sunday's food-poisoning incident was there in black and white.

Oh God, Imogen thought, forcing herself to close the newspaper. What were they supposed to do now?

Then, slowly, as she sat down on a stool, her panic turned to confusion. The story itself was quite vague, and the people involved hadn't been named, but there were details about the shop history and their lease that were oddly specific. Things only another person who worked in the Arches could know. Someone had set out to try and ruin their business, and it seemed likely they were right on Vivien's doorstep.

Acting on a hunch, she walked into Finn's surf school, with the newspaper in her hand.

'Finn. Do you know anything about this?' she asked him, showing him the article.

Finn looked at her blankly, then took the newspaper from her. He glanced over it. 'Oh dear, this isn't good, is it?' he said.

'I know the incident the other day shouldn't have happened, but did you really have to talk to the local press?'

'It's nothing to do with me.'

'Really?' Imogen said, disbelieving. 'It's just it seems strange that you're the one person who I know has been really annoyed about it. And perhaps you stand to gain something from seeing us go down?'

'I don't know anything about it,' Finn said with a shrug, 'and I don't know why you think I'd benefit from seeing Vivien's suffer. We rely on each other down here, and support each other's businesses. It's always been the way. It's the very reason I felt let down the other day.'

'But there were things in the article that only one of us business owners could know.'

'You're not going to let this go, are you? OK then, Imogen. Find the evidence, and I'll happily hear you out.'

'I will,' Imogen said. 'Because it's not fair to do this to us.'

Chapter Fourteen

'So you add in fifty grams of cream now,' Bianca told Anna, leaning over her workspace and pointing to the large silver mixing bowl.

Anna listened carefully to the Italian instructor, and tried to steady her trembling hand. Here she was, a complete novice, in the presence of Bianca Romeo, a culinary legend. She didn't want to mess this up. Bianca nodded her approval, and moved on to the next table.

Bianca was an elegant, charismatic woman in her mid-thirties, whose passion for food was evident in every word she said. Paying attention to the quantities, Anna mixed the ingredients together carefully, making sure she followed the recipe exactly.

Over coffee in the reception area that morning, Anna had met her four classmates, an international group – Georgios, a rotund middle-aged Greek; Sian, a friendly art-school graduate from Ireland; and Ria and Hiro, honeymooners from Japan.

Bubbling with nerves and enthusiasm, they'd then filed

into the room, high-ceilinged and elegant with large, tall windows, faded frescoes on the walls and ornate decorations on the white ceiling. Bianca had welcomed them to the class, and then got straight to the point. 'Unless you are ready to make the highest quality of ice cream, you won't receive a certificate – and your course will have been a waste of your time and mine.'

She'd then divided the class up into pairs, and Georgios had made a beeline for Anna's table.

'You are good at this, eh?' came Georgios' booming voice from Anna's side, accompanied by a nudge in the ribs. 'I knew I picked a good partner. I can tell you are an expert cook,' he laughed.

'You can?' Anna said, smiling in surprise. 'I've certainly never made gelato. This is all new to me.' She weighed out the sugar and tipped it into the bowl. 'What about you, Georgios? Have you ever done this before?'

Anna glanced over at him – he was dressed awkwardly for the kitchen, apron over a formal dark suit and unbuttoned shirt, his tie done up loosely.

'Never,' he said. 'But it is time to try something new,' he added with a shrug. 'In Athens . . . I'm sure you've heard. Things are not so good.'

Anna nodded: it had been hard to miss the updates on the news lately.

'Don't worry,' he said, with a grin. 'Yes, there are problems with the economy – big problems. And my shoe shop – I used to sell high heels for ladies, *beautiful* shoes! You should have seen them, Anna.' The volume of his voice rose with his excitement as he described them. 'Silk – the finest materials . . . ' As Giovanna threw him a stern look and he seemed to come back down to earth. 'Anyway, this is just dreams now,' he whispered to Anna. 'We don't have customers these days.'

'I'm sorry to hear that,' Anna said, thinking how heartbreaking it must be to close a shop you had invested so much in.

'But with every crisis, a new opportunity,' Georgios continued. 'It's not going to be easy, I know that. My wife, she always tells me I'm a disaster in the kitchen. But I have this,' he said, pointing to his head. 'A good mind, for the business. In a year – just you see, Anna, I will have a gelato empire going. I have made good money before, and I'll do it again. It's just hard work. We'll go out with our children to the Greek islands, maybe Naxos, and set up a gelateria for the tourists,' he said. 'Fantastico!'

'So, how are we doing here?' Bianca appeared by their sides, and Anna jumped a little. 'Anna, is Georgios distracting you from your practice?'

Anna shook her head no, not wanting to get Georgios into trouble.

'I want to taste some delicious vanilla gelato here by the end of the day. And if you keep on chatting I don't know how you're going to have time to make it.'

The door to the class swung open, and Bianca and Anna turned to look. A young man of about thirty, in jeans and a checked shirt, walked into the room, as relaxed as if it were his own home. Anna's breath caught as she got a better look at him, his warm brown eyes and dark hair. It was the same man – just with clothes on this time. She'd caught a glimpse of him through her half-open door at Giovanna's that morning, making his way to the bathroom in a towel. He didn't appear to have seen her watching.

'Signora Bianca,' he said, greeting the instructor with a smile and a kiss on the cheek. He began to chat to her in lilting Italian, as if he already knew her.

'Matteo,' Bianca said, in a restrained, professional tone. 'While we're in the class, we'll talk in English – it's easier for everyone here. You can work with Sian, over there by the window.'

Matteo went over to join his new partner. Anna breathed a sigh of relief when he didn't acknowledge her and returned her gaze to the recipe. She stripped the seeds out of the vanilla pod she and Georgios had been given, then put them in the bin, adding the pod to the mixture.

'Anna, I'm sorry, my dear,' Georgios said, with kindness in his voice, 'but I think we just did that part wrong.' She looked at the precious vanilla seeds in the bin, when they should have been in the mixture. Darn it, she thought. What a fool. She'd thrown the best bit away.

'I'll ask her for another one,' Anna said, going to the front of the class and apologising for her mistake. When she got back to the counter, Georgios had turned the ice cream maker on.

'Did you heat it all up first?' Anna said.

'Was I supposed to?' Georgios said, panicked.

'Yes,' Anna said. She quickly switched the machine off and tried to save the mixture, but what was left was a sad, gloopy mess. The only place for it was in the bin.

'Now, everybody,' Bianca said, calling the class to order. 'Let's look at your grand creations. And more importantly, let's taste them!'

'I'm sorry, Anna,' Georgios said, clocking her disappointment, verging on despair. She wanted the ground to swallow her – and their ice cream disaster – up. Why was it so much harder here, when she had managed perfectly adequately with a simple recipe in her kitchen? They'd created a flat, flavourless mess of an ice cream that she was ashamed to show to anyone.

Bianca was at Sian and Matteo's counter, and as she took a spoonful of ice cream from their maker, she squirmed in delight. 'Now that really is delicious,' she said. 'Come on, everyone, try this one.'

Reluctantly, Anna made her way over, got a fresh spoon and tried the mixture. It was good. It was really, really, annoyingly good.

'But you have an advantage –' Bianca added, talking to Sian – 'with this Italian on your team. And did he tell you he comes from one of Italy's most famous ice cream-making families?'

Matteo dismissed the comment. 'Ah, enough of that, Bi. You know they didn't teach me a thing. So I'm starting from the beginning like all of you.'

He looked kindly around the class and caught Anna's eye for a moment. If his family were so good at making ice cream, Anna wondered, then what was he doing here?

'Not bad,' Bianca said, tasting Ria and Hiro's ice cream. 'There's real potential here – you just need to make it a little bit sweeter.'

Anna hoped for a moment that Bianca might decide to stop there, decide that she had tasted enough. But she turned next to Anna and Georgios'.

'So, this – wow,' she frowned, as if Anna and Georgios' lack of expertise somehow offended the ice cream-making history of the region. 'This is quite a mess, isn't it?'

'As appearances can sometimes be deceptive, I will, of course, try it,' she said, but she winced as soon as she put the spoon into her mouth and tasted the concoction.

'It is the first day,' Bianca said, her voice softening a little. 'And really this is what first days are for. So, all of you –' she turned to the other members of the class – 'make your most horrendous mistakes now – as Georgios and Anna have been so unafraid to do – and then, please, please, make sure that what you do for the rest of the week is much better.'

Anna shrank into her size six sandals, and wished she could disappear.

'You're staying at Giovanna's too, aren't you?' Matteo asked, as the two of them left the class with the other students.

'Yes, I am,' she said, feeling a blush rising to her cheeks. So he *had* seen her that morning.

'Well, why don't we walk back together, in that case?' he said warmly. His English was almost flawless, with a slight American accent, as if he'd honed his skills watching films rather than studying grammar in English classes.

'Sure,' Anna said. She could do with some company after today. The humiliation of her ice cream going so badly wrong still stung. Cooking was something she was supposed to be good at. Had she been wrong to think she could handle the course?

Matteo seemed to read her mind. 'Don't feel bad about it,' he said. 'That's just what she's like, Bianca. She pushes people really hard. That's how she gets the results she does.'

His words soothed Anna. Perhaps he was right.

'How do you know her?'

'I grew up here. She's my sister Carolina's best friend: the two of them were always teasing me when I was little.'

Anna smiled. 'And now? If you're from here, how come you're staying at the house?'

'My family moved to Siena, so now it's my turn to be a tourist,' he laughed. 'No better city in the world to do it in.'

'I think I agree,' Anna said. 'Every corner I turn here there's something else beautiful to look at.'

'Or beautiful to eat,' he said with a smile. 'One thing I can tell you're going to enjoy. Have you got ten minutes?'

Anna nodded. 'For once, I'm not in a hurry for anything.'

'Great, let's get some food to take back for dinner out on the terrace. I told Giovanna I'd treat her.'

Anna walked with Matteo along a cobbled street until they reached a bustling neighbourhood shop, with huge joints of ham and boar hung up outside.

'Come in,' Matteo said, sensing Anna's hesitation. 'And try some of this.' He asked the rotund, bearded shop owner to slice off a segment of white cheese for Anna to try. 'Buffalo mozzarella, fresh.'

Anna smiled with delight at the taste and the way it melted in her mouth. 'Now, that's good,' she said, laughing.

'And what do you think?' he said. 'Shall we take some of this meat too?' He pointed to the bewildering array of cured and smoked meats in the glass cabinet.

'They look delicious,' Anna said. He nodded again and before she knew it Anna had a small plate of samples for them to try.

'I'm not going to need to eat dinner at this rate,' Anna said, laughing.

Anna came back into her hotel room, and closed the door behind her. She, Matteo and Giovanna had shared a delicious dinner up on the roof terrace, and she felt a warm glow from both the conversation and the red wine they'd drunk. With Matteo there to translate, she'd been able to talk much more freely with Giovanna, and to ask questions about her children and grandchildren, getting a picture of the life she'd had growing up in Florence.

Anna took her laptop out of her wooden chest of drawers,

loaded up Skype and pressed to video-call Jon. She couldn't wait to tell him about the trip so far.

'Hi,' Jon said, his picture coming into focus. 'How are things going?'

'Good,' she said. 'Well, today was a bit of a disaster, but it's all better now.'

'A disaster?'

'Not volcanic levels,' she said, smiling now at what had seemed so awful earlier. 'I just made some really rubbish ice cream.'

'Is that all?' Jon said.

'Yes, silly now I say it. Anyway, how are things over there?'

'All fine,' Jon said. 'Still raining. Oh, and Ed and Jess never made it on their honeymoon.'

'Oh, no – that's terrible. What happened?'

'The travel company went bust. Ed's back at his job and apparently Jess is sulking in the flat in her pyjamas watching reruns of Desperate Housewives.'

'Poor thing,' Anna said. 'I can't blame her. They were really looking forward to the time away. She must be fed up.'

'She's taking it out on Ed, apparently. He was supposed to be organising the insurance, I think. Anyway, not the rosiest start to married life by the sound of things.'

'What bad luck. How's everything else? How's Alfie?'

'Everything's fine. Alfie's good, he's enjoying nursery and has a new best friend there called Poppy. Always a hit with the ladies.'

'Sweet,' Anna said, picturing Alfie's smiling face. 'Give him a hug from me, will you? And how's work going?'

'Busy,' he said flatly. 'I've been working late, thought I may as well do it while you're away. And you? How's Italy?'

Anna couldn't find the right words to explain to Jon all of the new things she was seeing and doing.

'It's good,' she said. 'Listen, you look tired. You should probably take advantage of being at home and get an early night. I'll need one too, if I'm going to be any better in class tomorrow.'

'OK,' Jon said. 'Well, goodnight then.'

'Love you.'

'Me too.'

Anna reluctantly shut her laptop and put it on the chest of drawers. She looked out of her small room's window. The piazza was alive with couples eating together by candlelight and drinking wine. If only Jon were here too, then he'd understand.

Chapter Fifteen

Today's news is tomorrow's fish-and-chip paper, Imogen told herself, praying that it would turn out to be true in their case. It was difficult to tell whether it was the dismal weather or the food-poisoning scandal that was keeping people away from Vivien's.

It was mid-afternoon and the elderly man who rented out striped deckchairs on their strip was Imogen's sole customer, sipping at a mug of hot tea and waiting for the worst of the storm to pass. Imogen was beginning to wonder if summer was ever going to take hold at all. It was June and they'd barely had a glimpse of sunshine so far. Were they destined to have more weeks of grey clouds and the pattering of raindrops on the windows?

'Grim out there, isn't it?' the man said, voicing Imogen's thoughts. She nodded and forced a smile.

Imogen wished she could escape. Life on the island had suited her a lot better than this. But she owed it to her grandma, to her dad – and to Anna, she reminded herself sternly – not to give up. She couldn't let Anna come home from Italy to rumours of poor hygiene standards. She needed to build up some positive PR for Vivien's to balance out the negativity of the newspaper article. And she needed to do it quickly.

Positive mental attitude, she told herself, as she tidied away the spoons. When Anna got back it would only be a matter of time before they had a product they could feel really proud of. In order for the public to know about it, they needed to line up some really strong promotion.

She glanced up at the wall above the counter, where she'd framed some of the photos from Vivien's album – children playing on the beach in front of the shop, and parents relaxing in deckchairs alongside them. They would need something that conjured up the spirit of summer. Ice creams = sunny childhood daydreams. But when the sky was grey, what could she and Anna do to remind customers of those hazy warm days?

A gentle tune rang out in her head. The tinny notes that used to make her and Anna's ears prick up, send them running back to their parents for ice cream money to spend.

That's it, Imogen thought to herself. Festivals, beaches, picnics in the park. She had just the plan Vivien's needed.

Her thoughts were interrupted by the front door opening. 'Room for one more?' Jess said, smiling and walking in.

'I think we can squeeze you in.'

'Saw that article,' Jess said, taking a seat on one of the stools at the counter. 'What a nightmare.'

'Tell me about it.'

'Oh, don't fret. No one even reads local press any more.'

'I hope that's true,' Imogen said.

'And on the plus side, this place really does look a lot better.'

'Thanks,' Imogen said. 'It's scrubbed up pretty well. What are you still doing here, anyway? I thought you'd be sunning it up in Antigua by now.'

'Talking of nightmares, that bloody travel company!' she said. 'We had hundreds of pounds of honeymoon vouchers, that people had bought us on our wedding list – and now, with it going bust those gifts are all gone. The moment Ed's work got wind that our Antigua plan was down the pan they jumped at the chance to draft him in to do some more work. So it's just me. Here. New wife on staycation.'

'That's terrible,' Imogen said. 'Would you hate me if I said it's nice to see you, and I'm actually quite glad you're still here?'

'Yes, I would,' Jess said. 'So to make up for it I want a big cup of hot chocolate, please. Still here in rainy Britain and all on my own too. Even Anna's buggered off.'

Imogen went over to the kitchen to make Jess's drink.

'Not completely on your own,' Imogen said a moment later, handing her a warm mug.

'Sorry,' Jess said. 'It's great that you're here. It's just been an awful week. Anyway, how's Anna? She enjoying Italy?'

'I've had the occasional text,' Imogen said. 'It sounds like she's having a brilliant time.'

Jess smiled. 'Good, she deserves it, doesn't she? All these

years of cooking obsession might finally amount to something other than her creations ramping me up a dress size or two.'

'Yes,' Imogen said. 'Bet she's top of class right now, don't you? Teacher's pet.'

'Definitely,' Jess said, idly stirring the hot chocolate with her spoon.

'Jess,' Imogen said. 'Seeing as you're here . . . '

Jess raised an eyebrow suspiciously.

'Can I just run something by you? If you wanted to find a van, where would you start looking?'

'A van?' Jess said with a smirk. 'Are you planning on going somewhere? Anna always said you were a bit of a hippy.'

'It's not for me,' Imogen explained. 'It's for the business. An ice cream van. I've decided it's time – I mean it will be, when Anna gets back – for us to go mobile. What do you think?'

'A van.' Jess pushed her unruly shoulder-length curls back behind her ears, weighing up the idea. 'Like an old-school ice cream van?'

'Exactly.'

'I like it. There's a friend of Ed's down in Worthing who does up old vans, most of them VWs and stuff, but I bet you could find something there.'

'Brilliant,' Imogen said, lighting up at the idea.

'Depends how much you know about car engines though,' Jess said. 'Some of them still need a fair bit of work.'

'Oh, I'm pretty practical,' Imogen said. She'd changed a few tyres, and fixed her beach bike more than once.

'Great,' Jess said. She scribbled down the website of the

place on a napkin. 'Here you go. Ask for Graham. It's probably best if you go down there in person, so you can see the van and work out what's right.'

'Dreams on Wheels,' Imogen read out, smiling at the name. 'That's what it feels like, Jess. This way, we can take our ice cream dreams on the road.'

'Just don't let on to your sister that I've been encouraging you,' Jess said. 'Not sure she'll take kindly to me helping you with this madcap scheme.'

'I won't say a word,' Imogen said, already reaching for her mobile and bringing up the website. 'And there's nothing mad about this, I assure you.'

Imogen took Anna's bike and cycled over to the address that she'd found online. She came to a stop in the gravel outside Dreams on Wheels, and leaned it up against the brick wall. The garage owner slid out from his position under an orange VW van and turned his head to greet her. His face, ruggedly handsome, his hairline receding slightly, was streaked with oil, and he was wearing dark blue overalls.

'You must be Jess's friend. Imogen, was it?' he said, coming all the way out from under the van and slowly getting to his feet.

'Yes, that's me.' Imogen said with a smile. 'The ice cream lady.' He reached out an oil-covered hand for her to shake – then, clocking her hesitation, pulled back, wiping his hands on his overalls.

'Best not, eh?' he laughed.

'Now, I have to say it felt like a stroke of luck when you called. You see, I've got an old ice cream van – from the seventies, it is – that I've been trying to shift for a while. It's not right for the ordinary customer, of course, but it might fit the bill for you. Just needs a lick of paint – come and have a look.'

Graham led Imogen round to the back of his workshop and past a row of vans, an old yellow school bus and another van with 'Girl Guides' written on the side.

'I can offer you a pretty reasonable price, if you're interested. Seven hundred should do it, as it's been here a while and to be honest I could really use the space. It's a good little runner, still got the freezers inside there and everything.'

Imogen's eyes adjusted to the dark at the back of the garage and she could make out the van in front of her. Yes, it looked faded, but it had four wheels and a brilliant ice cream model on the top. Perfect.

'That's the one,' Imogen said. She could just picture it – with 'Vivien's' written in script on the side – selling ice cream at festivals, by other south-coast beaches, at local parks. When Anna got back she would fall in love with it just as much – she wouldn't care less about the other things that had happened while she'd been away.

'I'll give you four hundred for it,' Imogen said. In her satchel was five hundred pounds in cash, the last of the money their grandmother had left them to start up the business. OK, so she and Anna had had it earmarked for ingredients, but just as soon as they got the van out there they could make that money back in a week.

'Four hundred and fifty,' Graham said firmly, but with a smile in his eyes, 'and you've got yourself a deal.'

Chapter Sixteen

Giovanna had laid out an array of delicious-looking breakfast pastries on the roof terrace, and Sian and Matteo were both sitting at the table drinking coffee.

'Morning, all,' Anna said with a bright smile, sitting down with them. 'I didn't realise you were staying here, Sian.'

'Got here late last night,' she replied. 'I was in a hostel nearby, a right dump. I was feeling pretty desperate about it actually, but then Matteo recommended this place to me and luckily there was a room available.'

Anna smiled, and took a seat at their table. The terrace overlooked the pretty square, and just a hundred metres or so away was the distinctive silhouette of the Duomo, the cathedral that was the city's primary landmark. She reached towards the pastry plate and took a cannoli, a rich cream horn, and as she took a bite, the flaky pastry dissolved on her lips. It was still warm, fresh from the oven.

'Mmm,' Anna said, in undisguised delight. 'These are incredible.'

'Pretty good, eh?' Matteo said, pouring her a coffee.

'I think everyone in Italy knows about Giovanna's pastries.'

'How do you know her?' Sian asked.

'She was our neighbour, before we moved to Siena. My mother and father decided they wanted a change and they set up a gelateria there instead. They said it was getting too competitive here, too political.'

'And you?' Anna asked, taking a tentative sip of her drink, which was still hot. She flinched a little – it was stronger than she was used to.

'Siena was fine for when I was studying,' Matteo said, pushing a dark curl out of his eyes. 'My parents wanted me to do something different, so I started training to be an accountant. But it wasn't for me. Not at all,' he laughed. 'I wake up and I think about food, I go to sleep and I think about food. I even dream about ice cream! How could I possibly do anything else?'

Anna smiled in recognition. She wondered for a moment how she'd stayed in her marketing job as long as she did.

'When I realised that,' Matteo continued, 'Bianca's school was the obvious place to train. I hope that when I've finished I can go back to Siena and start up on my own.' He smiled kindly, his eyes crinkling a little at the corners. 'But, listen, I didn't mean to tell you my whole life story.'

Sian was listening to Matteo with rapt attention, and Anna noticed she'd barely touched the pastry on her plate.

'What do you make of Florence so far?' he asked them both.

'It's beautiful,' Sian said.

'Yes, even more so than I expected,' Anna added. She couldn't stop marvelling at the elegance in every fountain, each feature of the tall townhouses. It was as if even the most unimportant of structures had been crafted as a work of art, not a functional object.

'Did you know there's another reason Florence is the perfect place to study ice cream making?'

'There is?' Anna asked.

'Yes, the famous Ice Cream Festival.'

Anna thought back to her guidebook, wondered if she'd overlooked something. There was going to be a festival of ice cream going on right here in Florence? How had she missed hearing about it?

'Next week,' Matteo said. 'It starts the day after we finish the course. You're going to see the city transformed.' His eyes lit up as he talked. 'Sorbets, ice creams, granitas – you name it, you'll be able to taste it here.'

Anna grinned with excitement. 'What an unexpected treat,' she said. She'd have a day to enjoy it before getting her flight home.

'Sounds like the perfect way to celebrate after our hard work on the course,' Sian said, tying her blonde hair back with a hairband. 'But I'll be back on a plane to Dublin by then.'

'Plans,' Matteo said, with a cheeky glint in his eye. 'The best thing about plans,' he went on, 'is that you can always change them.'

Sian smiled. Anna suddenly felt awkward, as if she shouldn't be there. Was there something going on between Matteo and Sian that she hadn't spotted?

'Right,' she said, checking her watch. 'Half past eight. I'm going to walk in a bit early, go the long way by the river. I'll see you in class.'

'Today,' Bianca announced, 'we'll be learning to make a fig and almond ice cream.' From her expression Anna could tell that this was one of her favourites, and as soon as she caught sight of the figs on her table – plump and ripe, almost bursting with juice – she could understand why.

'This one looks good,' Sian whispered to Anna. After the terrible ice cream she'd made the day before, Anna had been relieved to be paired with her, and could already see Georgios and Hiro struggling with the ingredients list at the adjacent bench.

'Today we get serious,' Bianca said. 'We don't have much time, only a week, so I'll be working you hard on this course, and I expect to see results. Only those who have produced three ice creams of the highest standard will receive the certificate on Friday.'

Anna thought of yesterday's mess, and how far that ice cream was from being a contender. But today, she vowed, tightening the strings on her apron, was a whole new day.

'Right. Now, we only have thirty minutes for this,' Bianca said, 'so let's get started.'

Anna glanced over at Matteo and Ria enviously: they

seemed so organised, and in just a couple of minutes, they had their workspace set up and ready to go. Matteo was peeling the figs and chopping them into small pieces.

Anna and Sian got to work, and had soon prepared plenty of fruit for their ice cream, along with some sliced almonds. They chatted as they worked, and Anna found it all came more naturally than the day before. After fifteen minutes they had a mixture ready to freeze in the ice cream machine.

'Looking pretty good,' Bianca said, as she passed their table. 'I think I may have underestimated you, Signora McAvoy.'

It was supposed to be their afternoon treat, but as Anna huffed and puffed her way up the steep steps of the Duomo – Florence's grand cathedral – later that day she was beginning to wonder if she wouldn't rather be back in the classroom.

'Keep up!' Bianca said, as her class trailed behind her up the stone staircase. 'We're almost halfway there.'

After a successful morning of ice cream making, Bianca had suggested that they finish an hour early and take advantage of the beautiful summer's day by going on a class trip. 'I'll be the first to say that ice cream making is important,' she had told the class after their brief lunch break, 'but I can't have you here in Florence for a week without seeing one of the most beautiful sights in the world.'

'And what happens at halfway?' Hiro asked.

'You're about to find out. Just step through this doorway.'

Bianca motioned to a gap in the stone to her left, and then led the way through.

Anna kept focused on Matteo in front of her, trying not to think about how high up they had climbed. As she followed him through the opening, she found they were on a circular platform leading around the inside of the dome. Beyond the low wall that kept them from falling, she could make out people on the cathedral floor below, tiny dots. She felt a wave of nausea, and gripped the edge.

'Are you OK?' Matteo asked, looking back at her.

'Sort of.' Anna smiled. 'I'm terrified of heights.'

'Try not to look down,' he said, putting his hand on her arm reassuringly. She allowed it to linger there. It felt good, his touch, and physical closeness meant something different over here, she reasoned.

'And why would you? Look up, Anna.' He pointed to the frescoes on the cathedral's ceiling, in vibrant blues and gold leaf, a depiction of heaven.

'Wow,' she said, forgetting all about her previous fear.

'Do you like it?'

'Beautiful enough to make you forget how high up we are,' she smiled.

They went halfway around and then back through another doorway, to more stairs. Anna stopped at a small window on the way up the next flight, and pointed at a collection of metal padlocks attached to the grate. 'What are these?'

'They're to, how do you say . . . to remember,' Matteo said.

'Look,' he pointed at where people had inscribed or painted their initials onto the metal. 'You come here with someone who matters to you, and leave a lock as a reminder. So it will always be there.'

Anna thought of Jon. He wasn't the keenest traveller – he'd only been out of Britain once before, on a stag outing to Amsterdam. But perhaps she could persuade him to come here. Maybe they could retrace her steps and put their own padlock up here. She warmed at the thought.

'Nice, aren't they?' Matteo said, with a smile. He glanced up at the empty staircase ahead of them. 'They've gone ahead. Let's catch up.'

Anna picked up her pace, and in a couple of minutes they reached the top. She stepped out onto the outdoor platform at the top of the Duomo, and emerged to a view that took her breath away. It was a clear, sunny day and she could see for miles, across the city, past the sparkling river and out into the Tuscan countryside.

'So what do you think?' Bianca said, pointing at the view. 'Worth the walk, isn't it?'

Anna made her way over to the edge, where her classmates were standing and taking photos. She distanced herself from them slightly so that she could look out at the view.

'Yes,' Anna said. 'It's stunning.' Matteo came and stood beside her.

'It looks to me,' he said, 'like your vertigo might be cured.'

Chapter Seventeen

Jon opened the door in a pair of boxer shorts. 'Imogen,' he said, surprised.

'Sorry, Jon.' Imogen was still holding Anna's borrowed key to the flat in her hand. 'I didn't think anyone would be here.'

'Come in,' he said, still looking embarrassed. 'I know, normally I'd be out, but I'm working from home today.' His hair stood up in tufts and spikes, as if he'd just woken up.

'I won't be a minute,' Imogen said, walking past him. 'I just need to pick something up.' She went through into the bathroom, found her washbag right away and slung it into her satchel. She could hear the TV on quietly in the background. Doesn't sound much like work, she thought to herself with a smile.

She put her head around the doorway to the living room, where Jon was sitting on the sofa.

'If you're at a loose end, I'd love a hand at the shop today,' she said, adopting her most winning expression.

'Hectic day ahead, sorry. How's it been going down there?'

'Good,' Imogen said. 'Better. It's all change at Vivien's.'

'What, with Anna's course?'

'More than that,' Imogen said. 'Come and take a look.' She nodded towards the window.

Jon followed her cue and got to his feet. She cleared the steam from the window and they both looked out.

'Imogen, what on earth's parked in front of our house?' he said, pointing down at the van in horror.

'It's less a case of what it is,' Imogen said proudly, 'more what it's going to be.'

At the café later that day, the list Imogen was writing was getting longer:

Glastonbury
Secret Garden
Isle of Wight
Sussex Food and Drink Festival

Once they had quality ice creams to sell, the more people they could take them to, the better. When she arrived at the shop after visiting Anna's flat, she'd scrubbed and cleaned the new van so that it was ready to paint. Now she had the more pleasurable task of dreaming about all the places she could visit in it. She checked out the prices for pitches online and noted them down.

Imogen went to the shop's own website and uploaded some photos of the van for the blog post she was writing. Visitors to the site would be able to see the van being decorated at various stages, then find out where they could come and buy from it. The screen loaded as the photos went up.

She should put a link through to TripAdvisor too – everyone used that nowadays. She opened a new window and tapped in the URL for the review site and searched for Vivien's.

A one-star review dominated the page. *Oh Christ*, she thought. *Someone give us a break, please.* Shocked, she forced herself to read it:

Vivien's Heavenly Ice Cream Shop, Hove Seafront

I've reluctantly given this one star, simply because they don't give you the option to grade it as none. Why they call it 'heavenly' is beyond me – it's more like the place below, if you ask me! I used to love this shop back when the old lady ran it – you always got a warm welcome. But since her granddaughters have taken it over it's gone badly downhill. Not just the décor – although God only knows what was going through their heads when they chose that – but the customer service is terrible. There's barely any choice of drinks or snacks, so it's hardly worthy of the ice cream shop label.

Imogen braced herself as she read the final sentence.

Appalling. Spend your hard-earned cash elsewhere until someone else takes it over. 0/10

FROM: TheRoadLessTravelled

The words stared out at Imogen – *Appalling. Terrible . . .* There was a tiny flicker of relief that the poisoning incident hadn't been mentioned – but it was still a damning review, the first that many potential customers would see. She flicked to another restaurant review site and saw the same comment posted – then another, and another – all under the same name, with not one positive review to balance them out.

Were they written by the same person who had spoken to the press, or was someone else now trying to break them? All Imogen knew was that if they were to stand a chance of bouncing back from this disastrous week, she had to find out.

'Ta-da!' Jess said, putting her iPad down on the counter at Vivien's. 'I think I've got it. What do you think?'

Imogen looked at the logo that Jess had designed. 'Vivien's' was written in a swirl, in a sweeping vintage script. It was simple but stylish – and would look a treat painted on the outside of the van.

'It's perfect,' Imogen said.

'Why, thank you,' Jess replied. 'Didn't even have to burn any midnight oil. It came to me right away.'

Imogen fell quiet.

'Why the long face?' Jess asked.

'Oh, it's nothing. I just read a crappy review for the shop online. It's nothing worth worrying about.'

'There are some nasty people out there, but try and forget

about it,' Jess said. 'And if you ask me, painting my fabulous logo onto the van is the best possible way to do that.'

'Tell me you've got time to help me?' Imogen said. 'I've prepped the van, cleaned and scrubbed it. But I'm not an artist.'

'I'm all yours,' Jess said. 'For a limited time only. I wore my best clothes especially.' Jess's curly hair was tied up in a topknot and she was in worn jeans and a faded T-shirt.

'Thank you,' Imogen said. 'You're a godsend. Right, what do we need . . . ?'

She opened a cupboard under the sink and took out the cans of car paint she'd bought, candyfloss pink and pistachio to match the retro interior of the shop. 'Reckon we've got pretty much everything here.'

'Let's go, then,' Jess said eagerly.

Outside, they turned the stereo up loud and got to work. Jess was drawing out the design ready for them to paint.

'Ooh, what's going on here?' Evie said, poking her head out of her shop door.

'Meet the newest member of our team,' Imogen called out over the music, pointing to the van.

'I like it,' Evie said. 'Does it play a tune?'

Jess reached inside and pressed the button that sent the summery music ringing out. Evie laughed in surprise. 'Terrific,' she said.

'Yes, only we'd better not do that again,' Imogen said, 'because we've got nothing to sell yet.'

'You will soon enough. Anna will be back next week, won't

she?' Evie said, leaning back against the doorway. 'And you can take it out on the road then.'

'Believe me, I'm counting the days,' Imogen said.

As the sun set over the sea and the air cooled, Imogen finished the remainder of the painting on the van. Jess had gone home, but had painted enough for her to take over the final stages.

'This yours?' came a male voice.

Imogen's heart sank. Finn.

'Yes,' Imogen said. She got up from her crouched position to standing and looked him in the eye.

'Don't you think you might be running before you can walk?'

'Look, Finn,' she said assertively, wiping down her paint-covered hands on the front of her overalls. She thought of the nasty review she'd read. Could Finn have written that too? She hesitated, then decided it would be better to try and make peace.

'I'm sorry about what happened the other day,' she said, as calmly as she could. 'But what more can I do? I've taken the ice cream off sale and until Anna's back we're sticking to the ready-made stuff – the van is for when we have her new ice creams ready.'

'I hope, for your customers' sake, that you'll be testing them properly.'

'Of course we will,' Imogen snapped. 'I don't interfere with your business, Finn, so how about you don't—'

Finn cut her short. 'Imogen, you already *have* interfered with my business – it's strange that you don't seem to realise that. I had to give half of my class a refund. Usually in Granville Arches we look after each other, we trust one another – but I guess things have changed. Maybe you're right – we should just let each other get on with what we do.'

'That sounds good to me.'

'You can get him on for just a minute, can't you?' Imogen said to her mum. She was sitting in the top floor bedroom at Vivien's house, tucked up under the duvet. 'I really need to talk to him.'

After the day she'd had, there was only one person who might be able to make her feel better.

'It's not the time,' Jan said. 'Your dad's very tired.'

'Still?'

'He's no better,' Jan said. 'In fact . . . Well, I wasn't going to mention this to you until Anna was back. But actually he's quite a lot worse.'

'Worse?' Imogen said. 'What's going on, Mum?'

The line fell silent for a second.

'We had a visit last night, from Françoise and Martin. They're insisting on trying to push forward the date for the house sale again. But it's more than that. Françoise is trying to persuade your father to let her make a bid for the business.'

'What?' Imogen said, sitting upright. 'She can't do that.'

'She said there've been bad reviews and publicity about

the shop – and she's arguing that it'll go bankrupt under your ownership,' Jan said.

'What right does she have to interfere?'

'None, I know, but that doesn't seem to be stopping her. Imogen, I don't know what she's capable of. But she and Martin are having a damn good try at breaking your father's heart.'

Chapter Eighteen

'It's lovely, Imo. Just so pretty – the sun's out – not like at home.' Anna walked, chatting on her mobile as she went, across the cobbled square in front of the Uffizi Gallery, where she and Sian had spent their lunch break looking at Renaissance masterpieces – Leonardo and Botticelli, the originals right there in front of them. She'd left Sian sketching in one of the rooms.

'And the people are really friendly,' she went on. 'You know I used to be funny about travelling on my own, do you remember? But I've hardly been alone since I arrived.'

'I told you,' Imogen replied. 'And you're enjoying the course?'

'It's fantastic. And there's an ice cream festival starting next weekend – I'm here just long enough to go to it,' Anna said, full of enthusiasm. 'It's only once a year, Imo. Isn't it amazing timing that I'm over here? Some of the country's top ice cream makers are going to be here – there's going to be all kinds of experimental flavours, apparently it's . . . Oh look, I am rambling on, aren't I? How are things with you, the shop?' Anna remembered what her sister had said about making and selling the ice cream herself: it sounded like she was really coming into her own without her elder sister there crowding her.

'Oh fine,' Imogen said, sounding chirpy. 'Everything's going well. Now you enjoy yourself out there and bring us back some flavours we can wow our new customers with.'

'Sure I will,' Anna said. 'I definitely will.' She was about to hang up the phone, but a thought nagged at her. 'Listen, Imogen – weird thing to ask, I know, but you haven't heard from Jon, have you? Only I've been calling him at work all morning and he hasn't picked up.'

'I saw him yesterday,' Imogen said. 'I popped by the flat and caught him in his pants.'

'In his pants?'

'Not as dodgy as it sounds,' Imogen reassured her. 'He was working from home. Try him on his mobile.'

'OK, I will. See you soon, Imo.'

'Bye.'

Anna hung up and walked back slowly towards the ice cream school. Energised by the beautiful art she'd just seen, she felt inspired about getting to work on a new creation. The theme that Bianca had set today was fruit sorbets, and she and Matteo, teamed up for the first time, had opted for fruits of the forest, succulent red berries that tasted perfect in the ice. With Matteo's snippets of knowledge, and Anna's careful tasting, the flavours were working beautifully together. The fourth day on the course had been Anna's best yet.

She arrived back at the class at the same time as the others, and there was a buzz as everyone retook their seats. 'Top of the class, eh?' Georgios said to Anna with a hearty chuckle as he passed her workstation. Yesterday Bianca had offered her that coveted placement for her coffee ice cream and she'd been glowing with pleasure ever since. It didn't mean much, really – there were only six students, after all, but it was the reminder Anna needed that doing the course was going to be worthwhile.

'You next,' Anna joked, with a smile. It was hard not to see that Georgios' progress had been the slowest, but he always launched into the tasks with gusto, and Bianca hadn't given up on him yet.

'Hey, back to work, you,' Matteo said, giving her a good-natured nudge and motioning for her to add the prepared fruit to the sorbet mixture. His brown eyes met hers.

'And what next?' Anna said, squinting at the recipe book and trying to make out the final instructions. After another delicious breakfast on the terrace that morning, coloured by a leisurely chat with Sian and Matteo, she'd forgotten to bring her glasses. She could barely make out the words. It was normally she who read recipes out to Imogen, so she jumped in surprise as a gentle voice came over her shoulder. 'You test the sugar level now,' Matteo said, 'with the – what do you call it – the monitor thing.' Something about the tone of his voice made her feel suddenly conscious of how close he was to her. She could feel the warmth of his breath on her neck as he spoke, and smell the clean, but faintly musky, scent of him.

'Right, let's do that then,' Anna said, the words rushing out. She should say something about Jon. Any moment now, she would explain that she had a boyfriend, and make sure that was clear.

They finished the preparations together, and Anna barely said a word. When they had finished, she put the bowl in the fridge. As she made room for it she spotted another bowl in there, in addition to the one they'd prepared together that morning. 'What's this?' she asked.

'I made that at lunchtime,' Matteo said. Then, laughing, 'Don't call me teacher's pet, please . . . I just had a bit of free time. And I wanted to experiment.'

She took out the bowl, peeled back the clingfilm and looked at the sorbet, a pale green colour. 'Kiwi?' she guessed, and he nodded. 'And *melone*,' he said. Anna thought he made '*melone*' sound like the most exotic and delicious of all fruits, the way it tripped off his tongue. 'Melon, I mean,' he corrected himself.

'Try it,' he said. He dipped a spoon into the sorbet and then passed it to Anna. She took it, and braced herself for the cold on her tongue – over the day's ice preparation she'd grown used to the chill in her mouth that ran right the way down to her toes. Even on a hot summer's day like this one, when the air outside was stifling, and only the floatiest of summer dresses, like the lilac one Anna had chosen that morning, would do.

But it wasn't the cold that she noticed. It was the flavours – the delicate zing of the kiwi first, and then the more subtle flavours of the melon underlying it. Deeper still was another taste, mint perhaps, that made the whole sorbet deliciously full-bodied.

She was conscious that a smile had spread right the way across her face, her spirits reacting to the exquisite combination. Her expression was mirrored by Matteo's. He grinned, watching his creation working the intended magic on Anna.

She didn't want the mouthful to end, savoured the final, minute crystals of ice and the way every part of her mouth responded to it.

'You like it?' Matteo asked. Anna nodded. 'Just wait until the festival – this is nothing. You're going to taste things you never knew existed. Why don't you come out with me and a few friends tomorrow night? Elena, and Caro, Saverio – you'll like them, and they speak a bit of English. We can show you around.'

'I'd like that,' Anna said, with a rush of excitement.

It was Friday, and their course was drawing to a close. Anna prepared herself for the final day of study by eating another breakfast of pastries up on the terrace, this time with Giovanna for company. She wondered where Matteo and Sian had got to, and concluded that they must have got an early start.

'Did you see?' Giovanna said, pointing down beyond the low terrace wall to the lively city square below. Stalls were being constructed on the cobblestones, and people were chattering animatedly around them. A big banner had appeared overnight:

FIRENZE − FESTIVAL DEL GELATO

The city was alive with festival colours. 'It looks beautiful,' Anna said enthusiastically.

'More than that,' Giovanna replied. 'It is *delizioso*.' She put two fingers to her lips to illustrate the point.

Anna was looking forward to the day and the evening ahead. Unless there were any major culinary disasters, they'd be receiving their end-of-course certificates, and then the whole class would be going out for a meal with Bianca in what she had assured them was one of Florence's finest restaurants. After that, Anna thought, with a glow, she'd have time to explore the ice cream festival with Matteo and his friends.

Anna was only sorry Sian wouldn't be able to make it due to her early flight − over an evening chatting and drinking prosecco by the river, they'd become close, and she'd be sorry to see her friend go.

After breakfast, she got her things ready for class, and walked out into the piazza. The clock tower showed half-past eight. Jon would probably only just have woken up, but she was longing to hear his voice after failing to get through to him at all the previous day. She got out her mobile and dialled his number.

'Anna?' he said, answering after just one ring.

'Hi, Jon,' she said, instantly relaxing at the familiar sound of his voice. 'How are you?'

'It's lovely to hear from you. But listen, I'm just about to head into a breakfast meeting. Is it important?'

'No, nothing urgent,' she replied, trying to brush off the disappointment she felt. 'I just wanted a chat, to catch up a bit. We haven't spoken for a while.'

'Of course. Everything's fine. Sorry to ask, but do you think this could wait till tomorrow?' Jon said. 'I'm really pushed today. But I'll come and pick you up from the airport. It's nine p.m. you're getting in, right?'

'Nine twenty,' Anna said. 'I emailed you the flight number. I can't wait to see you again.'

'OK, darling. See you then.'

'I love you,' Anna said.

'I love you too,' he said quietly, like he always did in the crowded office. 'Have a safe journey back.'

At the end of their final day on the course, Bianca had given the whole class certificates and insisted they deserved a round of applause. 'Now to celebrate,' she'd said. 'Tonight we are going out to dinner, and you're going to have the best food you'll taste here in Florence.'

The accademia's students and their proud teacher settled down at a cosy, family-run trattoria with red-and-white chequered tablecloths, wooden furniture and a menu full of hearty pastas, pizzas and risottos. Anna was relieved to find that Bianca hadn't meant best in a Michelin-starred sense – her budget would never have stretched to that.

Anna ordered a pizza, which arrived laden with fresh artichokes and mushrooms, stone-baked to perfection, and, starving after a day of hard work in the kitchen, she took a big bite.

She'd been pleased with her experiment that day, a fresh and light quince ice cream – in fact it was probably the best one she'd made all week. But in spite of her culinary success, she hadn't been able to relax. She couldn't put her finger on what was wrong, but there was something in Jon's tone that had unsettled her. She couldn't wait to see him and Alfie again, so why did it seem as if she was further down his list of priorities right now? Was she being too demanding? She resolved to give him space when she got home. If there was an issue he'd tell her in his own time.

'Congratulations,' Bianca said, raising her glass of red wine. Anna, Georgios, Sian, Matteo, Ria and Hiro clinked their glasses with her over the table. Anna smiled. They'd survived the course and, better still, mastered some truly mouth-watering recipes they'd all be taking home to their own countries.

'To the best teacher,' Georgios said, raising his glass again. 'To *bella* Bianca!' he smiled. They all joined him enthusiastically for the second toast. Despite Bianca's occasional harsh criticisms, Anna could tell she really cared about her students, and in just a few short days she'd brought out the best in all of them. Right now Bianca was glowing.

After the meal, the group congregated on the pavement outside the restaurant and exchanged contact details, hugging their goodbyes.

'Thank you,' Anna said to Bianca, separate from the rest of the group. 'The last week has been such an inspiration.'

'You're ready, then?' she said. 'To get going at home, in your shop?'

'I think I am.'

'You'll send me pictures,' Bianca insisted. Then she whispered, 'He's a good catch, you know –' she nodded over at Matteo, who was helping Sian into a taxi – 'and I think he might have . . . How do you say it? A soft spot for you.' She gave Anna a wink, and before Anna could answer, Georgios had swept Bianca up into a bear hug.

Sian's cab pulled away and Matteo walked over to Anna. 'Are you ready to go?' he asked. 'I said I'd meet Saverio, Elena and Caro over by the Duomo.'

'Sure,' Anna said, trying to forget what Bianca had just told her. 'Let's go.'

Anna and Matteo walked slowly across the square, the festival buzzing around them. 'They'll be here any minute,' Matteo said. Anna thought she detected a little nervousness in his voice. She tried to think of something to say to make the atmosphere between them more relaxed.

'Ciao, Matteo!' A young couple and another woman in her twenties came around the corner and greeted both their friend and Anna with kisses on the cheek. They chatted easily in Italian, and Anna caught the occasional word and wished she could understand it all better. She was relieved when one of the women turned to her and said shyly, 'Hi, I'm Caro. You're English, aren't you? Pleased to meet you. I badly need to practise my English!'

Excitedly chatting among themselves, the group made their way to the first ice cream tasting of the festival. Matteo handed Anna an almond gelato in a chocolate-trimmed waffle cone and she licked it, enjoying the coolness of the ice on the steamy summer evening. The flavour developed after a moment – there was a subtlety to it that made it irresistible. In her own happy bubble, she continued to eat and for a moment didn't realise that Matteo and his friends had moved on to the next stall without her. As she hurried to catch them up, she felt more determined than ever to produce outstanding ice cream when she got back home – if only so that she could eat it herself. Cornettos and Viennetta were never going to cut it now she'd tasted this.

'Anna, *cioccolato!*' Matteo said, turning towards her with a taster spoonful for her to try. 'But this isn't any ordinary chocolate,' he said with a wink.

Anna took a bite and after the comforting swirl of chocolate, other flavours sparked in her mouth – chilli, with a real kick to it. 'Wow,' she said.

'Good?' Matteo asked.

'Fantastic,' she replied, laughing with the pure joy of the delicious discovery.

'It's Mexican, the ice cream of the Aztecs.'

Matteo asked for some more tasters, and there was a surge from behind, as new punters joined the crowd. Anna's leg pressed against his for a moment. Conscious of the closeness, she looked up and her eyes met his, his gaze lingering naturally. Anna's phone buzzed in her pocket, and she was relieved to have an excuse to look away. She took it out, pleased that Jon had found time to call her back. She could explain to Matteo now that her boyfriend was calling. But instead of

Jon's name, she saw it was a text from Jess:

> In case you're wondering: nice olive oil, and a packet of those crunchy
> biscuit things, please. Can't wait till you're back. Jess xx

She smiled at the message. 'A friend,' she explained.

It was nearly two in the morning, and Anna had a flight to catch in the morning, but she wanted to stay exactly where she was. Saverio had driven them all up to a lookout, with a panoramic view of the city and a dark sky full of stars stretched out above them. The five of them were leaning against the white Cinquecento car they'd squeezed into on the way up, glasses in their hands.

'More limoncello?' Matteo asked.

'I suppose a little bit wouldn't hurt,' Anna said with a smile, offering her glass, traces of the sweet spirit still on her lips. The others in the group were discussing what music to put on the car stereo.

Matteo filled her glass, and their eyes met again. 'Anna, I've been wanting to say something. Since the first day—'

A blast of music came from the car stereo, cutting him short. Matteo's friends laughed and found the volume switch to turn it down.

'There's no need,' Anna said gently. She thought of Bianca's words, and felt a wave of guilt and confusion. She should have been honest about Jon from the start. She'd done the wrong thing coming here tonight.

'It's my last night here, Matteo. Let's just enjoy it.'

Chapter Nineteen

CLOSED DUE TO A FAMILY EMERGENCY

Imogen Blu-tacked up the sign on the front door and shut the shop at midday. It wasn't as if they'd be missing out on that much business, she told herself. Her only customers that morning had been a group of stoned twenty-something students, marvelling for what seemed like hours over the intricacies of the hundreds and thousands on Fab lollies.

She couldn't just wait around in the shop, knowing that Françoise was pressurising her dad and it was making him feel worse. She threw her small rucksack onto the passenger seat of the ice cream van and climbed into the driver's seat.

She started the engine, and drove on to the main road. She didn't know quite what she was going to do when she reached her parents' cottage, but if Françoise was still around, she was soon going to wish she wasn't.

Forty-five minutes later, Jan opened the door to their family home.

'Are they still here?' Imogen demanded.

'Are who here?' Jan said, looking wary. 'Do you mean your uncle and aunt? If so, then yes, they are.'

Jan peered around her daughter and out into the driveway, spying the ice cream van parked there. 'Imogen, what is that in our driveway?'

'Nothing,' Imogen said. 'I mean, I'll explain later. Let me come in and talk to them.'

'OK,' Jan conceded, standing back. 'But,' she said, voice dropped to a whisper, 'please don't cause a fuss. Your father's upset enough as it is.'

Imogen strode through into the kitchen, where her uncle and aunt were sitting around the table with her father.

'Hi,' she said. Her father looked tired and a little dazed. She leaned down to hug him hello but he barely seemed to register her presence.

'Aunt Françoise,' Imogen said, turning to face her. 'Could I have a word?'

She glanced over at Martin for protection, and he gave his wife an apologetic shrug. Françoise reluctantly scraped back her chair and followed Imogen into the living room.

Imogen closed the door behind them.

'What have you been telling Dad?' she said, furious.

'Only the truth,' Françoise retorted. 'What everyone in Brighton is saying. It was even in the newspaper, I hear. That you are running Vivien's business into the ground, and ruining any reputation it ever had.'

'That's not true,' Imogen said. It stung that some of it – maybe – was. A bit. 'We've been working all hours trying to get this business off the ground. Anna's on a course now so that we can improve the product we're selling. How dare you interfere like this!'

'I'm just looking out for your father and Martin's best interests,' Françoise hissed back. 'And right now, it's pretty clear that your shop needs some new direction. I've given your father a business plan of my own, with Martin's approval. It's Tom's decision whether he wants to talk to you and Anna about it. But I've let him know I feel your grandmother's shop would stand a better chance in mine and Martin's hands.'

Tears of fury welled up in Imogen's eyes. 'How could you?' she said. 'You know how upset he's been since Granny's death.'

'And you think watching his mother's business going down the drain is going to help, do you, Imogen?'

Imogen was momentarily speechless. What she'd said had made no difference at all.

'You're clearly determined to ruin this for me and Anna.'

'I think you're being a little dramatic,' Françoise said dismissively.

'I don't think so.'

Imogen turned her back on her aunt and walked out of the room and into the kitchen. She took a deep breath and tried to keep her cool, for her dad's sake.

'Sorry for dropping in like this,' Imogen said. 'I shouldn't have come.' She kissed her mum and dad goodbye. 'I have to head off now, but I'll be back in a little while.'

'OK, dear,' her dad said, still distant. 'Well, it's always nice to see you.'

Jan gave her daughter a hug and whispered in her ear: 'We'll sort this out, don't worry.'

Imogen left the house and started the van's engine, pulling out of the driveway. On the main street she indicated left at the roundabout, to take the A-Road back to Brighton. She could still see Françoise's face in her mind, ruthless and determined. 'How dare she!' Imogen said out loud, reliving the moment.

She pressed on the gas and shot out on to the edge of the roundabout, instantly stalling. Panicked, she restarted the engine. For a moment there was hope, then it sputtered and died.

Cars honked and flashed their lights at her, but no matter how many times she tried, she couldn't start the engine up again.

'What were you thinking?' Jess said, when she arrived twenty minutes later.

Imogen was signing the AA's man clipboard to become a member so that she could get towed back to the Arches. 'You're lucky you got this far,' Jess continued. 'I thought you were going to get that thing serviced before you drove it again.'

'I had to go,' Imogen said. Tears pooled in her eyes, but she fought them back. 'I thought it would be fine.'

'Well, no point worrying about it now,' Jess said. 'They'll tow it back for you. Now let me give you a lift home.'

'Thanks,' Imogen said, getting into Jess's car.

'What was so urgent that you had to shut up shop and drive over here anyway?' Jess said, as they pulled away from the kerb.

'Family stuff,' Imogen said. 'It's a long story.'

'And our hurry is?'

'In a nutshell, Dad's been depressed since Granny died, and now our aunt is trying to manipulate him.'

'Sounds nasty,' Jess said, wrinkling her nose. 'Manipulate him how?'

'She's trying to convince him we're not capable of running the shop, so that she can put her own bid in for the business.'

'She'll never manage that.' Jess said.

'I want to believe you. But you don't know my Aunt Françoise.'

'Anna told me she can be quite determined when she wants something.'

'And some,' Imogen said, leaning back in her car seat and raking her hands through her hair. 'God, Jess. I've made such a mess of everything. And now we're going to need more money to repair the van. Anna's going to kill me.'

Chapter Twenty

On the bus seat next to Anna, a generously proportioned Italian mamma adjusted her wide-brimmed hat, purple with an arrangement of fake flowers on top. She chattered away animatedly with a woman in turquoise across the aisle, and from the odd word Anna caught, it seemed like they were talking about a wedding. Her attention drifted away from their lively conversation to the scenery out of the window.

She watched as the spectacular landscape went by, the same cypress trees and yellow houses that had signalled her arrival in Italy just a week ago. She felt a pang at the thought that she was leaving it all behind – perhaps forever. But it was only a holiday, she told herself. It was silly to think of it as anything more than that.

Anna had never thought of herself as the adventurous type. When she and Imogen were kids it had always been Imogen who was experimenting on insects, building dens with their dad and mixing deadly looking potions. She was more likely to be in the house, usually cooking – she'd always thought she'd rather be pottering around the kitchen than camping under remote desert stars or trekking through the rainforest.

But as she neared Pisa Airport, passing by the houses and churches of a small town, Anna wondered if the story she'd always told herself – about who she was and what she wanted – was still true. Italy had opened her eyes – to adventure, and a world full of energy, and a life lived with food at the very heart of it.

Thinking of the journey ahead, and of what she was leaving behind, her senses were revived by a memory: the taste of kiwi and melon. Matteo's sorbet. It was almost as vivid now as when she'd taken the spoonful. The mingling of fresh fruity sweetness with a sharp tang, a flavour people would travel across a country for. She'd never tasted it before – and doubted she'd ever find that exact flavour again.

Unless. She fumbled in her handbag, past her mobile, lipstick and fake Prada sunglasses. Inside was a folded sheet of paper, the one she'd encouraged her fellow students to write their contact details on. She glanced over the names quickly until her eyes came to rest on Matteo's – he'd put both his email and Facebook details on there.

It could be worth staying in touch, she thought, with just the tiniest flash of guilt. Jon wouldn't be happy about it – but he didn't really have to know. It would only be so that she could request that recipe from him, maybe get his advice in the future. Business – she needed to compile a dozen or so top-notch recipes for the relaunch of Vivien's. She typed Matteo's email address into her iPhone and pressed Save.

*

Jon took Anna in his arms the moment they stepped through the door, and kissed her gently on her mouth, her neck. He put down her suitcase in the hallway. He'd been there to meet her in the arrivals hall at Gatwick, and while they'd driven back to the flat she'd filled him in on all the details of Florence and the course – flavour by flavour, she'd talked him through the ice creams she'd made.

'I've missed you,' he said, nuzzling into her shoulder.

'Me too.' She kissed him back. 'Shall we?' she nodded towards the bedroom, and he didn't need much encouragement to follow her.

Jon slowly unbuttoned her blouse and ran his hands over her bra, then her bare stomach. Her skin tingled instinctively, and her hands found their regular place on his arms, his chest. Her brain was only semi-engaged, still caught up in memories of sunshine and cobblestone piazzas, the delicious tastes she had just left behind. But as Jon kissed down her shoulder and gently took her blouse off, those thoughts began to shift and she found herself back in Brighton again. Yet with that came not the relaxation of being home, but thoughts about the shop.

'Jon,' she said, between his increasingly urgent kisses. He pulled away and looked at her with a mixture of impatience and distraction. 'Uh huh,' he said, still fiddling with the clasp on her bra.

'Maybe I should call her,' Anna said, reaffixing the hooks at the back and shuffling back a fraction on the bed. 'Imogen. Check that everything's been going all right.'

'Really?' Jon said, furrowing his brow, his cheeks colouring a little as he spoke. 'You've only just got back, Anna, and we've been apart for a whole week.'

'Sorry,' Anna said, trying harder now to silence her doubts and relax. Imogen had reassured her on the phone that everything was going OK, and she should trust in that. 'You're right,' she said. 'Where were we again?' she smiled, and he brought her back into his arms.

An hour later, Anna came around from the doze she'd fallen into in Jon's arms. Squinting at the clock she saw it was just after 7 p.m.

'Jon,' she said, waking him gently. 'We must have fallen asleep. It's nearly time for dinner.'

He moved his head on the pillow slightly, beginning to stir. 'Dinner,' he echoed, and his eyes opened. 'I don't think we've got any food in,' he said apologetically. 'Fancy a meal out tonight?'

'Absolutely,' Anna said, sitting up with the duvet wrapped around her, feeling snug and protected. 'How about Gianni's?'

They had always liked Gianni's – romantic and candlelit, the Italian restaurant tucked away in the Lanes was off the tourist trail, instead packed to the rafters with Italian families and Brighton locals most nights. She and Jon had gone on their second date there, and it remained a favourite of theirs for special occasions. And tonight – a taste of Gianni's pasta or pizza would keep the holiday high going a while longer.

'You know what,' Jon said, propping himself up on his elbow, 'I feel more like curry tonight. Is that OK?'

'Curry,' Anna said, forcing herself to forget the meal she'd imagined. 'Sure. Curry it is.'

'Poppadom?' Jon asked, snapping one of the crisp discs in half.

She took it from him, and Jon spooned out a dollop of mango chutney onto his. They were the only customers in the restaurant, a quiet basement room around the corner from the flat, and their twenty-something waiter was being particularly attentive.

'I'm absolutely starving,' Jon said, with a smile.

Anna scanned the menu, longing for a risotto juicy with sun-ripened tomatoes, or fresh tagliatelle flavoured with delectable truffle sauce . . . A chicken jalfrezi, she decided. That would do. She was with Jon, she reminded herself. That was what mattered. Back home, with the man she'd missed the whole time she was away.

'Madam,' the waiter said, eyes bright, 'are you ready to order?'

'The chicken jalfrezi and some garlic naan, please,' Anna said. 'And a Cobra beer.'

'And you, sir?'

'A chicken tikka for me, and plain naan,' Jon said, putting the menu back down.

He looked from the waiter back to Anna. 'I feel better now that's on the way.'

'Have you been eating OK while I've been away?' Anna asked.

'Oh yes. I mean, not full meals like usual, but I'm still alive, as you can see. I suppose Imogen said something to you?'

'No,' Anna replied, puzzled. 'About what?'

He shook his head. 'Oh, nothing. She just caught me unawares the other day. I had a day working from home, and she came by.'

'Oh yes, she mentioned that,' Anna said. 'Something about you in your pants? Sorry, I should have mentioned she still had a spare set of keys.'

'Would have helped,' Jon said, looking slightly embarrassed.

'That's good, though, that you're able to get some time working from home now.' Anna said. 'It'll help when Alfie's ill, that kind of thing.'

'Yes,' Jon said. 'Should do. Alfie was asking after you, by the way. He's still going on about that instant ice cream you two made together.'

'Lovely. I missed him. Anything new to report?'

'He's still drawing a lot, or "mark-making". That's what they call it nowadays, apparently. Oh, and he can't wait to see Hepburn again. Although I have to admit I was happy to let Imogen take him and give me a break from his whining.'

The naan bread arrived and Anna tore off a corner and began to chew on it. 'Maybe he was lonely,' Anna said. It felt almost as if she'd never been away.

*

'Anna,' Imogen said, 'we need to talk.'

Anna had come down to Vivien's early on Monday morning, excited about starting work again, only to find her sister standing behind the counter with an anxious expression on her face.

'Some things happened when you were away.'

'Some things?' Anna said, taking a seat. *Things* – that could mean good things, couldn't it? There was no reason why not. Apart from the look on Imogen's face, that is. 'What kind of things?'

'To start with, I bought a van.'

'Right,' Anna replied. 'But after paying for the course, we hardly had any money left. How did you get hold of a van?' Irritation rose up in her – she and Imogen had made an agreement when they first started not to make any major purchases without consulting one another.

'I used the rest of the money from Granny V,' Imogen confessed.

Anna felt her cheeks blaze red, her annoyance now impossible to conceal. 'That was the money we put aside for ingredients, Imogen. You knew that.'

'But it seemed like a great opportunity,' Imogen said. 'A real vintage ice cream van. Jess did the logo . . . and we painted it together, and . . .'

'Why do I sense a "but" coming?' Anna said.

'It worked fine when I first drove it, and now it just needs a bit of work to get going again. Then we'll be able to take your ice creams on the road . . . to festivals.' Imogen's words were coming out in a rush. 'But then something happened, and I tried to drive it and it conked out and . . . '

'Oh God. So you not only bought a van, without talking about it with me first, but you're telling me it's a *dud*? Imogen, just tell me now, because I don't think I can cope with you dragging it out any longer. What else happened when I was away?'

Imogen talked her sister through the food-poisoning debacle, the article and damning online reviews and the feud with Finn. After that, Anna hoped that they might finally have covered everything.

'And that's it,' Imogen said, biting her lip.

'I don't believe you,' Anna said.

'That is almost it,' Imogen said. 'There's also some family stuff going on that you should know about.'

'Family stuff?'

'Dad's still depressed and Aunt Françoise has been trying to bully him. She's been badmouthing us to both him and Uncle Martin, so that they'll put pressure on us to sell up. So she can set this place up as some chichi little restaurant,' Imogen explained.

'That's awful,' Anna said. 'Poor Dad, stuck in the middle of all that. I'll call Mum, see what we can do to smooth things over.'

'Good luck with that,' Imogen said. 'Talking to Françoise is like negotiating with a pitbull.'

'We have to try, for Dad's sake,' Anna said. 'Now tell me. Is that really, really it?'

'Yes,' Imogen said sheepishly. 'Only I guess there are some consequences we'll need to work around.'

'Consequences.'

Imogen wrinkled her nose.

'We don't have any more money left,' Anna said, as reality gave her a sharp kick.

'For basic ingredients – fine. But not the kind of specialist, seasonal stuff we'll need for the new recipes you were telling me about.'

'How could this happen?' Anna said, her ice cream dreams slipping away with each word from her sister. 'We had thousands of pounds, Imo, and now . . . nothing but a freezer full of ice lollies to show for it.'

Jess and Anna were sitting in the shop after closing time, eating scoops of freshly made hazelnut and pretzel ice cream. 'A lot of bad luck,' Jess said. 'But it's just teething problems, isn't it?'

'I wish I could be as confident about it as you,' Anna said. 'It's all such a mess. To be honest I can't really take it all in. I've only been away just over a week.'

'You're annoyed with Imogen, aren't you?'

'I can't help it,' Anna said. 'You know I love Imo, but seriously, how has she managed to lose control of every aspect of the business in only a few days?'

'Tricky. Doing this stuff with family,' Jess said.

'I'm wondering if we just did it all too hastily, without

really thinking through whether we could work together. It's one thing getting on as sisters, but running a business together is different.'

'You can't go back on it now, though. You've made your bed.'

'Have we? In a way we've only just got started, and what we have done would be better off forgotten. The reputation of the shop's been damaged, and our budget is going to be really tight.'

'What other option do you have? You and Imogen have invested so much in this place.'

'My Aunt Françoise wants to buy it,' Anna said. 'I was completely against it at first. But now? I don't know.'

'You've just got back,' Jess said. 'Give it time for all of this to settle. For what it's worth, Imogen really has been trying. And I think the van will be great once it's going again. God, who'd have thought I'd end up painting an ice cream van on the south coast rather than sunning it up in a four-star beach resort?''

Anna smiled. 'It was good of you to help out. The logo is perfect, and I agree about the van. I think. Even if it's not actually going to go anywhere for a while.'

'I really enjoyed it, actually,' Jess said. 'Getting my hands dirty was a nice break from the office,' she added, taking another spoonful of ice cream. 'This stuff is delicious, by the way.'

'Wow,' Anna smiled. 'From you, I know how high that praise is.'

'Take my word for it,' Jess said. 'This is something worth investing in. A better bet than mine and Ed's honeymoon, for starters. I'd better go. Promised Ed we'd have a quickie after work, before we get dinner on.'

'Now there's romance,' Anna said with a smile.

'I take it where I can get it,' Jess laughed.

They kissed each other goodbye, and Jess walked out of the shop, a spring in her step.

An hour later, when she'd finished cleaning, Anna opened up her laptop to check her emails and see what else she'd missed. Among the spam and suppliers' emails, there was a personal message waiting for her:

To: Anna
From: Matteo

Hi, Anna,
How are you?

Italy is very quiet without you, but I've been filling my days in my favourite way – with plenty of ice cream. I tried out a prosciutto and parmesan one this week – delicious.

The parmesan ice cream is nothing new, it's actually based on a recipe over 150 years old, so I can't take the credit for that, but the prosciutto addition gave it something really special. I have started working in a friend's shop and we had queues out into the square yesterday!

Anyway, tell me, what flavours have you been trying out –

something like Wimbledon, all those strawberries and cream?

Your friend,
Matteo x

Anna smiled, in spite of her worries. In a moment, Matteo had reminded her what the shop was all about – not just balancing the books, but sharing the true pleasure of ice cream.

She typed back a reply.

From: Anna
To: Matteo

Hi, there,

Actually it's funny you should say that, today I tried something different. A hazelnut ice cream with chunks of chocolate and pieces of pretzel – covered in a caramel sauce. The saltiness and sweetness worked deliciously together. My friend Jess gave it the thumbs up (and she's a tough customer!)

One idea I'd like to try – don't laugh (I didn't laugh at your prosciutto, and, man, that sounds gross). Have you heard of Earl Grey tea? I'm planning to make a sorbet out of the tea, and see how that works. I'll let you know.

I'm not sure if you can get tea bags out there in Italy, so I'm attaching the recipe for the hazelnut and pretzel ice cream for now. Maybe you could try it out yourself?
Anna

Chapter Twenty-One

The atmosphere in Tom and Jan's living room was bordering on toxic. Anna and Imogen were sitting on one sofa, with Françoise and Martin directly opposite, their dad sitting awkwardly on the armchair and Jan hovering over them with a teapot.

'Well, thanks everybody for coming,' Jan said. 'It seems like there may have been a few misunderstandings lately and I thought we should try and sort them out, sooner rather than later.' When everyone had shaken their heads no to more tea, she perched on the edge of Tom's armchair. He seemed to be gazing beyond the walls of the house into a place none of them had access to. Imogen wondered if he was even able to take in what they were saying.

'By misunderstandings, Mum,' Imogen said, the argument the other day still fresh, 'you mean that Françoise has been trying to bully Dad.'

'I have been doing no such thing,' Françoise said, putting her cup and saucer down on the side indignantly. 'I have merely been trying to protect your family's interests, Imogen.

And perhaps if you'd made those a priority in the first place, I wouldn't have needed to say anything.'

'Sorry,' Anna said politely, 'but that's not really fair, Aunt Françoise. Imogen and I have been trying really hard to make the shop work. All new businesses have their teething problems.'

'It does seem as if you've had more than your fair share,' Françoise said. 'And Martin certainly hasn't enjoyed hearing about all the bad publicity, damaging your grandmother's reputation and legacy. Have you, Martin?'

'It hasn't been quite like that,' Martin said awkwardly. 'I mean I have to admit I was unhappy when Françoise showed me the newspaper article. In all the years Mum worked they didn't have any problems with food safety and it seemed a shame to have people think badly of the place.'

'And this is what convinced Martin that the shop would be better off in our hands,' Françoise said.

'Come on,' Martin said to his wife, in hushed tones. 'That's not exactly what I said.'

Imogen was fuming. Anna put a hand gently on her sister's arm to hold her back from letting loose and kept her own voice steady as she spoke. 'We're both sorry about what happened. It was an accident, and one we've learned from. It won't happen again.'

'No, it won't,' Françoise said, determination in her voice.

'Granny V left the shop to us,' Imogen said, feeling her cheeks colour, 'and she trusted us to run it. You can't buy something that we don't want to sell.'

'I think this is another misunderstanding,' Françoise said, her expression all innocence. 'You see, I know that – and I'm not trying to force you to do anything. But Martin and Tom have a right to know what you're doing to their mother's business. Then it's their decision if they want to talk to you about it.'

'You know what, Françoise,' Tom said, sitting forward, startling Imogen with the unexpectedness of his voice, 'I think it's about time I spoke up here.'

Françoise crossed her stocking-clad legs defensively.

'Because I don't think you do have Martin and my best interests at heart. Not really. If you did, you wouldn't have come here insisting that we sell Mum's house to people who plan to flatten it before we've even had a chance to scatter her ashes.'

'Oh, Tom,' Françoise pouted, 'I'm sorry you're upset, but someone needed to be practical. We'll have the inheritance tax to pay and—'

'And *now*,' he said, raising his voice to cut her off but keeping calm and controlled, 'you seem intent on making me and my brother – and I'm sorry about this, Martin, but I've gone long enough without saying what I think – doubt the abilities of Imogen and Anna.'

Françoise fell silent, and Martin glanced around awkwardly, his eyes refusing to settle on any one point.

Jan placed her hand on her husband's arm, and gave him an almost imperceptible nod, encouraging him to go on.

'What you don't seem to realise,' he continued, 'is that I

– that we –' he moved his hand to take hold of Jan's – 'will always trust our daughters to do the right thing.'

Imogen looked over at him. He looked bolder and stronger than he had in weeks. *Go Dad*, she thought to herself.

'No matter what mistakes they make, and no matter how their ideas might differ from ours. They are determined and capable, and we couldn't be more proud of the women they've grown up to be. Their grandmother had faith in them, and I get the feeling that you, Martin, do too.'

Martin shuffled awkwardly. 'Of course I do. Listen, I don't want a fuss,' he said. 'It was just intended as a point for discussion, really . . . '

'If you think for just one moment, Françoise, that you are going to persuade me to turn on my own daughters,' Tom continued, 'then I have to say I don't feel you're welcome in this house any more.'

Anna and Imogen got back into Anna's car in the late afternoon. They travelled in silence until they got onto the A-Road, both still stunned by the events of the day. Eventually Imogen spoke up. 'Well, I don't think any of us were expecting that.'

'No,' Anna said. 'He really put her in her place, didn't he?'

'He was brilliant. Do you think this means that the old Dad is back?'

'Hopefully. It certainly looked like it today. But we shouldn't expect too much. These things take time.'

'Well, she was totally lost for words. When I talked to her

the other day, my anger only made her more resolute. But when Dad spoke up just now she totally crumbled.'

'With any luck, this is the last we'll hear of it. Françoise has to accept that Granny left the business to us, and leave us to it.'

'And there's no part of you that's sorry?' Imogen said.

'What do you mean?'

'I mean that while we both know Françoise is a nightmare, she was also a potential buyer. I'm not deluded, Anna. I know how annoyed and disappointed you've been since you got back and heard about everything that's happened. I can't blame you, and I would understand if you didn't want us to go on working together. Or if you wanted to sell up altogether, come to that.'

'I'm sorry, Imo,' Anna said. She stopped at traffic lights, her hands resting on the wheel, and turned to face her sister. 'You're right. I did doubt you. Us.'

Imogen swallowed her pride and tried not to feel hurt. Anna was only confirming what she'd already suspected, after all. 'I had such high hopes when I was out in Italy, for what the ice cream shop could be, what we could make it,' Anna went on. 'I came back feeling really inspired. So to be confronted with all this . . . all this *reality*, nothing but problems we need to fix, that was difficult. It doesn't mean I love you any less – you're still the best sister I could ever wish for.'

'I understand,' Imogen said. 'And thanks for still loving me.' She smiled. 'I don't know why I thought I could do it on my own. It was really hard. Far harder than I'd ever imagined.

And the truth is that while I'm committed now, I still miss the way my life used to be. It was all so simple.'

'Don't you go giving up on me now,' Anna said. 'It feels like we're finally starting to make some progress. I'm trained up, and with Dad's show of strength just now, at least we won't have a family feud threatening to undermine the progress we're making.'

'But what progress?' Imogen said. 'Thanks to me, money is going to be tight, really tight.'

'We'll think of something,' Anna said. 'Now, where am I dropping you off – back at home?'

'Can you leave me by the shop? I know you've only just forgiven me and everything, but I'm paranoid I might have left the door unlocked.'

Imogen said goodbye to Anna, and took the steps down to the seafront. In the fading light of dusk, the West Pier looked eerily beautiful. The Granville Arches stretch was quiet this evening. She looked over to where the AA men had towed the van the other day, a short walk from the shop. Its silhouette was unmistakeable, with the ice cream cone model on the top.

As she approached it, Imogen saw that the bonnet was open, and a man was leaning into it.

'What on earth do you think you're doing?' Imogen called out, acting on instinct.

The man stood upright and took a step towards her. Imogen squinted to make him out – grey T-shirt, jeans, dark-blond hair . . . His face was lit from the side by the glow coming from the surf school.

'Finn?'

'Yes,' he said calmly. 'Were you expecting someone else?'

'I wasn't expecting anyone to be interfering with our van,' she said. 'It's our property.'

'I'm not sure I could do much more damage to it, to be honest,' he said, wiping his dirty hands on his jeans.

'That doesn't seem to have stopped you from trying,' Imogen said. 'What gives you the right . . . ' She felt a flush of annoyance come to her cheeks.

'Imogen,' he said, 'maybe you could stop jumping to conclusions for a minute.'

'OK,' she said, taking a breath. 'Tell me what the legitimate reason is why you're tinkering under the bonnet.'

'I don't know why I bothered,' Finn said, shaking his head. 'But I saw the van getting towed back the other day, and – well, I was an apprentice in a garage once. I thought maybe I could work out what went wrong.'

'Oh,' Imogen said, words deserting her.

'And I think I have, if you're willing to listen. Shall we go inside?'

Imogen followed him into the surf school, feeling sheepish. The walls were lined with boards of different shapes and sizes, and in the corner there was a small kitchen, with an old kettle and lots of mugs hanging up.

'Right,' he said. 'First things first, can I offer you a cup of tea?' he asked. 'Or something stronger?'

'A beer would be good,' Imogen said.

Finn opened a bottle of beer from the fridge, and passed it to her.

'It's always easier to apologise when you have alcohol nearby, I find,' Imogen said. She braced herself. 'I was wrong about you,' she added. 'And I'm really sorry.'

'Thanks. Apology accepted. So, can we talk like normal people now?' he asked tentatively, taking a seat.

'Yes,' Imogen said. 'Yes, please,' she continued. 'It wasn't you, was it, who leaked the story to the press? I can see that now.'

'Of course it wasn't,' Finn said. 'That's the last thing I'd do.'

'I read the situation badly. I wasn't thinking straight. What with one thing and another it's been a weird time. The article, my aunt being a nightmare. Someone posting horrible reviews online.'

'Oh, you're got one of those, have you?' Finn said. 'Nasty.'

'Yes,' Imogen said. 'They're posted on a few sites, too. It would be OK if they were balanced out by some more positive ones, but at the moment we haven't had enough customers for that. I imagine it's the same person who leaked the food-poisoning story to the press.'

'Any idea who it could be? Now that you've ruled me out, I hope?'

'Our Aunt Françoise was trying to make life difficult for a while, but it's really not her style. Other than that . . . ' Imogen thought back on the past weeks, and tried to look at things objectively. She'd been so caught up in accusing Finn she might well have missed something. 'Actually there is someone we've upset.'

'And that is?'

'Sue.' Imogen recalled her face with vivid clarity. 'The woman who used to help my grandma out in the shop.'

'Ah, yes. I remember her,' Finn said. 'She was there quite a lot, but never really seemed to be doing much.'

'Exactly,' Imogen said. 'That's what we suspected, which is one of the reasons why we didn't offer her the job back. That, and we don't have any money to pay her.'

'And now she's got an axe to grind,' he said. 'Sounds a likely candidate.'

'I don't know how I've missed it till now,' Imogen said. 'What do you reckon we should do?'

'If you want my honest advice, I wouldn't do anything.'

'Really? But what she's doing isn't fair.'

'She reported something to the press that was – and don't hate me for saying this – true. She vented some of her understandable anger online. Everyone gets the odd nutter giving them a bad review. You guys are moving forward, you're training up, and positive word of mouth will follow, just wait and see. That's what matters.'

'I should just ignore it?' Imogen said, taking a sip of beer.

'It's up to you. But probably, yes. You'll get through it,' Finn said. 'And she may well run out of steam soon.'

'You may be right.'

'All I'll say is that if you're willing to let a few negative reviews throw you off, then you might as well jack it in now. You've found out already that when you're running your own business you need a thick skin. Andy and I lost money for the first three years, but we kept going, and it was worth it.'

'So you're saying we need to toughen up?' Imogen asked.

'I think you're pretty tough already,' Finn laughed. 'Just use it when you're working from now on, not on your neighbours.'

Imogen smiled. 'Thanks for being OK with all this.'

'It's nothing,' he said. 'A misunderstanding.'

They stood in silence for a moment.

'And if you'll let me,' Finn said, 'like I said, I can sort out the van. Shouldn't cost much for the parts.'

'I'd appreciate that,' Imogen said, with a feeling of immense relief.

The moon was full in the sky, and after checking that the front door of the shop was locked properly, Imogen walked the long route home via Brighton Pier. The fresh air cleared her head, and the beach was full of people partying around campfires and barbecues. The beers she'd had with Finn had left her with a warm buzz, and she fell into step with the sound of the bongos.

She remembered the full-moon parties in Thailand – dancing till dawn with old friends and new ones she'd met, learning how to juggle. Those parties would still be going on, out in the islands, all the way across the world. She tried to stop wishing herself back there.

Chapter Twenty-Two

Anna looked at the TripAdvisor page for Vivien's, and spotted two recent one-star reviews. The usernames were new, but the tone was unmistakably familiar:

> This used to be a caring, friendly establishment, but since the new owners started, it's become really stuck-up – <u>avoid</u>.

'This is her again, isn't it?' she said.

Imogen read slowly over her shoulder. 'Definitely,' she said, annoyed. 'There's no doubt about it. Different name, but you can tell – she's even used some of the same phrases later on. *Appalling* – that's one of her favourites.'

'It's clearly Sue,' Anna said, turning on her stool to face Imogen. 'I don't know how we missed it. How do you think she heard about the food-poisoning stuff?'

'I don't know, but people talk, don't they? It could be that she knows Jill and Jeffrey, the couple who were affected.'

'That's possible,' Anna said. 'Look, I know we said we'd

ignore this, but I feel like we need to do something. What if it gets worse?'

'I agree,' Imogen said reluctantly. 'I mean I doubt she'd have the courage to do anything that doesn't involve skulking behind a computer screen under a fake name, but you never know.'

'But what do we do?'

Imogen picked up the address book and flicked through it until she found Sue's name. There, as she'd hoped, were Sue's details. 'Her address is in here,' she said, pointing at it.

'So, what, are you suggesting we go round and confront her?' Anna said.

'Kind of,' Imogen said. 'Don't get annoyed, but I'm actually suggesting *you* go round and confront her. I know it's partly my fault we're in this mess, but I think it's going to have to be you, for the sake of the business.'

'Me?' Anna said, a surge of adrenalin running through her. 'Why? I can't!'

'You can,' Imogen said. 'You've got a far better record than me at conflict resolution.'

'You're serious, aren't you?' Anna said. 'You're going to make me go over there on my own.'

'You know what'll happen if I go,' Imogen said. 'I won't be able to hold back from telling that woman what I really think of her – which we both know will only make things worse.'

'OK,' Anna said, steeling herself, and scribbling down the address on the menu pad. It wasn't far from Vivien's house

– she could be there in ten minutes. She ripped off the sheet of paper and put it in her wallet. 'Wish me luck.'

'Luck,' Imogen said.

On the walk over, Anna mentally rehearsed what she was going to say. Calm and polite, she told herself. As long as she stayed like that, things would be OK.

She checked the address again as she arrived at the entrance to Sue's road. Number 3a. She took a deep breath, went to the door and pressed the buzzer.

The door opened a crack, held back by the chain. Sue's eyes peered through the gap.

'You,' Sue said bitterly. 'Nothing to say to you.'

She closed the door in Anna's face. Anna stood there on the doorstep. How was she supposed to reason with a woman who was so set on hating her and Imogen? She considered turning to go, then pressed the buzzer one more time. If her grandmother could find something to like about this woman, then there had to be a way for her to do so too.

'I thought I made myself clear,' Sue said, talking through the gap again.

'Five minutes,' Anna said. 'That's all I'm asking. Just hear me out.'

The door closed and Anna heard the clanking of the chain as Sue undid it. 'Five minutes. And I'm only doing this for your grandmother's sake.'

Sue stood back and Anna passed her and went through into the hallway. 'Through there,' Sue said, motioning for her to go through into her compact living room.

Anna sat down and tried to remember what she'd planned to say now that she was actually here.

Sue sat opposite her on a flowered armchair next to her gas fire. On the mantelpiece were framed photos of her family – a young man and woman in a wedding photo, and a baby girl in a pink bonnet. Despite her cold expression, Sue looked somehow softer here in her own home.

'I'm sorry, Sue, about what happened,' Anna started.

Sue raised an eyebrow, unimpressed.

'I mean, I'm sorry about what we did, letting you go. I know our grandmother thought a great deal of you – she told me so herself.'

'She did?' Sue said.

'Yes. And if there hadn't been two of us working at the shop already, we might have come to a different decision.' A white lie never hurt anyone, Anna reassured herself.

'It was all a bit brutal,' Sue said. 'And sudden, I must say. When I heard that the business was staying in the family, I assumed my job would be safe. Thought you would look out for me, just like Vivien did. Didn't expect to be tossed aside like a bit of rubbish.'

'We didn't mean to make you feel that way.' Anna thought back to how she and Imogen had reacted after Sue left the shop, with relieved laughter. It seemed callous now. 'I'm sorry. We had to make a plan for the business, and there was hardly any money left over after we factored in the essentials. It was a business decision, pure and simple.'

'Well, let me tell you, I know all about hardly any money

left over,' Sue said. 'This thing –' she pointed to the gas fire next to her – 'barely had it on this winter. And what little Jamie used to bring round to me –' she glanced up at the picture of the young man on his wedding day –'that's gone now that he's inside.'

'That must be hard,' Anna said.

'Yes. But not as hard as the judgements,' Sue said, shaking her head. 'Neighbours staring. I know they're talking about me too, thinking that I'm a bad mother. Looking at his wife, Sally, the same way. Even little Carrie-Ann's had stick at school for it – seven years old, and she's getting a hard time about her dad's stealing.'

Sue's hands were clasped in her lap. 'It was wrong what he did,' she said. 'But he's not a bad man, Jamie. Six months out of work – with a mortgage and a child to support – it did something to him.'

Anna nodded, listening.

'It wasn't right what I did either,' Sue said. 'I know why you're here. The reviews I wrote. But I was angry.'

'I can see why,' Anna said.

'Your grandmother,' Sue said, 'she was the first person round here not to judge me. When the news came out, all the neighbours were gossiping in the corner shop. Thought I couldn't hear them, but of course I could. And you know what your grandmother did?'

Anna waited for her to go on.

'She was straight round here, knocked on my door. Gave me a card, and a soft toy for Carrie-Ann. Said she was thinking of us all. Two weeks later, she offered me the job.'

That was Granny V, Anna thought to herself. That was her all over. And today had shown that she and Imogen still had a lot to learn from her about compassion.

'I didn't know her well,' Sue said, 'but there was something special in that woman.'

'She had a good heart,' Anna said. 'How much longer is it, until Jamie gets home?'

'Two months,' Sue said slowly. 'Sally's got a job working school hours at the deli now. That's made things a bit easier. It's Jamie's chances when he gets out I'm worried about.'

'I'm sorry there's not more we can do to help,' Anna said.

'Things change,' Sue said. 'Maybe I should have understood that better from the start. It's not you and your sister's fault. Not really. Seemed like an easy answer, but let's face it – life's not often that straightforward, is it now?'

'No,' Anna said, the complex reality of the situation sinking in. 'It really isn't.'

'Hi, Mum, is Dad there?' Anna said. 'I wanted to check in with him, after everything that's happened.'

'Yes, love,' Jan replied, sounding more positive than she had in a while. 'I'll just put him on.'

'Hi, Anna,' her dad said. 'How are you?'

'I'm fine. And you, how did things go after we left the other day?'

'It wasn't exactly comfortable, as you'd expect. But Françoise and Martin left politely.'

'Thanks for sticking up for us.'

'You don't need to thank me,' Tom said. 'I was only doing what any father would do. Martin's been letting that woman run riot over his life since the day they got married, but I'll be damned if she thinks she can interfere in our family too.'

Anna smiled to herself. 'You sound better.'

'Well, it's up and down, but that argument certainly woke something up in me. And it feels good to feel something.'

'You must miss Granny V a lot still.'

'Of course I do,' Tom said. 'Her calls every day. The home-made biscuits she'd send over in packages, do you remember those?'

'Yes. I miss those too.'

'It still feels incomplete without her here, in our family. Like there's a gap where she used to be. It was difficult being in her house, all that space that she used to fill with her chat and her laughter. It seems so big and empty now. But the house is one of the last things we have of her, and I've made it clear to Martin that I want us to keep it for a little while.'

'He agreed?'

'Yes,' Tom said. 'He's called off the plan with the developers. Whenever we're on our own we can work things out. It's when Françoise is around that the problems start. Anyway, for now at least she'll be keeping her nose out of your business at the shop. Should be smooth sailing for you two now.'

'Yes, something like that,' Anna said. How could she gloss over things, pretend that everything was OK? He deserved to know how things really stood, financially. 'I wanted to talk to you about that, actually,' Anna said, taking a deep breath. 'As you know, we've had some issues getting started, but what I didn't mention is that we're running lower on funds than we expected.'

'Didn't Mum leave you something to start up with?'

'Yes,' Anna said. 'But we've been getting through it much faster than we thought. I'm thinking of getting a loan to tide us over.'

'Sounds sensible,' he said, without hesitation. 'Most small businesses do it at some point, don't they? I'm sure whatever decision you make will be the right one.'

'OK,' Anna said, feeling relieved at her father's reaction. It was as if he'd somehow given her permission to take what had felt like a risky step. 'Thanks, Dad.'

After speaking to her dad, Anna talked her plan over with Imogen, then called up and made an appointment with the building society. She met with the same small business advisor as before, and the woman was understanding about the challenges they were facing. She couldn't offer a large loan, but what the bank could lend would be enough to help them get back on their feet again. Once more, Vivien's stood a fighting chance.

As she stepped out into the bustling high street, Anna took out her mobile and dialled Imogen's number.

'Time to get sourcing the figs and vanilla pods,' Anna said.

'Really?' Imogen said, sounding excited.

'Yes, we've got a new loan. But promise me, this time . . . '

'I will buy nothing—' Imogen said, in a sombre tone— 'I repeat nothing – not even fancy wafer cones – without consulting you.'

'Correct.'

'In other news,' Imogen said cheerfully, 'the van's fixed, and it barely cost us a penny. Finn did it. Do you fancy taking it for a test drive?'

'I'd love to. And now that the heat's off, I think I actually mean that. But I'm going to meet Jon after work – I want to fill him in.'

'OK, see you in the shop tomorrow and we can start buying in some stock. Thanks, Anna. I know we'll get there.'

'We will,' Anna said, feeling for the first time in days that it might just be true.

She wandered slowly through the Lanes in the direction of Jon's office; she was really looking forward to sharing some good news about the ice cream shop with him. Lately, it seemed as if all she'd done was talk to him about everything that had been going wrong with it.

The concrete-and-steel offices of his brand management firm, EnVision, were easy to spot beyond the low-rise Georgian houses. She walked up to the entrance and stepped through the revolving glass doors that led to the reception.

'Hi,' she said to the young receptionist. 'Could you call up to Jon Garrehy please? It's Anna, his girlfriend.'

As the receptionist checked her phone list, Anna glanced around at the reception area, dotted with bright reclining chairs and beanbags. She suddenly felt a little out of place in the formal suit she'd worn to her meeting at the building society.

'I'm sorry, I can't do that,' the receptionist said finally.

'Are you sure? It's not normally a problem.'

'I'm afraid I can't help you.'

Anna undid one of the buttons on her jacket. She felt hot and awkward.

'Why's that?' she said. 'I've never had any issues before, and I used to drop by here quite often. I know it's a personal visit, but . . . '

The phone started to ring.

'It's not that,' the receptionist said, smiling apologetically as she went to take the call. 'Jon Garrehy left the company three weeks ago. He doesn't work here any more.'

Anna stood, bewildered for a moment, then slowly walked back out into the street. She took out her phone and called Jon's mobile. There must be some kind of a mistake. The receptionist had been new, so she could easily have made an error.

'You've reached the answerphone of Jon Garrehy. Please leave a message.'

Anna pressed the red button, then immediately tried

again. When the same thing happened, she put her mobile away in her handbag and took a deep breath. There must be some explanation, she told herself, and there was no point trying to work out what was going on before she spoke to Jon. What she needed was a walk to clear her head. She found herself heading in the direction of the Pavilion Gardens.

She sat down on a park bench, overlooking the grand white pavilion that she'd worked for so long to promote. Jon had mentioned that his work situation had changed, but that was all. He certainly hadn't said anything to suggest he had left the company. She tried his mobile one last time, then hung up again at the message.

After a few minutes, she got up to leave, and as she did she spotted a callbox. She stepped in, brought up Jon's mobile number on her own phone and tapped it in on the buttons of the callbox.

After a couple of rings, he picked up. 'Hello, Jon speaking.'

She held her breath, tried to stop any sound from escaping. Her mind raced. Why had he ignored all of her calls only to pick up now when her real number was withheld?

'Hello?' his voice came again.

In the background was a young child's laughter. She'd have recognised it anywhere.

Later that evening back at home, Anna waited on the sofa, with the TV on and the volume low. When she finally heard Jon's key turn in the lock, she felt sick with nerves.

'Hi, sweetheart,' he called out. He came into the living room and bent down to give her a kiss. She moved just a fraction so that his kiss landed on her cheek.

'What's up?' he said, taking a seat next to her.

'I'm confused,' Anna said. 'I feel like what I thought I knew doesn't make sense any more.'

'What do you mean?' Jon said.

'I came by your offices today, and they told me you didn't work there any more.'

Jon loosened his tie a little. 'Oh,' he said. 'They mean full-time. I told you my role had changed a bit, love. I'm more of a freelance consultant now, so I'm out at meetings rather than at my desk all the time. I work for more than just EnVision now. I haven't really had time to fill you in on all that, have I? You've been so busy with the shop.'

Anna furrowed her brow. 'So this afternoon, you were with a client?'

'Yes,' Jon said. 'Until just now. Huge opportunity, if it comes through.'

Anna felt torn: there was so much that still didn't add up, and yet she didn't want to accuse him of lying.

'Any reason I'm getting the Spanish Inquisition here?' Jon said with a laugh. 'I mean you're looking pretty smart for going to work in an ice cream shop, now I think about it.'

'I went to get a loan approved,' Anna said. 'For the business.'

'You've what?' Jon said, wrinkling his forehead. 'You're putting more money into that place?'

'Yes,' she said calmly. It was one of the few things at the moment that she felt completely confident about. 'We are.'

'Imogen's spent nearly all of the funds your grandma left you, and this is how you're dealing with it?'

'It's our decision,' Anna said numbly. 'Mine and Imogen's.'

The way she'd felt that afternoon, hearing his phone ring and ring, came back to her in stark clarity. 'How come you didn't pick up when I called you today?'

'I told you,' he said, curtly. 'I was in a meeting.'

'With *Alfie*?' she snapped.

Jon was staring at her blankly, but not a single word came out.

'Aren't you going to say anything?' Anna said, after the silence between them had stretched out for what felt like forever.

'They sacked me,' Jon finally admitted.

'What?' Anna said, disbelieving. Jon had got up every morning, without fail, since they'd moved in together, and got dressed in a suit. They'd talked about his meetings together over dinner in the evenings. What he was saying didn't tally. 'When?'

'A month ago. I didn't know how to tell you.'

'A month ago . . . so almost half of the time we've been living together, you've been lying to me?'

'I suppose so. I didn't mean to. I just didn't know how to tell you the truth,' he said, his face showing the strain. 'It never seemed like the right time.'

'OK,' she said, putting a hand to her forehead, trying to make sense of the situation. At least now she knew what she was dealing with. 'We'll get through it, Jon. You'll find a new job, or we'll work something out. It's all right.'

'It's not,' he said, his eyes dropping down so that they no longer met hers.

'What do you mean?'

'I needed somewhere to go, Anna. I needed a home, and this didn't feel like my home. I wanted to be somewhere I could feel like me again.'

'Like you again?'

'I don't know what to say,' Jon said. 'I don't know what it all means. But that place, where I could be myself, was with Alfie. And with Mia.'

PART THREE

Lessons Learned

Chapter Twenty-Three

'It's a vendor's pass,' Imogen said, showing her Glastonbury ticket to a guard on the perimeter fence.

'Haven't seen one of those before,' he said, eyeing the neon-orange lanyard Imogen had handed to him.

'All of the food and drink vendors have them,' Imogen said, starting to lose her patience. Did he think she'd brought along the ice cream van just for fun, to try and sneak her way into the music festival with it?

'I'll have to check it out with my supervisor,' the man said, stomping off in his khaki wellies, sending mud flying all around with each footstep.

Imogen had set off just after midday. She'd loaded the van with camping essentials borrowed from friends who were regular festival-goers, then filled the van's freezers with ice creams and sorbets and put in bags of cones and wafers. She just had to hope that the hot weather held – if it was another rainy year, not only would there be the risk of another health-and-safety nightmare, but she was pretty sure that people would be heading towards the organic burger vans, not feasting on ice-cold sorbets and granitas.

It was 6 p.m. as she waited for the security guard to give her the go-ahead. The roads on the way up to Somerset had given her a pretty clear run until the last couple of miles leading up to the site when the gridlock had started. She'd got through it, the long wait in traffic with all the other festival-goers who'd come up early, by blasting out the tunes on her radio.

Anna had worked hard all morning in the shop to get the ice creams ready in time for Imogen to take away. She'd seemed tired, and Imogen had offered to help, but Anna insisted she wanted to do it on her own.

'You're good to go through,' the security guard said, handing Imogen back her lanyard and waving her through the gate. 'Nice van, by the way.'

Imogen revved the engine and immediately stalled. She felt a flicker of fear – perhaps she should have got the van checked by a qualified mechanic before setting out on such a long journey? She tried the ignition again, and this time, to her immense relief, it caught. With a noisy rev the engine kicked into life and the van juddered through the gate along pockmarked muddy ground.

And she was in! As she entered the festival ground, she felt a rush of excitement about the weekend ahead. Yes, she'd be working, but outside the confines of the shop she immediately felt freer. A field of white wigwams spread out to her right and to her left, smaller tents and food and drink stalls had started setting up. A woman in a luminous vest took a look at her lanyard and waved her through towards the field where her pitch was. She double-checked the details. It was perfectly positioned – a short walking distance from the Jazz World stage where festival-goers would be lazing in the sun and were most likely to snack, and about ten minutes from the larger Pyramid stage where the headline acts would be playing, guaranteeing plenty of human traffic.

Imogen parked the van and got out, doing a gentle stretch to release the muscles that had tightened while she was driving. She looked back at the vehicle that had just completed its first long-distance trip under her ownership and felt a glow of pride. Painted in vibrant pastels, with a bold logo and an ice cream on top of the roof, it was now both pretty and functional. Plus there wasn't another van on the road like it. She'd had a few admiring toots from cars and lorries on the way up.

Now she was here, it was time to explore. She locked the van with her things inside, pulled on her wellies and straw cowboy hat, and walked off to familiarise herself with her new surroundings.

She strolled across the fields and after a while reached the stone circle, a raised area of land towards the back of the site, its signature large stones reminiscent of a miniature Stonehenge. A group of men and women in their twenties were sitting in the middle of the semi-sacred space, singing along to a badly played guitar.

'Room for one more?' Imogen asked.

'Of course,' a woman with dreadlocks replied. 'Do you sing?'

'No, but I can play the guitar,' she said, sitting cross-legged with them on a blanket.

'Thank God for that,' the woman said, laughing. 'Hand it over, Rich.' She took the instrument from her friend and passed it to Imogen, ignoring his protests.

'Any requests?'

'"One Way or Another",' someone called out.

Imogen strummed the guitar, tuning it up before playing the opening chords. As she played the field slowly filled up with more groups of young people starting the festival early. The crowd she was with passed a two-litre bottle of cider around between them, singing a little louder with each swig.

'Keep playing,' one of the men said when Imogen attempted to lay down the guitar.

'OK, just one more,' she conceded. 'But I can't stay here all night. I've got an early start getting the van set up for customers in the morning.'

'What is it that you're selling here?' said a handsome guy with thick stubble and a woolly jumper. 'You seem like one of us. You're not here on some kind of capitalist drive, are you?'

Imogen laughed. 'Hardly,' she said. 'I'm only selling ice creams.' His expression softened a little. 'My sister makes them. We've got a little shop together in Brighton.' The guy smiled at that, a lazy, sweet smile that caught Imogen's attention. 'Nice,' he said. 'I'm Brodie, by the way.'

'Imogen,' she said.

'"All Along the Watchtower",' a drunken friend of Brodie's shouted out, impatient to carry on the singalong.

'OK, you asked for it,' Imogen said, merrily strumming out the opening chords.

The howls of drunken singers echoed out into the starry evening.

Imogen woke up in her van feeling as if something had died in her mouth. It was furry, her temples throbbed, and she was desperate for a wee. Rather than coming back early as she'd planned, she'd ended up staying out drinking cheap cider with Brodie's friends until the early hours of the morning. Pulling her sleeping bag more closely around her, she tried to ignore the pressure on her bladder, but it just got worse. Reluctantly, she wriggled out of her sleeping bag, pulled on a fleece and opened the door to the van. She swung her legs out and put on her wellies, bracing herself for a visit to the nearest Portaloo.

She trudged through thickening mud and tried to block out the pain in her head. The sun was peeping up above the horizon, faintly lighting her path to the plastic cubicle. As she inhaled the smell of urine mixing with toilet chemicals she felt certain for a moment that she was about to get reacquainted with the cider she'd downed with that guitar-loving bunch last night. Holding her breath, she opened the Portaloo door and closed it behind her.

A couple of minutes later, she surveyed the campsite as she walked back to the van. A few people were still scattered about who had clearly been up all night, but on the whole the place was quiet. Fields stretched for miles around, and she was caught up for a moment in the sheer beauty of the Somerset countryside: lush green fields and trees – it was pretty. Still not Thailand, but it wasn't bad.

That afternoon, Imogen scooped out an Earl-Grey sorbet and passed it to a pretty blonde festival-goer: she looked like a younger Holly Willoughby, and in a pristine flowery dress, she must have only just arrived.

She took the girl's money with a smile and turned to the next customer.

'How can I help you?' she said cheerfully.

'Can't believe you had Sarah Canelli here at your van,' the next woman in line said.

'Sarah who?'

'The girl you just served. Didn't you recognise her? She hosts that celebrity street-dance show. Goes out with . . . Oh, I forget. Very famous though – my daughter's always on about her.'

'Really?' Imogen said, interested. She barely watched TV these days. 'Well, a celebrity visiting can't be a bad thing, I suppose.'

'It can make all the difference, can't it?'

'Regular customers can too,' Imogen said with a smile. 'So what can I get you?'

'A strawberries-and-cream ice, please.'

The morning went like clockwork, despite Imogen's faint

hangover. The sun beat down on the Somerset fields, and the temperature soared towards 30 degrees, bringing a steady stream of customers over to the van. At midday, she stripped down to just a vest and swept her long hair back into a ponytail.

Feeling cooler, she turned to the next man in line. She recognised him at once – the cheeky glint in his eye. He was the guy from the guitar singalong the night before. Brodie.

'What's a granita?' he said, reading the menu and bringing his eyebrows together in puzzlement.

'I'll make you one,' Imogen said. 'On the house.'

She crushed the flavoured ice and put it into a tall plastic cup for him. He took greedy sips until the cup was practically drained, then nodded his approval.

'Give us a try of that,' a dreadlocked girl said as she appeared by Brodie's side. He put a spoonful into her mouth and then followed it with a lingering kiss.

Imogen fought back disappointment. She was here on business, she reminded herself. That was all.

Chapter Twenty-Four

Jon was looking in the fridge when Anna stepped into the kitchen. From behind, in a striped navy and white dressing gown, he looked identical to the man she'd fallen in love with.

'I made a chilli,' she said, sitting down at the kitchen table and taking the weight off her feet, 'and put it in the freezer the other day. We could have that tonight.' Bad as things were, Anna thought, a decent meal always helped. Didn't it?

'Sure,' he said, turning to face her. 'That would be good. Thanks.'

'It's OK,' she said. 'Do you want some wine? I'm not quite sure I can get through this evening without some.'

After Jon's revelation about Mia two nights ago, Anna had been in shock. The kind of shock that makes having a conversation not only pointless, but impossible. They'd resolved to sleep on it – Anna in her bed and Jon in the spare bedroom. One night had turned into two. They'd stepped around each other silently, like cohabiting ghosts. Anna hadn't slept much either night: she'd lain there staring at the ceiling, trying to stop the thoughts – the nagging doubts that maybe, somehow, this was her fault.

She poured a glass of red. 'Do you want to sit down?' she said. 'And maybe you can tell me what's going on. Because a couple of nights of insomnia haven't helped me understand this any better. Are you and Mia back together?' It hurt to say the words. 'Or are you having some kind of crisis, Jon?'

Jon's eyes were fixed on a space on the table between them. He was running his finger absentmindedly over a spot Alfie had drawn on with felt-tip pen. Anna hadn't managed to get it quite clean afterwards.

He looked up a fraction, but not far enough to meet Anna's eyes. 'I don't know, Anna. This work thing has really knocked me for six. And it seemed like you were so consumed in the business, pouring all your energy and money into it, going away . . . I didn't feel I could talk to you about what was going on.'

Anna took a deep breath. 'Please don't try and make this my fault. So, what, Mia . . . she had more time for you?'

'She knows me,' Jon said. 'We've been through so much together, Anna. With the marriage, with Alfie. She felt like a safe harbour when I needed one.'

'Look, I understand you needing to talk to someone,' Anna said, her hurt and anger proving difficult to repress, 'and I'm sorry you felt I wasn't there for you. But Jon – did that mean you had to sleep with her?'

Jon looked away. 'I know it was wrong, Anna. And I'm sorry.'

'It certainly was wrong,' Anna said, hot tears starting to gather at the corners of her eyes. 'I *trusted* you, Jon. I've always trusted you, every time you've gone around to drop Alfie off, each time you've talked to her on the phone. That time we had to come back from the hotel because Alfie was ill – only, now I remember, he wasn't . . . by the time you got there he was miraculously cured. Was there always something going on? Was any of it, you and me, ever real?'

Anna thought of Alfie, remembered when she'd held his hand playing crazy golf down by Brighton Pier the previous weekend. Would that be the last time? The last time she'd hear his warm laugh, once a tiny baby's chuckle? She looked at Jon and thought of the future she'd dreamed of with him. Had it all been fiction?

'Of course it was real,' he said, sounding hurt. 'And it *is*,' he insisted. 'Anna, I made a stupid mistake.'

She raised an eyebrow at his wording.

'OK, mistakes, plural. But I've learned my lesson, Anna. I got confused about what I wanted, but now I know better than ever what matters to me. I've told Mia that what happened won't be happening again. You're the one I love – and I think part of why I did what I did was actually because I missed you. I know that sounds crazy, but I felt I was losing you to something that you cared about more than me. But you're all I want.'

'I love you, Anna,' Jon said, looking her in the eyes now. 'I knew all along that I loved you. Maybe it was too much for me to accept that I really deserved this good thing that we have. I think I tried to destroy it. And Mia was the easiest way to do that. I'm an idiot, Anna. But I know now that what I did was wrong. Let me make things right again.'

He reached out a hand and covered hers. As angry as she still was, she let it rest there for a while.

Chapter Twenty-Five

Imogen shut the ice cream van at nine on Saturday night, and headed over to the Pyramid stage to catch the headline act. Pulling her cardigan around her, she looked out across the crowd: teenagers in cowboy hats, a Welsh flag flying high, the lights around the stage glaring brightly. She got her camera out of her bag, fixed on the lens, and, dancing along to the music, started to take photos. In the warm summer's night she let the crowd, and the rhythm, carry her along.

'What do you think of these guys?' the girl next to her shouted over, above the sound of the music.

'Amazing,' Imogen replied with a smile. She let the music wash over her and enjoyed the feeling of being part of the crowd. Here she was, on her own, in the middle of a field – and she felt complete.

There was nothing around her but nature and people. The night was lit up by stars and the little lights of dance tents in the distance. She thought back to March, when she'd got the call from Anna. Back then she'd never anticipated staying in the UK as long as she had already. Even when she committed to help start up the shop, she'd been sure she would use the return leg of her ticket and go back to Thailand within a few months. But at some point, she had mentally closed the door on going back to Asia. Why? So what if it hadn't worked out with Luca. He wasn't the reason she went out to the island in the first place, and he certainly wasn't a reason for her to abandon her dreams. For all she knew, he and Santiana might have moved on by now anyway.

The island had made her feel alive and young, in a way that working in the shop never would. Yes, the van gave her a get-out, but if she stayed in Brighton the majority of her days would soon be routine, managing the business. She'd studied photography for three long years, and for what? To give up without even trying to make a go of it?

Bass throbbed through her body and she moved with it. She was pretty sure she wasn't done with travel, and adventure. Not at all.

She kept dancing until 2 a.m., and then walked slowly back to the van through the stone circle, still buzzing with the excitement of the bands she'd seen.

'Imogen!'

She turned at the sound of her name.

There, standing by the entrance to the wigwam camp, was Finn.

'Imogen,' he called out again, a smile brightening his eyes as he beckoned her over.

She made her way towards the field entrance.

'What are you doing here?' he asked kindly.

'I was about to ask you the same thing,' she replied, smiling in surprise.

A fire was burning dimly beside him and he was surrounded by spacious tents. The whole scene looked much more inviting than the prospect of going back to hers to sleep in the van or her damp tent.

'I'm helping a friend out with his stall,' he said first. 'And you – did you bring the van here?'

'Yes,' Imogen said proudly.

'It made it all the way?' he said, raising his eyebrows in disbelief.

'Yes – and hardly complained at all,' she laughed.

'I'm pleased my botch-job held out. Couldn't have coped with the guilt if you'd broken down before you were past Stonehenge.'

Imogen smiled, and then silence fell between them for a moment. In the distance, there were the sounds of people sitting around campfires talking, scrambling to find the zips on their tents and laughing, but in their tiny patch of field there was no sound at all.

'And your friends?' Imogen said finally.

'Passed out now,' Finn said. 'I was just putting out the fire, and then I'm going to head inside myself.'

'They look comfy, those wigwams,' Imogen said. 'Can I look inside?'

'Go ahead,' he said, lifting the white canvas flap of the one nearest them.

Imogen wolf-whistled as she spotted the fairy-lit interior

and camp beds. 'Check you out, glamping all the way. Beats freezing your butt off in an ice cream van, I'd imagine.'

'Yes, maybe. Andy was the one who organised it and I'm sharing this with him. Said he's too much of an old man to deal with tents any more. We've even got proper toilets,' he said, pointing over at a posh-looking mobile block of WCs.

'And Andy's where?' Imogen said. 'I thought you said everyone had gone to sleep?'

'In the end he found a better offer,' Finn laughed. 'Met a nice girl this evening, and it turns out he didn't mind roughing it for just one night after all.'

'Lucky Andy.' Imogen laughed.

'I completely understand if you're not interested,' Finn said, pausing. 'But Andy's romantic success does mean that bed's free. If you really would be freezing in the van. There's a spare duvet and pillows you could use – and I'd be miles away on the other side of the tent, so you probably wouldn't even have to put up with my snoring . . . '

Imogen mulled it over. It was a crazy idea, really, she barely knew Finn. But then again – it did look comfortable in there.

'OK,' she said, lighting up at the thought of a good night's sleep and a proper toilet to go to. She stepped inside the wigwam, and felt instantly warmer. 'I'd like to take you up on that.'

'Cocoa?' Finn said, getting out a camping stove after he'd put out the dying embers of the fire. 'Not very rock 'n' roll, I know.'

'I'd love some,' Imogen said, getting settled on the bed. 'How've you been enjoying the festival so far?'

'It's been great,' Finn said. 'Haven't seen most of these guys for ages, and so it's been brilliant to catch up over a few beers, see some good music. It's funny, there was a time when we'd spend all our time together, but then – well, things change a bit, don't they? Work, or people getting married.'

'Yes,' Imogen said. 'I know what you mean. People settle down and forget to do anything interesting.'

'That's isn't quite what I meant,' Finn said, laughing.

'Sorry,' Imogen said. 'I might be projecting a bit. I just remembered tonight, how important it is to keep doing the things that make you feel alive.'

'And what is that, for you?' Finn asked, curious.

'This,' Imogen said, patting the camera in her bag. 'Taking photos.'

'Have you taken many here?'

'I've been working at the van a lot, but I did get to see some bands tonight,' she said, taking the camera out. She flicked through the other photos on her memory card until she got to the most recent set. 'Would you like to see?'

'Sure,' he said, moving over to sit next to her.

'This one, well, the light show didn't quite come out how I expected, but I actually really like the effect,' she said. Finn nodded his agreement. 'And then I got a nice close-up of this group of teenagers in the crowd.'

'I like it,' Finn said. 'You can tell they're going to be living off memories of that night for a long time, can't you?'

'Exactly,' she said. 'That was what I was trying to capture. And then there was . . . Oh, it's skipped. This is just some stuff from Thailand.'

'Hang on, don't flick over them, go back,' Finn said, steadying her hand. 'Those look amazing. Are they underwater shots?'

'Yes,' Imogen said, feeling suddenly shy. 'Those are from my other camera. Underwater photography is what I do. What I *did*.'

'They're stunning,' he said, taking the camera she offered him and looking through the pictures slowly. 'You should do something with these. Exhibit them, sell them . . . '

'Thanks. That's the plan,' Imogen said. 'Although life has sort of got in the way lately.'

'It can be a pain like that,' Finn said with a smile.

Sipping at her hot chocolate as Finn continued to look at her photos, Imogen starting to get sleepy.

'Thanks for showing them to me,' he said, passing her camera back. 'Brighton must seem pretty tame by comparison.'

'There are things I miss, yes. Although getting out here for a break has been great.'

'Talking of which, tomorrow, White Stripes or Arcade Fire?' Finn said. 'Which are you going to?'

'Arcade Fire,' Imogen said, 'no doubt.'

'What a waste,' Finn said.

'You really think so?' Imogen said with a smile.

'I could tell you, at length, my reasons,' he said. 'But you look really tired, and it bums me out when my audience falls asleep.'

'You're right,' Imogen said, cosying up underneath the thick duvet, 'Let's save that one for another time.' She was grateful to be under a proper blanket on the cold night.

'Do you want a T-shirt or anything to sleep in?'

'I'm OK,' she said, kicking off her shoes and bringing her legs up into the bed.

'Do you think, when you've finished at work tomorrow, we could check out some of the festival together?'

Imogen thought sleepily of the money she'd made that first day, stashed away in a plastic bag in the bottom of one of the fridges. The wad of notes she'd got in one day was as much as she'd expect to make over the whole weekend.

She smiled up at Finn drowsily. 'I don't see why we shouldn't have some fun.'

'Great,' Finn said.

Imogen's eyelids grew heavier, and the last thing she noticed before they closed was the fairy lights in the tent still twinkling around her. And Finn's voice, saying 'Sweet dreams.'

Chapter Twenty-Six

'Where did that smile come from?' Anna asked Imogen the following Saturday. Imogen was sitting up at the counter, browsing through a magazine.

'Nowhere,' Imogen said. 'Am I not allowed to be in a good mood these days?'

'It's been a while since I saw it, that's all, and you've been glowing all week,' Anna said, pouring herself a cup of coffee from the machine. 'Did something happen at the festival?' she asked. 'I mean, I know you said you sold out of our ices, but surely even that can't be the reason you're grinning from ear to ear?'

'It was good to have a change of scene,' Imogen said. 'Re-energising.'

'OK,' Anna said. A weekend's camping certainly seemed to have done something to Imogen. The sun had lightened the streaks of gold in her hair, but it was her positivity that was the most obvious change.

'Oh, and I have some good news to tell you,' Imogen said brightly.

'Fire away,' Anna said. 'I could do with some of that.'

'Have you ever heard of Sarah Cavelli? Or Canelli?'

'Canelli,' Anna said. 'Of course I have – everyone knows her. She's on the front cover of *Heat* this week. What about her?'

'She's only our biggest fan,' Imogen smiled. 'I saw on Twitter this morning she was raving about the Earl Grey sorbet she had at Glastonbury from our "gorgeous vintage van".'

'You're kidding!' Anna said, her mood lifting.

'I know. Nice bit of free publicity, eh?'

'Just what we need,' Anna agreed.

'So why do you still look depressed, sis?' Imogen asked. 'Or tired, at least. Dark shadows. Late night?'

'Yes, a late one,' Anna said, wishing her lack of va-va-voom wasn't so obvious. 'Although not as rock 'n' roll as you. Up till one making three new batches: Pimm's sorbet, Wimbledon – which is a strawberries and cream ice cream – and a fresh-tasting cucumber sorbet.'

There was nothing like having a train wreck of a romantic life, Anna thought, to make you productive and focused in the kitchen. After her chat with Jon last week, she'd turned to cooking to give her space to think everything over. Jon had looked so pathetic and broken sitting there. Her mind was still in a fog – her trust in Jon, in *them*, had been shattered. None of that could be fixed overnight. But to just walk away, from what they had, from Alfie? She couldn't bring herself to do it. She had to see if there was something there worth saving.

'Wow, you have been busy,' Imogen said.

'I know,' Anna said. She'd normally have shared her worries with Imogen, but right now it helped to act normal. 'So, what do you reckon? I'm calling them "The British Summertime Collection". I've got some wafer cones to serve them in today.'

'Sounds good,' Imogen said. 'Sounds delicious. But what are you going to do with it all? I mean, you know how it's been round here. Who's going to eat it?'

'Freebies,' Anna said. 'I've been mulling it over for a while – some of the ice cream places in Italy give away samples, and it makes a lot of sense. How do we persuade customers to come to our shop if they don't know what we sell? Jess said she'd help me out. You don't mind keeping an eye on the shop on your own for a while today, do you?'

'While you're working up a sweat walking up and down the beach with freezer bags? Fine by me.'

A few minutes later Jess arrived, and Jess and Anna sorted through the ice creams and put them into freezer boxes, strapping them on to themselves.

'I feel like a packhorse,' Jess said, laughing. She picked up a bag of wafer cones and the two of them headed out and over to the beach, treading carefully on the pebbles in their flip-flops.

'I'm glad you brought the sunshine back with you,' Jess said, her dress floating prettily in the breeze. 'Makes this a whole lot more fun.'

'I try,' Anna said. It was wonderful to see the seafront come to life at last, as locals enjoyed the longed-for sunshine. 'I think I can see our first targets.' She pointed over at a young family who had brought a picnic and set up a rug. Their two children, toddlers, were laughing and playing with a ball.

'Free ice cream! Come and get your free ice cream!' Jess bellowed out. Her complete lack of shame, which had caused Anna a good deal of embarrassment over the years, was making her the ideal partner today.

The larger of the two toddlers looked up at them and pointed animatedly. 'Would you like two?' Anna asked their mum.

'Anything to quieten these two down,' the woman said, taking a couple of cones gratefully.

Then – 'Over there,' said a girl of about nine, pointing over at them. 'They said "Free ice cream"!'

Within fifteen minutes, Jess and Anna found themselves surrounded by children and parents clamouring to try their wares. A couple of hours later, the boxes were empty.

'That's everything gone,' Anna said with a satisfied sigh, closing her freezer box and taking a seat on a bench facing out to the sea. 'I reckon we deserve a break, don't you?'

Jess sat down next to her and smiled, tipping her straw sunhat back slightly so that the rays could warm her face. The British Summertime Collection had been a hit. They'd talked to all of the families who came to try the ices and handed them flyers for the shop.

'We did OK, didn't we?' Jess said, her cheeks already a little rosier for the early July sun.

'Even better than I expected,' Anna said.

'I'd say Vivien's is well and truly back in the game!' Jess laughed.

Jess gave her a hug and Anna relaxed into her friend's arms. What Anna needed now, more than anything, was to forget about what was happening with Jon. Thankfully the shop was the perfect diversion – and even if they weren't making any money yet, she'd seen today that her and Imogen's instinct had been right – there was definitely a local market for gourmet ice cream. The people who'd tried their samples had loved the home-grown, fresh and seasonal tastes in Vivien's ices.

'So, why is it, Anna . . . ' Jess said, her face suddenly serious, popping the bubble Anna had felt safe in. ' . . . Look, I don't want to step out of line here . . . but I thought today went amazingly – so why don't you look happier ?'

'Oh, I'm fine,' Anna said, brushing away Jess's concern. 'It's been a hectic couple of weeks, that's all, sorting out everything that went wrong.'

'Right,' Jess said, waiting for her to say more.

'Jess, it's fine, honestly.' Anna assured her. 'I mean Jon and I have had our ups and downs lately, but what couple doesn't?'

'As long as you're OK,' Jess said. 'Remember I'm always here for you, if you want to talk.'

'I appreciate that. But really, there's nothing to say.'

*

On the specials board: Pear and Ginger Sorbet.

The following Friday, Jess popped into the shop early before work, as Anna was getting ready to open.

'Jess,' Anna said, stirring her mug of tea, 'I've had an idea. After we gave out those freebies last week, business has really lifted. We've had customers flooding in, in fact.'

Jess got up and gave a bow. 'There's no need to thank me,' she said, smiling.

'All the same, I'm very grateful,' Anna said. 'Your loud-speaker voice definitely helped draw attention to us. It's got me thinking . . . this stuff really makes a difference, doesn't it? Maybe we should hold a local event.'

'Oh, right,' Jess said, curious. 'Like an in-shop promotion, that kind of thing?'

'Something community-based. A lot of people never stray this far down the seafront unless they're coming for a reason – like they've heard about Finn's surf school. But once they do make it down here, they tend to come back. The other Arches shop owners have been great so far – Evie and Finn, and the couple who own the newsagents. Maybe if we did something together, a party on the bandstand perhaps?'

'Love it,' Jess said, her face lighting up. 'I could ask Dan's band to come along – you know, the band from our wedding? They do the odd free gig for friends, local stuff – as long as they get to flog a few CDs, they're happy. And there's the Brighton Community Brass Band – you could start up with them. They're a big hit with the oldies and I bet they'd per-form at the opening of an envelope.'

'Perfect,' Anna said, jotting the ideas down in her notebook.

'We could have a barbecue on the beach too,' Anna said. 'I reckon Finn would be up for organising that, and that would ensure plenty of his surfing crowd came along. Hopefully Evie could make us some bunting, or make some cakes to sell – she's pretty good like that. It would be a day for the community to come together and enjoy the sunshine, making a feature of this part of the seafront.'

'What are you guys plotting?' Imogen said, taking off her jacket and hanging it up.

'A party,' Jess said. 'Although I shouldn't really be plotting it at all,' she added, checking her watch, 'as I'm late for work. Still in holiday mode. See you guys later.'

'"Summertime Under the Arches",' Anna said, trying out the phrase as Jess rushed out of the door. 'An event where all the local businesses chip in and get involved.'

'Nice,' Imogen said approvingly. 'Why don't we strike while the iron's hot – have it the weekend after next? I could call Finn about it. He's away in Cornwall on a surf camp for a couple of weeks, but I could ring him, see if he has any other ideas.'

'Really?' Anna asked. 'So, what, are you guys friends now?'

'Not exactly,' Imogen said. 'But I suppose I may have read him slightly wrong. I bumped into him in Glastonbury and he actually seemed kind of OK.'

'Wonders will never cease,' Anna said, smiling.

'No point holding grudges,' Imogen said. 'Summer's here, so we may as well make the most of it.'

Grabbing a teaspoon, she took a scoop of Anna's freshly made pear-and-ginger sorbet. 'Now this isn't bad at all.'

At home that evening, Anna was sitting in Alfie's room with him, cross-legged on the floor. He was dressed in a yellow T-shirt with a giraffe on it that she'd bought him the first time he stayed over, piling coloured building bricks on top of one another.

'Alfie buildin' a house,' he said triumphantly, placing a green brick on top of the others. His cheeks glowed with a sense of achievement. 'Building a house for Anna.' Hepburn shuffled in through the door and waddled his way over to Alfie, narrowly dodging the brick tower, and nuzzling his head against Alfie's side. Alfie collapsed in giggles. 'Hep-urn,' he said, breathless with laughter. 'Tickling me!' Anna pulled Hepburn away gently and brought him onto her lap, from where he proceeded to lick her face enthusiastically.

'House for Anna and Hep-urn!' Alfie laughed, adding one more brick to the pile.

Anna smiled. Spending time with Alfie brought her right into the present like nothing else could. When she was reading him a bedtime story, or collecting stones with him on the beach, everyday stresses lessened or lifted altogether. She couldn't help but get caught up in his bright and uncluttered way of seeing the world, this capacity for make-believe.

Jon peeked around the door. 'Everything all right in here?' he said with a smile. 'Because it sounds crazy. Dinner's almost ready.'

'We're fine,' Anna said, looking up at him. She saw the warmth in his expression that she'd fallen for on that very first night they spent together.

'Good,' he said. 'It'll be about five minutes. Nothing for us yet, I'm afraid, Anna – unless you're keen on some chicken nuggets?'

'I think I'll wait for ours,' Anna said.

Jon closed the door and Anna turned back towards Alfie. With one swift move, Hepburn leapt off her and darted out, knocking the bricks in every direction.

'Oh NO,' Alfie said, his giggles bubbling up.

'It's OK, sweetheart,' Anna said. 'It just means we get to start the game all over again.'

She swept the bricks up so that they were all within reach of his tubby arms.

'Now, what shall we build next?' Anna said, putting a finger to her lips as if she was thinking up a plan.

'A-Nother house,' Alfie said.

'A different one?'

'Yes,' Alfie said, putting down a yellow slab as a base. 'This house is where Mummy and Daddy live.'

The words hit Anna like a jolt.

Maybe it wasn't Alfie who was playing 'Let's pretend'. It was her.

*

Once Alfie was in bed, Jon got his and Anna's dinner ready, plates of steaming spaghetti Bolognese.

'So, how did it go today?' Anna said. 'You had a meeting, right?'

'Oh . . . yeah,' Jon said, dishing up. 'Nice guys, and it sounds like an interesting agency. Not sure it will lead to anything though.'

'OK. Well, still worth a shot.'

Jon shrugged. 'Hopefully. By the way, I've been meaning to tell you that Alfie's going to be staying a bit longer than usual next week.'

'That's fine,' Anna said. 'You know I love having him around.'

'Mia's bringing him around on Thursday. She has some fundraising event or other to run that evening.'

'OK,' Anna said, forcing herself not to react to Mia's name. The thought of seeing her again – now – after all that had happened, made Anna feel sick.

'You don't have a problem with that, do you?' Jon said. 'I mean I could meet her somewhere else, if that's easier.'

It was all too soon.

'It's OK,' Anna said. 'I mean –' something inside her gave, a thread snapped – 'I'd rather never see Mia again, if I'm honest – but I can be adult about this, if she can.'

'Come on, Anna,' Jon said, 'there's no need to be like that.'

'Isn't there?' she said, glaring at him. She felt dizzy all of a sudden and needed some space. 'I'm going to have a bath.'

As she left the kitchen, her head was spinning. She sat down on the bench in the hallway, next to a pile of post she'd dumped there during the week without sorting through it.

She saw now that a colourful postcard was nestled in among the bills and she pulled it out. A bright blue sky shone out behind terracotta-toned buildings and a sparkling river. There in the centre of the photo was a bridge she instantly recognised: the Ponte Vecchio in Florence.

She flipped the postcard over.

Anna,

she read in elegant black handwriting

Tell me you haven't forgotten about Florence, and about the power of ice cream, just yet.

She smiled in spite of herself, as she read the words in Matteo's warm, Italian-accented voice.

Hugs,
Matteo

She tucked the card away inside a book and put it on the shelf, her own slight feelings of guilt about her friendship with Matteo mingling with the anger she felt towards Jon. One point was clear – the last thing she needed right now was daydreams, sunshine memories that had nothing to do with her real life.

Once in the bathroom, Anna locked the door behind her. It was the first time she'd pulled the lock across – normally she liked to leave the door open a crack so she could talk to Jon through it while he pottered about. But things felt different now.

She sat down on the wicker chair by the bath, letting the water run hot, and pouring a citrus bubble bath under the tap.

She waited for the bath to fill, and absent-mindedly picked up the embroidered cushion from the chair, running her fingers over the stitching. It was one of the few things she'd chosen to take from her grandmother's house. She could remember Vivien making it, sewing and half-watching *Downton Abbey*. For a moment she felt as if her grandmother was in the room with her.

When Vivien was living around the corner, even when Anna was in her crummy rented flat, she had always felt at home in Brighton. And yet now, in her own home, with the man she was supposed to be in love with in the next room, she had never felt more alone.

This doesn't feel right, Anna thought, as she watched water fill the bath. She hugged the cushion into her chest, and the words she said out loud were hushed by the running water. 'But I can't just give up, Granny V. Can I?'

Chapter Twenty-Seven

On the specials board: Blueberry Sorbet

It took her a little while to admit it to herself, but from the moment Imogen had fallen asleep chatting to Finn in that fairy-lit wigwam she'd started to feel a glimmer – just a glimmer – of attraction to him.

It was Sunday morning, and she and Anna were getting things ready for the bandstand event, but she was conscious of the fact that Finn was just a few metres away. She'd be seeing him later for the first time since they'd been in Glastonbury together, a fortnight ago. She'd spent longer than usual in front of the mirror that morning, adjusting her hair, threading in a small plait, and putting on an old-gold necklace with her red tank top and jeans, to dress them up a bit.

'Right, here's the bunting,' Evie announced, as she breezed into the ice cream shop. Brightly coloured fabric triangles were wrapped around her neck, and she had the other lengths of bunting pulled tight so as not to tangle them, with her arms spread wide. 'Up all night I was with this, you know,' she said, a smile on her face. 'I hope you ladies appreciate it.'

'It's beautiful,' Anna said, dashing over, and cooing over the mixture of lace and colourful fabrics that Evie had picked out and sewn together with strings of blue ribbon.

'Why, thank you,' Evie said, giving them a bow.

'Are we putting that up on the bandstand?' Imogen asked, taking a length into her hand and running her fingers over the fabric.

'There's one long one for the bandstand,' Evie said, pointing to it, 'and another for your van. You're selling out of the van today, aren't you?'

'Yes,' Imogen said. After the shaky beginning, the van was really beginning to come into its own as part of the business. And today it would mean they'd be able to sell ice cream from right in the middle of the party.

'You know what?' Evie said. 'It's a shame your grandmother's not going to be here. Nothing Vivien liked more than bringing people together.'

'You're right,' Imogen said. 'She would have loved this.'

'Did I ever tell you about the Bring and Buy sale we hosted out here on the front?' Evie said. Imogen and Anna shook their heads. 'It was when they were threatening to close the children's ward at the hospital. We had stalls lined up full of jumble that your grandmother sorted through and priced up ready to sell on. We had hordes of people down here – kids and their parents, local actors and politicians, the newspapers. Vivien had a way of getting word around.'

'Did you make much money?' Imogen asked.

'About five hundred pounds, I think,' Evie said. 'Can't quite remember now. But the real outcome was that the local press coverage drew attention to the campaign. This was before you had social networking and all that, of course, and it wasn't easy getting people to take notice. The next week over a thousand people marched in protest, along the front here, and the government was forced to change their plans.'

'What a great story,' Anna said. 'Whatever Granny V was doing, she made it fun to be part of. I miss that.'

'I guess it falls to us now,' Imogen said. 'We should make today a great event in her honour.'

'Sounds good to me,' Evie said.

Anna checked her watch, then glanced back at Imogen and Evie, excitement and nerves dancing in her brown eyes. 'It's nearly midday,' she said. 'We start in an hour. Shall we go out and get things set up before the rabble arrive?'

'Why don't we start over there?' Imogen said as they stepped out onto the seafront, pointing towards the bandstand. 'String the bunting up. Hang on, I'll just grab a ladder.'

She returned a moment later, and Evie propped the ladder up against the wrought-iron.

'I'll do it,' Imogen said, taking hold of the end of the bunting and climbing the first couple of rungs.

'You most certainly will not,' Evie said. 'I've made this, and I'll put it up myself – won't have you taking all the glory.' She laughed good-naturedly. 'I'm as fit now as I ever was. My old bones haven't given up yet.'

'What's going on here?' Imogen heard his voice before she saw him. Deep, sure and steady. A tingle ran from the back of her neck right down her arms. 'Looks like you're really putting Evie to work.' Imogen turned to see Finn's smiling face.

Evie gave him a glare from her position balanced precariously at the top of the ladder, her hands overflowing with bunting. 'I've had this argument once already,' she said.

'She insisted,' Imogen said.

'Why doesn't that surprise me?' Finn said.

Imogen's eyes met his. Warm and smiling. She melted a bit inside, but did her best to hide it.

Evie continued to tie the string of bright triangles to the metal curves of the bandstand as Imogen held the base of the ladder steady. The sea breeze sent the flags fluttering.

Inside the bandstand, the community brass band tuned up in the golden glow of the July sunshine, and the sound of the trumpet carried on the wind.

'A summer of music,' Finn said quietly to Imogen. In an instant the day that they'd spent together at Glastonbury flooded back. The lazy morning out by the jazz stage, their wander together through the circus field – getting their fortunes read in the tarot tent, then making it back to the main stage to see the final day's headline act. Being with him, talking, laughing, had felt so easy. 'Seems like only a minute ago we were at the festival, doesn't it?'

Imogen looked at Finn, her hair whipping across her face in salty strands.

'Finn,' came a masculine yell from the surf shop.

'Andy. I think that's my cue,' he said. He touched Imogen's shoulder gently. 'But I'll catch you later, I hope.'

She nodded, and then he was gone.

Evie, looking down from the top of her ladder, raised an eyebrow and smiled. 'Is there something I've missed?'

By mid-afternoon the seafront party was in full swing. Throngs of revellers surrounded the bandstand as Jess's wedding band played their way through Motown classics. The opening chords of 'Heard it Through the Grapevine' rang out and couples swayed along to the beat. At the front of the crowd a small space cleared, and young children were soon bopping along, twirling each other round. At the back Imogen joined the others in belting out the lyrics with joyous, summery abandon.

Imogen was on her break from the van, and she could see Anna working hard dishing out the ices. Last night they'd made an enormous vat of chocolate-and-macadamia ice cream, which was to die for, and also a choice of summery sorbets – blueberry and a fresh, zingy and gloriously simple lemon and mint.

One of their customers strolled past Imogen, scooping a chunk of chocolate out of the tub she was carrying. 'This stuff is amazing, Paul. We really must get down to this part of the seafront more often. And did you see the new range they had out there – "Hepburn's Glorious Ice Cream for Hounds"? Dog ice cream! Brilliant.'

Imogen felt a glow inside on hearing the words. From where she was standing, today was looking very much like a success.

'How are you doing?' Finn said, reappearing by her side. She gave a little jump of surprise and then smiled.

'Good, thank you,' she said. 'We're giving Glastonbury a real run for its money, aren't we?'

'Indeed,' he said, laughing. 'The barbecue's been stormed! And with all the new custom, we've also had quite a few people sign up for surf lessons over the next couple of weeks. I thought I'd let Andy take over for a while.'

'Has it tired you out?' Imogen asked.

'Not really,' Finn said. 'I just wanted to come over here and talk to you.'

'Talk to me about what?' Imogen said coyly.

'Come here,' Finn said. He took her by the hand, and wove them both through the crowd and back towards the Arches. They carried on walking, the sun beating down, until they reached an arch that was empty and unused, with some deckchairs stacked up in the corner.

'Take a seat,' Finn said, grabbing two of the deckchairs and opening them, putting them out facing the beach. Squinting at him with suspicion, Imogen sat down on one, relaxing as she took in the view.

'I shouldn't really be here,' she said. 'I told Anna I'd only be a few minutes.'

'This won't take long,' Finn said.

Imogen sat back in the chair, and enjoyed the familiar

feeling of the sun's heat on the bare skin of her arms and legs. If she ignored the piercing screech of seagulls, she could almost imagine herself back on the island.

She opened her eyes slowly and saw a couple of dogs bobbing up and down in the surf, barking as they tried to catch hold of a large ball their owner had thrown.

'I was just wondering . . . ' Finn started, and it was then that Imogen saw he wasn't as confident as he usually seemed. There was a slight, only just noticeable, tremble in his voice. For the first time in his company that day, she relaxed.

'Yes,' she said calmly, raising an eyebrow.

' . . . if you might be free later, when all of this is over,' he said. 'It's just – I enjoyed the time we spent together the other weekend, Imogen. And to be honest, for the last couple of weeks in Cornwall, all I've been thinking about is seeing you again.'

She scrutinised his face, doubting that he could really be serious, but saw nothing there but kindness – and warmth. He touched her hair gently, smoothing it back behind her ear.

His hand came to rest on her tanned shoulder, and he brought her gently towards him, kissing her on her lips. She moved in closer, and felt the smoothness of his skin. Her hands found the steadiness of his upper arms, his chest. For a moment the whole world, apart from the two of them, dissolved away. The distant sound of the waves, and the band playing, was the only soundtrack as she lost herself in his kiss.

After a moment, they were interrupted by Imogen's phone buzzing in her pocket. She tried to ignore it, but as soon as the ringing stopped, a message buzzed through. With an apologetic look, she checked it:

Crazy queues down here, Imo. Give me a hand? A x

Imogen pulled gently away from Finn's embrace. 'Sounds like Anna needs me,' she said.

'Don't let me keep you,' he said, smiling. 'I know better than to stand between you two and ice cream.'

'You know where to find me later,' she said.

'Yes. And I'll be there.'

Chapter Twenty-Eight

'So it went well today?' Jon asked.

'Really well,' Anna said. They were sitting opposite each other in a café in the Lanes where they'd arranged to meet once the event was over. 'Hundreds of people there, and most of them bought our ice creams. A really nice community spirit. Just a shame Granny V couldn't have been there to see it.'

'Sounds good,' Jon said.

'It was a shame you and Alfie couldn't make it,' she said softly.

'Yes, it was. I just dropped him back with Mia.'

'It's just . . .' Anna hesitated. 'Couldn't you have brought him down with you? It's not far from the Sea-Life Centre. He would have enjoyed it.'

'I didn't really feel like it today,' he said. 'All those people.' Anna steeled herself. The tension in the flat had been getting steadily worse over the past few days. Something had to give.

'Look, Jon, it feels as if you're being off with me. Is there something we need to talk about?'

He looked uncomfortable and shifted in his chair. 'No, it's fine. I'm just tired.'

'You might want to, but I can't pretend any more,' Anna said.

'What do you mean?' Jon said, weakly.

'You. Me. Something's changed and I'm finally ready to accept that. But I think I deserve some honesty about how you're feeling. I know we said we'd give this a second chance, but I'm not convinced that we can. Do you still have feelings for Mia?'

Jon paused. 'Alfie deserves—'

'Don't pin it on him,' Anna said. 'That isn't fair.'

'OK,' Jon said. 'I've been doing a lot of thinking. When Mia and I separated, I was furious. She'd damaged my pride by cheating on me, and it's taken me a long while to see that what happened was partly down to my behaviour too.'

'So what . . . Do you feel more at peace with things now?'

'Kind of. I feel like I was too quick to give up. I didn't put Alfie's needs first, and I want to do that now. I'm ready to take responsibility for what happened back then, for neglecting him.'

'You're a good father,' Anna said. 'You've already shown that.'

'But I could do more. Anna, Mia and I both feel that Alfie would benefit from having us together. And more than that, it's what I've realised I want.'

Anna heard his words but couldn't take them in. She felt as if any control she might have had over the situation had been pulled away from her in an instant.

'I'm sorry, Anna, I know it's not exactly what I promised you. But I've been given a second chance at happiness, and I want to take it.'

'You're serious, aren't you?' Anna said, choking the words out. '"*Not exactly what you promised*"? Pretty far from it, Jon. So this is really it, then. We're breaking up.'

'I'm sorry. I know I wasn't clear about what I wanted,' Jon said, 'but that's because I wasn't sure myself. I thought that you and I could make a go of it. I really did, Anna.'

Anna couldn't think of a word to say in reply.

'I was serious when I said I wanted to make things work,' Jon said.

'And yet now, just a few days later . . . ' Anna began. 'It's over.'

'Anna, there you are!' Jess said over the phone.

'Hi,' Anna said. She was standing outside in the street by the café, after saying goodbye to Jon and asking him to clear the flat of his things.

'I thought you said you were going to come back down with Jon,' Jess said. 'Where are you?'

'I'm still in the Lanes,' she said, struggling to hold back her tears. 'Change of plan.'

'Crap. Really? I was hoping that the fun didn't have to end just yet.' Anna could hear the buzz of the seafront in the background 'It's still pretty busy down here.'

'Listen, Jess,' Anna said. 'I can't promise you fun – and I

mean any at all – but if you're still up for a drink I'd love some company. Let's meet somewhere they serve wine.'

'Sure,' Jess said. 'Wine, I can always do. See you in Smokey Joe's in ten minutes.'

Anna made her way through the narrow streets towards their favourite bar, still in a daze, and settled in a corner booth. She sat there for a while, staring out of the window, her conversation with Jon running through her mind again and again.

'What's up?' Jess said, almost as soon as she came in through the door. 'You sounded weird on the phone.' She sat down. 'God, you look terrible. Have you been crying?'

'Jon and I just broke up,' Anna said. It all seemed so much more real as she said it out loud.

'What? Why?' Jess said. Anna got the barman's attention, with the questions still hanging in the air. 'The usual,' she said.

'Because I'm an idiot,' Anna finally replied. 'He's back together with Mia. He was cheating on me with her when I was away in Italy, and I was stupid enough to give him a second chance.'

'Bloody hell,' Jess said. 'Well, first things first, you're absolutely not an idiot. Let's get that clear. Jon – yes, idiot. With Mia a close second. Or perhaps they're joint first. Christ, I should have known it was a mistake inviting them both to our wedding. Is that when this all started?'

'I don't know. I didn't really want the details. But I'm sure it would have happened anyway, wedding or no wedding.'

'So it sounds like you've known about this a while. Why didn't you say something earlier?'

'I don't know,' Anna said, as she took a full glass of wine gratefully from the barman. 'I wanted to fix it. And Jon seemed a mess. Long story, but he got sacked just beforehand and hid it from me. I didn't want you to judge him.'

'Fair enough, I suppose, although I hate to think of what you were going through on your own,' Jess said. 'Damn right I would have judged him. I could wring his neck right now. Who cares if he got sacked – that's no excuse. So he's moving out?'

'Yes, he's back at the flat right now packing his things. I wanted it all to happen quickly.'

'Better that way,' Jess said. 'Rip the plaster off.'

'Maybe. Although that's not the nicest way to describe the end of the most meaningful relationship of my life.'

'Sorry,' Jess said. 'Would it help if I said there were more fish in the sea?'

'No,' Anna said, draining her glass. 'It definitely wouldn't. Not at all.'

'Right. Scratch that, then. When this all sinks in properly, Jon is going to be kicking himself for ever letting you slip away.'

'I don't know,' Anna said. 'He seems pretty sure.'

'I can't see Mia ever changing,' Jess said. 'I know Ed thinks she has, but if she's got away with cheating on Jon once, I don't see what's going to stop her doing it again.'

'Well, I hope, for Alfie's sake, that you're wrong,' Anna said. 'He's been messed about enough as it is.'

'Poor kid,' Jess said. 'He must not know if he's coming or going.'

Anna bit her lip. 'I should have known better than to get involved with Jon when Alfie was still so young.'

'Look, Anna,' Jess said, 'however hard you try, you can't make this your fault. Alfie is Jon's responsibility.'

'It felt sometimes like he was mine too,' Anna said. She thought of Alfie's room, all the hopes she'd had that together she and Jon could be the family he needed. 'But maybe I was fooling myself.'

'You know how we can make everything OK?' Jess said, a hopeful smile on her face.

'Turn the clock back a month?' Anna said wearily.

'No,' Jess said. 'No Marty McFly needed. It's simple, albeit one hundred per cent temporary.' She raised her hand to call the barman back over.

'Oh, don't,' Anna said, shaking her head. 'Seriously. I'm getting too old for this.'

'Times of crisis call for drastic solutions,' Jess said, smiling up at the young man. 'Four tequila slammers, please.' Turning back to Anna, she said, 'And I hear it's our turn on the jukebox.'

Chapter Twenty-Nine

Imogen poured herself a cup of tea, the dark wooden floorboards in the kitchen warm underneath her bare feet. It was too early for the usual Sunday bustle, and birdsong was the only sound she could hear that morning, coal tits and sparrows congregating at Vivien's bird table.

She pulled a long-sleeved top on over her white vest, worn with pale blue pyjama bottoms, and walked into the living room, cradling the mug in her hands and settling on the sofa. Her head was fuzzy, and there was a slight ache in her temples, but last night had definitely been worth it.

As the party wound up the previous night, with people drifting away from the Arches happy after a day spent with good food and friends, she hadn't been able to stop thinking about Finn coming over to meet her later. His kiss had been on her mind all afternoon. At around seven, she saw him approaching.

'I'd say our work here is done,' Finn said, walking over to her with a wide smile.

'I agree,' Imogen said. 'We've sold out of ice cream –

including the dog variety, Evie's cake stall's been mobbed and she's had commissions for more bunting, and I'm pretty sure we've put Granville Arches on the map today.' She reached down to the small chalkboard hanging on the side of the van, scrubbed it clean and then wrote CLOSED in pink chalk.

'We sold a ton at the barbecue. We should do this sort of thing more often.'

She climbed out of the van and closed the shutter. 'Yes, although I had no idea how tiring it would be,' she laughed. She felt Finn's eyes resting on her as if he wanted to draw her closer to him. The chemistry that had been there that afternoon was still as strong.

'Let's take it easy tonight then. What's your view on fish 'n' chips on the beach?' he asked with a smile. 'Not the classiest of dates, I know.'

'Sounds perfect,' she replied, hoping that the excitement she felt wasn't written all over her face.

An hour later, Imogen and Finn were sitting on the beach eating chips out of newspaper, metres from Brighton Pier. They'd picked up a bottle of wine, which Finn was in the process of opening, and around them groups of friends crowded around small barbecues and campfires.

'This is nice,' Imogen said, stretching out her legs.

'Not quite Thailand . . . ' Finn joked. 'But the best I could do at short notice.'

'It's still the sea. And nothing beats being close to it, don't you think?'

'Apart from being *in* it, of course.'

'True,' Imogen agreed. 'When did you learn to surf?'

'As a teenager. We'd go out there most days – there wasn't much to do where I grew up.'

'I've always thought it looked fun, but I've never tried.'

'Do you fancy giving it a go?' he asked. 'I could teach you. I've got a day off tomorrow, in fact. There's a secluded little cove up the coast we could drive to. Perfect for beginners.'

Imogen looked out into the murky depths of the Atlantic – it didn't look warm, but that was what wetsuits were for, wasn't it? It had been a while since she'd done anything that got her adrenalin flowing.

She turned to Finn. 'I'd love to.'

They'd talked for hours, until the evening chill had set in and Finn had walked her home. They'd lingered for a moment on her doorstep, then he'd kissed her gently. 'I'm looking forward to tomorrow already,' he'd said. 'Get a good night's sleep and I'll be round at nine.'

Nine, Imogen remembered, leaving thoughts of the previous night and glancing over at the grandfather clock in Vivien's living room. She'd just have time for a quick shower.

She managed to get showered and dressed before the doorbell rang. She had a last look in the hallway mirror before answering the door. She'd put a purple top and jean shorts on over her bikini, and tied her hair back loosely with a slim, pale-gold scarf that flattered her fading tan. It would do. She answered the door.

'Morning, Imogen,' Finn said, his voice a little husky. He

looked even more gorgeous than usual in a checked short-sleeved shirt and jeans, sunglasses in his hand.

'Hi,' she said. 'Sounds like I'm not the only one feeling the effects of last night.'

'The tiniest bit,' he admitted. 'The sea will soon freshen us up. Are you all set?'

'Ready as I'll ever be.' She gathered her things and followed him across the road, closing the front door behind her.

They climbed into his van. Once inside, Finn leaned towards her and kissed her gently, lingering for a while. She could make out the warm scent of his aftershave, mingling with the subtle, clean smell of his hair and skin.

'I really enjoyed last night with you,' he said.

'Me too,' she said. 'Best night I've had in ages. Who needs flash restaurants?'

'There's always next time for that,' he said, putting the key in the ignition and starting up the engine.

'Who mentioned a next time?' she said with a smile. 'Anyway, I hope you're going to keep things strictly professional today. I'm only interested in you for your surf guidance, you know.'

'I wouldn't dream of crossing any boundaries,' Finn said. He glanced over at her, and gave her a wink.

'Now, that's exactly the kind of thing I was concerned about,' Imogen joked. 'You're taking me somewhere isolated, all on my own, aren't you? My mum warned me about men like you. How far is this cove, anyway?'

'About an hour,' Finn said. 'It's worth the journey. And I promise you I'll behave.'

As they drove, the streets of Georgian houses made way for green fields and pretty coastline. Imogen chose tunes to play from Finn's iPod and they chatted easily, Finn talking her through the basics of surfing. The time passed quickly, and it didn't feel as if they'd been going for as long as an hour when Finn stopped the van at a small car park on a cliff edge.

'Come out and look at this,' he said, opening his car door.

They stepped outside. Below them was a perfect horseshoe cove, completely empty of visitors and sheltered by rock on either side.

'Beautiful,' Imogen said, getting out of the van. 'Twenty degrees warmer and this might even give Thailand a run for its money.'

'It's great, isn't it? This is where I come when I get a day off. I know I'm not going to bump into any of my students, and there's peace and quiet to think. Let's get you suited up and soon the last thing you'll be thinking about is the weather.'

By the open boot of the van, Imogen stripped to her bikini and pulled a wetsuit on over the top. She tried to ignore the fact that Finn was standing just half a metre away, in a similar state of undress.

'I'm not looking,' he said, reading her mind. 'I promise. Although I won't lie, it's very hard not to.'

'Zip me up?' she asked, and he stood behind her to do up

her wetsuit. Gently he pushed her hair to one side and kissed her neck, sending a shiver through her.

She playfully swatted him away. 'Are you going to teach me how to surf, or what?'

'I love a keen student. Right, it's down this way.' He led her down a rocky path to the beach, carrying both of their boards.

When they got to the beach, Imogen braced herself for the chill and then took her board and headed out into the water. 'You want to go for it straightaway?' Finn asked.

'I can't stand waiting for things,' she said. 'I'll get the hang of it quickly enough.'

'OK, if you're sure. This one's good,' Finn said, pointing to a wave behind Imogen that was gathering momentum. 'Catch it and then get up to standing as quickly as you can.'

Imogen focused on the wave, waiting for just the right moment to get on to her board. She leapt up but her feet slipped and she tipped forward sharply, falling headfirst into the ocean, sea water rushing up her nose.

She clambered to get back up to the surface, but once she got there and opened her eyes she caught sight of the board she'd flown off ready to land on her head.

'I've got it,' Finn said, holding her board out of harm's way. Imogen gasped for breath. 'Are you OK?'

'I'm fine,' she said, brushing the wet strands of hair out of her eyes and taking her board back off him. 'Ready for round two.'

Another wave was building behind her. She prepared

herself and got up onto it, positioning herself further back on the surfboard this time. As she popped up to standing she held her arms out as Finn had shown her and kept her balance, cruising the wave into shore.

She turned back and looked at him. 'Did you see that?' she called out, jubilant.

'You did it,' he yelled back. 'Well done!'

After a couple of hours in the water, they went back to the van to dry off and change. 'Fancy a picnic?' Finn said. 'I think we've earned it.' He picked up a bag from the boot and she followed him over to a grassy spot overlooking the cove. He spread out a rug and then opened the bag, getting out sandwiches and wine.

'I'm impressed,' Imogen said, taking a bite of her sandwich, and pushing her hair back so that she wasn't accidentally eating strands of it any more. 'And grateful, as I'm absolutely starving. But that was fun. I think I might understand now how you got so hooked.'

'I'm happy to hear it,' Finn said. 'You took to it really well.'

'Did you like it from the start?'

'From day one. It's the only thing I could imagine doing as a job, and I've been lucky enough to make it one.'

He leaned back and rested on his arms. The sea was a moody mix of dark greys and greens, seagulls ducking down and skimming the surface of the water, emitting loud caws. The horizon stretched out before them, uncluttered. In that moment, it felt to Imogen as if they were the only two people in the world.

'So what do you think?' he said. 'I thought you might like it here. The same sea, but wilder here somehow.'

'It's beautiful,' she said. She could sense the energy of the water as it thrashed there in front of her, unsettled, fighting against an unseen force. 'Fearsome but beautiful.' Out to the right she could see waves smashing against the dark rocks.

Finn squeezed her hand gently. Their eyes met and he pulled her into his arms, kissing her softly and then more urgently, as they lay there side by side on the blanket.

Chapter Thirty

Anna closed the front door behind her and stepped inside her flat. She was home, and yet – just under a week since her break-up with Jon – everything felt different now. She went into the bedroom and sat down on the bed to rest her legs after another busy day at the shop. She knew, without looking, where the absences were – half the wardrobe empty, two shelves free in the bathroom cupboard where Jon's razor and aftershave had once been. In the living room, her DVDs and CDs slipping over to their sides now that they were no longer supported by Jon's collection. While the gaps took some getting used to, she was still grateful that his exit had been swift, and that he hadn't left the place littered with reminders. It was easier that way.

She'd slept badly since he'd gone, her mind racing with thoughts of what had happened, what she could have done differently, never coming up with any answers. She missed feeling his body close to hers in bed at night, that reassuring sense that if something went wrong he was there.

But the intimacy they'd once shared, the way a conversation

or a joke could leave her smiling for hours – when had she last felt that, really? Looking back, things had started to change as soon as she and Jon had moved in together, maybe even before. She'd been so focused on having everything just right that she hadn't given herself space to see that really, nothing was.

She got up and and went through into the third bedroom. Because that was all it was now – a small room that would work as a study, somewhere for her to do the accounts and other admin for the shop, maybe. She forced herself to see past the colourful chest of drawers and the tiny bed. Perhaps she could even start a new hobby, with the room as her base. Set up her PC and write – she could put together a cookbook of summertime recipes. Ice creams.

Her hand found the edge of the chest of drawers that Alfie had once run to touch in excitement. Her fingers lingered over the drawer handle, then she slowly opened the top drawer. Empty. The second drawer, the same. The third drawer . . . it looked empty at first, but then she saw it. There, at the back, was one of Alfie's T-shirts – the yellow one with a giraffe on the front that she'd given him.

Sitting down on Alfie's small bed, Anna held the tiny T-shirt to her chest. She remembered the last time she'd seen him wearing it, the way he'd smiled. Saying goodbye to Jon had been one thing – this was another. When the tears came she couldn't stop them.

On the specials board: Espresso Granitas.

The next day, a Saturday, Anna flicked on the lights to illuminate the shop. If the last couple of days were anything to go by she'd have to work quickly to get things ready. Within the hour there'd be a queue building up outside.

Since the seafront party they'd been swamped with customers – and Vivien's had been getting plenty of publicity in the local papers (positive this time) and tourist guides. The summer holidays had brought an influx of visitors to Brighton and many had the shop on their list of 'must-do's'. Word of mouth was spreading, and some tourists were even arriving with lists of flavours they wanted to try.

At this time in the morning, though, no one was after cones and tubs of ice cream. It was Anna's espresso granitas the adults came for – an early morning pick-me-up, with a dash of calorific joy. A generous layer of freshly whipped cream was sandwiched between two layers of the dark, granular, coffee-flavoured ice.

Anna switched on the till and smiled as one of her new regulars walked in through the door. Tall with wire-framed glasses, he ran a local estate agent and liked to surprise his colleagues with delicious treats from her shop.

'Morning, Daniel,' Anna said, wiping clean the menu board. She had two new ice cream flavours to add to the list today.

'Hi Anna. You look nice today,' Daniel said politely.

'Do I?' Anna said, straightening out her apron. 'Staying

up all night making ice cream will do that to a girl, I suppose,' she added with a smile.

She still felt raw inside from everything that had happened with Jon, but after her tears the previous night she'd started to feel something else, something she hadn't expected – a kind of freedom. Her flat was her own space now, tranquil and quiet, and her life was once again in her control.

'Well, whatever it is, it seems to suit you,' Daniel said.

After she'd managed the morning rush, Anna put on the radio, still tuned into the same familiar station, and checked the shop laptop. There were a few orders for local ingredients she needed to put in, so she quickly fired off some emails. Back in May, she'd never have believed that soon she'd be so busy with customers it would be hard to find a moment to catch up on orders. There had been days back then that she and Imogen hadn't had anything to do but twiddle their thumbs.

Halfway through typing an email, a message popped up on her Gchat:

Matteo: That pretzel ice cream is incredible, Anna. Our customers have been going crazy for it.

She felt a rush of excitement. Matteo was there, online, right now. And he'd enjoyed her recipe! She smiled and typed back a reply.

Anna: Damn, knew I shouldn't have shared my secrets so easily.

Now I definitely won't be telling you about the champagne sorbet
I've been concocting . . .

As she waited for a reply Anna thought again about the
postcard from him she'd tucked away in a book at home.
She smiled remembering Florence, the golden sun on her
shoulders, the smell of fresh pasta with a full-bodied red
wine . . .

Matteo: Sounds delicious. Concocting? *gets dictionary out* ;)

Anna: Sorry, making . . . How are you doing, Matteo? Still lots
of sunshine over there?

Matteo: The weather's beautiful. I'm in Siena, still working with
my friend and looking into starting my own shop. When are you
coming back to visit?

A shadow fell over Anna's hands on the keyboard, and she
looked up with a start.

'Imogen,' she said, shutting the window on her laptop
abruptly. 'What are you doing here?'

'It's where I work,' Imogen said with an easy laugh. 'I told
you I'd be in again today, didn't I?'

'No,' Anna said, feeling a flush rise to her cheeks. 'You
didn't.'

'Well, anyway,' Imogen pulled up a stool opposite her
sister, 'there's something I wanted to talk to you about,' she
said in a conspiratorial whisper.

'There is?' Anna said, furrowing her brow. 'Does it explain why you're acting so weird?'

'Me?' Imogen said. 'You're the one being all snappy, and secretive with the computer. But I'm not going to pry, because I have more interesting things to think about. I had a *really* good day yesterday.'

'You do look all sort of radiant, much as it pains me to say it. Am I sensing romance?'

'Yes,' Imogen said. 'Or at least I think so.'

'Anyone I know?'

'Yes, in fact it's someone very close to us.'

'*Finn*,' Anna said, smiling at the revelation. Imogen's smile instantly confirmed her suspicions. 'Nice. That should keep neighbourly relations smooth for a bit then.'

'Should do,' Imogen said.

'I can see you're dying to tell me all the details. Go on.'

'Right. So we got on really well when we were in Glastonbury together, but for some reason nothing really happened. There was just all this nice chemistry going on. Then we went out the other night after the party down here, and everything sort of clicked. It feels easy with him, chatting, even about serious things.'

'And yesterday?'

'He took me out to a beautiful isolated cove and taught me to surf. Then we spent the afternoon having a picnic and chatting.'

'Sounds blissful,' Anna said. She couldn't help secretly

admiring any man who could keep up with Imogen, let alone keep her interested.

'It was,' Imogen said. 'It is. I feel a bit deranged. In a nice way.'

'I may not be an expert in love – as evidenced by the wasteland my own romantic life is right now – but I'm pretty sure that's all good. When are you seeing him again?'

'Tonight, he's taking me out for dinner. Somewhere posh. I'm going to hit the shops now and get something to wear.'

'He sounds really keen,' Anna said. 'And he certainly seems like a lovely guy. You'll be gentle with him, won't you?'

'Of course I will,' Imogen said, rolling her eyes. 'What on earth makes you say that?'

Chapter Thirty-One

'I thought we could try something a bit more high-end this time,' Finn said, smiling as he poured Imogen a glass of champagne.

They were tucked away at a quiet, candlelit table in a French restaurant. Imogen had picked up a red dress in town and a black pashmina from one of the discount shops, and splashed out on some new black heels. She was glad she'd made the effort.

'I like it,' Imogen said. 'I'm not really used to restaurants like this, if I'm honest.'

'Maybe you'll have to get used to them, what with the shop taking off like it is.'

'It has been quite a summer,' Imogen said. 'And we seem to be making a bit of money now at last. Thank God.'

'You two have really made it work, haven't you?' Finn said, looking over the table at Imogen. 'I mean, I hold my hands up here, I was hard on you at the start . . . '

'You had good reason,' Imogen said gently.

'But you've done it. Over the last few weeks the shop's been packed with customers, and all I hear about these days is what's on the specials board, or which celebrity is raving about your ices.'

'Thank you,' Imogen said. 'It's still sometimes hard to believe that we've made it happen. That we've done something that our granny would be happy to see, and that actually seems to be pulling Dad out of the slump he's been in. It's always been Anna's dream to do something like this – she's been a foodie since she was a kid. She might have lost sight of it for a bit, but you can see it now, can't you – she's born to cook.'

'And what about you?' Finn said.

'What about me?' Imogen said, taking a sip of her drink.

'You've mentioned your sister, your dad, your grandma. All of their dreams are tied up with Vivien's being a success, and you've helped to make those dreams come true.'

Imogen felt warmth spreading in her chest at Finn's words and a smile came to her lips. Because it was true. Despite all of the hiccups – no, *outright disasters* – she had been responsible for along the way, she had done it. She had helped to make her family happy.

Finn's hazel eyes fixed on hers. 'What I mean is, is the shop *your* dream?'

Imogen thought about it.

'I don't know,' she said.

After dinner, Imogen and Finn walked along the seafront, his arm around her, holding her close and warding off the cool breeze. She felt good and a little tipsy from the fizz she'd been drinking. Everything felt so natural with Finn, as if somehow she already knew him.

'Do you ever think about the future, where you'll be?' Imogen said, looking out towards the sea.

'Are you getting all philosophical on me?' Finn laughed.

'I suppose so,' she said with a shrug. 'Just a little bit. But you were the one who started asking about dreams.'

'Feels a bit early for this conversation,' Finn said, looking at her and slowing his pace. 'But if you really want to know?'

'I do,' Imogen said.

'I suppose,' he said, 'I see myself here. If I'm lucky, with a wife I love, and a house full of kids who make a mess of the place, and make us laugh. I see my brother Sam – once the eternal bachelor – and his family now, my nephew, Heath, who's brilliant. I'm pretty sure he's happy. Happier than he was back then, at any rate.'

Imogen listened. Her head felt foggy: perhaps she shouldn't have had that last glass. 'That's what my dad says,' she said finally. 'He used to love travelling – he had this big motorbike he was inseparable from, and he went around Asia in the sixties, when it was more dirt tracks than internet cafés and banana pancakes. I would have loved that . . . ' she went on, thinking of the tales her dad had told her. 'But he said that for him it had an end date. When he met my mum, he knew. It was time for his life to change.'

'He sounds like an interesting guy,' Finn said. 'And your mum must be quite something.'

'That's one way of putting it,' Imogen laughed. 'I can't always see it myself. But she's the yin to his yang, he says. Are you close to your parents?' she asked.

'We all get along,' Finn said. 'Christmas, birthdays . . . They moved over to Dublin when we left home, so we don't live in each other's pockets. I think they did a pretty good job raising us though, and I'm grateful to them for that.'

'It's funny, isn't it?' Imogen said. 'That as you get older you realise what a tough job that must really be. That your parents are human too. They get some things right, and some things wrong.'

'Exactly. And that whatever mistakes you might judge them for, you'll probably make some a hundred times worse,' he smiled.

'Listen,' Imogen said. 'I don't know about you, but I'm feeling this conversation – or another one – or indeed,' she said, squeezing his hand, 'no conversation at all . . . might be more fun back at your place.'

Finn smiled, and pulled her towards him for a kiss. 'I'm not going to argue with that,' he said, and without hesitating for a moment, he put out one arm to hail a cab.

They climbed in, and Finn gave the driver his address. Then he turned to Imogen and kissed her again.

Finn and Imogen were so caught up kissing on the back seat of the taxi that they barely registered the car pull up outside of his home fifteen minutes later.

'Ahem,' the cab driver coughed, trying to get their atten-tion. The cab ride had flown by, and Imogen hadn't even noticed which direction they were travelling in. She reluctantly untangled her limbs from Finn's as he paid the driver, then they both stepped out on to the pavement.

'Wow, is this yours?' Imogen said, taking in the stylish, modern house perched on the edge of the seashore, with an uncluttered view of the beach and horizon.

'Yep,' Finn said. 'Come in, and I'll show you around.'

She hurried ahead of him, skipping up the staircase towards the front door.

Finn caught up with her and put a hand on her waist, opening the front door with his keys. He stood back so that she could go past him inside, and flicked on the low lights. Imogen took in the room in front of her. A spacious open-plan living and dining space with floor-to-ceiling windows that gave a spectacular view out over the sea.

'Nice pad,' Imogen whistled. 'Better than the wigwam, even.'

'Thank you,' he said. 'Can I get you a drink?'

'I'm good,' Imogen said, kissing him, then leading him towards one of the sofas. 'I get the feeling there are more interesting things we could be doing.'

The next morning, Imogen got to her feet and took down the dressing gown that was hanging on Finn's bedroom door, slipping it on. She looked back at him, fast asleep, his head making a slight indent on the pillow.

She stepped into the open-plan living room and looked around the flat. It had just the right balance of classy minimalism and cosy touches. Tasteful art prints hanging on the bright white walls, black-and-white prints of friends and family in frames. One of Finn's nephew's finger paintings pinned to the fridge – bright and colourful, there was a forest with a flock of red birds flying high above it. In the distance was a bright blue sea.

Everything about Finn was right. So why, in the light of day, did she want to leave?

'I don't get it,' Anna said, sitting opposite her sister at the shop. 'I honestly don't. He's really nice, Imogen.'

'I know that. He's great. That's not the problem.'

After leaving Finn's flat that morning, she'd got the bus back into town, and walked along the seafront with only the gulls and a few dazed clubbers for company. It had slowly started to dawn on her – she wasn't ready to settle. She wasn't ready to find someone like Finn.

'I love being with him, but if we are together, I'll end up staying here,' Imogen said.

'And would that be so bad?' Anna said.

'Anna, you know I never planned to stay in Brighton for good. It's different for you. You're older – don't make that face, you are – plus you're the one with the talent,' she said. 'You're amazing at making ice cream and you've got what it takes to make this place really special.'

'Not without you,' Anna said, closing the books of accounts she'd been working on. 'You've done so much for this place. I don't understand it. You seemed really happy the other day.'

'I was. I still am,' Imogen said, struggling to find a way to express how she felt. 'Finn's a really lovely guy. But I can't see myself working here at the shop without ever having given what I really love a shot. What makes me feel alive – the way that you feel when you're cooking – is taking photos. And the animals, the things I want to photograph, aren't here. They're—'

Anna bit her lip. 'In Thailand,' she said, looking defeated.

'Yes,' Imogen said. 'I'm sorry. I thought I could talk myself out of it. Or that liking Finn would be enough to change my mind. But it's not. If I stay here, I'd feel like I was giving up on something I desperately want to do.'

Back at Vivien's house, Imogen looked over at her mobile as it buzzed from the side table. She knew that it would be another message from Finn.

She should read it. Not just that – she should be jumping up to read it and reply. This was the man she'd had an amazing time with just last night, yet he was the one person who could hold her back from achieving what she wanted.

The day she'd got her acceptance to Bournemouth to study photography had been one of the best days of her life – for three years, she'd trained with experienced photographers and honed her technique. Then travelling had brought her skills to life. The moment she'd stepped off the plane into Bangkok's humid air, she'd hardly been able to stop – orange-clad Buddhist monks, floating markets, the tiny wooden spirit houses Thais placed outside buildings. She'd filled memory card after memory card, updating her blog constantly and building a following. And then, on the island, she'd discovered that beyond what there was on the surface of the planet, there was even more to see below. Her underwater project, what there was of it, was good. But it wasn't even half-finished, and there was nothing there that was ready to exhibit. If she was serious about becoming a photographer, she had to keep on going.

As much as she enjoyed being with Finn, it couldn't last. After a few months, she knew she'd grow restless. And he'd made it clear he wasn't going anywhere, that he was settled in Brighton. Staying with him, knowing that one day she'd want to leave – it wasn't fair on either of them.

Imogen's mind was made up. She wouldn't talk to him again until she'd rebooked her flight back to Thailand.

'Hello!' Tom said. 'Nice to hear from you, Imo. I was beginning to think something had happened to you and your sister. Are you becoming workaholics over there? I've heard about those people . . . '

'Anna and me are fine,' Imogen reassured him. 'What about you?'

'Getting better,' he said. 'Slowly. For now your mother's got me taking these awful pills, which make me drowsy. I can't stand them. But I've started to see someone, once a week. And it's helping, you know, to talk everything over. I thought I was old enough and ugly enough to deal with losing Mum on my own, but it looks like I'm not.'

'I'm glad you're feeling stronger,' Imogen said. A wave of relief came over her – her dad was getting better, and he was in safe hands. 'I love you, you know.'

'I do, sweetheart. I love you too. Now, why do you sound sad? I thought things were getting better with the shop?' He must have heard something in the tone of her voice. He'd always been able to see right through her.

'They are. It's doing really well, actually.'

'Wonderful,' he said, his voice lifting.

'The reason I'm calling is to let you know that things are changing a bit. Anna's going to be running the shop on her own from now on, and I'm going back to Thailand.'

'It's bitten you again,' her dad said.

'Yes. Yes, it has.'

'That darned travel bug.'

'I've tried to ignore it. But I can't.'

'Well, good for you,' he said. 'You're only young once, and it's over in a flash. We're all going to miss you. But I understand.'

'Thanks, Dad.'

'But I hope you'll let an old traveller give you one piece of advice,' he said. 'Something I had to think about myself once. Whatever you're going out there for, just make sure you're not leaving something more important behind.'

Imogen thought of Finn. The way they clicked, made each other laugh.

'Thanks, Dad. I'll keep that in mind. Can you put Mum on? It's probably better that I tell her myself.'

'Of course. *Jan!*' he called. 'It's Imogen on the phone.'

'Hello, dear,' her mum said a moment later.

'Hi, Mum. I'll get to the point. I'm going back to Thailand.'

'But you've only just *got back here.*'

'I know,' Imogen said, momentarily wishing she'd gone for the easier option and let her dad pass on the news. 'But I always said I'd go back at some point, Mum.'

'Oh, I know what you said, darling. But you say a lot of things. I didn't think you really meant it.'

'Dad understands.'

'Has he been encouraging you again, to go off to places where you'll be putting your life at risk . . . ?'

'Of course not,' Imogen said. 'It's my decision.'

'It's just . . . you're my daughter too, and I really don't think . . . '

Imogen heard the catch in her mother's voice.

'Mum,' Imogen said. 'Are you OK?'

'Yes, dear. Of course I am.' Imogen heard muffled sobs at the end of the line. *Oh God,* she thought, *this is actually worse than the yelling. No tears for thirty years and now there was no stopping her.*

'Are you sure?' Imogen asked.

'No,' Jan said, her voice faint where it had been bold only a moment before. 'I *worry* about you, sweetheart. I'll never understand why you have to put yourself in danger like you do. Diving and risking getting nitrogen whatsit. It's my job as a mum to look after you, and I want to do that right. But you make it so hard sometimes.'

'Mum, I'm twenty-three,' Imogen said, sitting down in an armchair. 'You and Dad, both of you are wonderful parents, in your own ways. But I'm not like you, Mum. Maybe I will be, one day, but I'm not yet. I don't want to settle down – there are things I want to do first. I want to make something of myself, become a photographer.'

'I don't want to stop you. Not really. 'It's only because I love you, you know,' Jan said.

'I know that, Mum. And thank you for that.'

Chapter Thirty-Two

On the specials board: Praline Indulgence

Anna was sitting on the same stool she had once sat on next to her sister, when they were little girls. She had a bowl of praline ice cream in front of her, the shop shutters halfway down and a subdued Hepburn for company. Even he seemed to realise that something had gone wrong.

She looked around the shop and thought of all the hurdles she and Imogen had faced so far – knew that there would be plenty more to come. Facing them together had made it all so much easier. Could she do it alone?

She heard a rap at the shutters and glanced up to see the bottom half of Evie, visible beneath the metal door, unmistakable in overalls and pink DM boots.

'Evie,' Anna said, her mood lifting a fraction.

'Yes, of course it's me, dear,' she said. 'Now, are you going to let me in?'

Anna raised the shutter to see Evie's smiling face. For a moment it felt as if part of her Grandma Vivien was standing there too.

'Are you OK, dear? You're very pale.'

'I've been better, if I'm honest,' Anna admitted. She and Evie sat down together in one of the booths.

'Man trouble?' Evie ventured. She covered Anna's hands with her own silver-ring-covered fingers.

'Yes,' Anna said. 'Plenty. But no. I've had my fair share of it lately, but it's not that today. It's the shop. Or rather, it's Imogen.'

'She's got itchy feet?'

'How did you guess?'

'Perhaps it takes one to know one,' Evie laughed gently. 'I travelled a fair bit in my time. I saw that same lust for adventure in your sister the very first time I met her.

'So let me guess, you're worried about all this,' she continued, nodding over at the counter, where during opening hours colourful ice creams filled the glass cabinets and waffle cones of all sizes were piled high. 'Running this place on your own?'

'Yes,' Anna said. 'That's about it.' She started to cry, quietly.

'Well, it's a lot of work, isn't it, going it alone. But you're a strong woman, Anna. There's so much of your grandmother in you.'

'Do you really think so?' Anna said, snuffling and wiping away the tears with the sleeve of her cardigan, glad that no one but Evie was there to see her.

'Oh yes, you're the spirit of Vivien. And a fighting spirit it is.'

'Do you miss her, Evie?' Anna asked.

'Do I miss her?' she said, eyebrows raised. 'There's not a day goes by that I don't miss your grandmother. Feels like a hole in my heart.'

And it was then that Anna saw it. Just a flash of pain in Evie's eyes, a sense that it wasn't just a friend, but a soulmate who had left her.

'There's no one like Vivien,' Evie said.

'I miss her so badly right now,' Anna said. 'She always knew the right thing to do.'

'Oh yes,' Evie said, smiling. 'But you know too. You just have to silence all the other voices and let yourself hear your own.'

An hour later, Evie and Anna were still sitting in the booth, with mugs of tea and Vivien's photo album between them on the table.

'Now, that one –' Evie said, pointing to a black-and-white photo held in place with photo corners – 'was from that summer in the sixties, you know, with the mods and rockers. Came down here, fighting about nothing and making a God-awful mess.'

Anna looked at the photo more closely. The window of the Sunset 99s was smashed in, with a pile of glass in front of Evie's shop next door was even more badly damaged, with the door hanging off its hinges.

'Petrified, we were that day. We hid out in the kitchen at the back of my shop and waited for the police to come and break things up. But they took forever to get here. And we could hear the youngsters doing God only knows what to each other out there. I mean, you know me and Vivien, we were never ones to shy away from danger. But this was something else – something we hadn't seen before. No one down here had.'

'Sounds awful,' Anna said. 'All that damage, for nothing. But I'm glad you weren't hurt.'

'Yes, we were lucky really. Although it didn't feel like that at the time – it cost us both a fortune to get the shops back to how they were'

'I can imagine. What about this one?' Anna asked, pointing to a photo on the opposite page. The shops' signs, which looked like they should be neon and bright, were dull and tatty. Vivien and her husband Joseph were standing in front of the shop with smiles on their faces, but something in their expressions seemed to suggest a different story.

'The eighties – business wasn't great back then. But we all stuck together, helped each other out. And of course having gone through it once you know, don't you, that it'll pass. That things'll get better again soon. They always do.'

'You just kept going, didn't you? Both of you,' Anna said. She looked at more photos: celebrations, street parties, shop revamps, fifties furniture, then psychedelic seventies prints, her grandmother's outfits reflecting the changes in fashion.

'We did,' Evie said. 'And so will you, sweetheart. You're a survivor.'

'I am?' Anna asked, unsure. The past weeks had taken their toll on her.

'Of course you are. Your grandmother was so very proud of you.'

The next morning, Anna started work with more vigour and enthusiasm than she'd had in days.

The night before, after talking to Evie, she'd decided she was ready to run the shop on her own. Emboldened by her new plan, she'd also deleted Jon's number from her phone, and finally got around to unfriending him on Facebook. She felt liberated.

She still missed Alfie desperately. Missed Jon too. But when she'd gone back to the flat the previous night, she'd realised it wasn't empty without the two of them. It was just getting ready to be filled with something new. Something Anna now had space for.

On her break Anna opened her laptop, and logged into her email. She found a new message.

To: Anna
From: Matteo

Dear Anna,

A hello from across the ocean.

Forgive me for writing. I know that you have your own life over in England, and really I should just leave you in peace.

But the truth is, I can't stop thinking about you.

I know you didn't want me to tell you how I felt when you were here. But now you can't stop me (ha!). When you walk into a room, it lights up. I want that in my life. I want you in my life.

Anna took Matteo's words in slowly. Hearing how he felt, directly from him, sent a rush of warmth through her.

You're thinking you should tell me you have a boyfriend. Don't worry, I already know. You never pretended anything different. Sian told me, but I had already guessed.

All the same I'm taking a chance. Because if I don't then . . . well. I figure I'll be a sad old man, wondering what could have been.

I hope you are happy. But if you're not . . . Or if one day in the future, you're not . . . I'm here. At the very least, I could make you a good ice cream to cheer you up.

I'm going to press Send. (I will not chicken out.)
Anna. I can't forget you.

Matteo x

Anna took a few minutes to digest what he'd said. Then she opened a new window and typed a message back.

To: Matteo

From: Anna

Hi, Matteo,

Thank you for your message.

Anna hesitated. That didn't sound right. She held down the Delete key until she had a blank screen again.

It was good to hear

Delete.

She began typing again:

Try this

Then restarted her message:

Mango and Raspberry Granita:

Ingredients . . .

When she'd finished typing, she took a deep breath and pressed Send.

Chapter Thirty-Three

On the specials board: Hepburn's Glorious Ice Cream for Hounds

On Thursday morning, Imogen walked across the pebbles on the beach in Kemp Town, where the shore was less busy and she could throw Hepburn's ball without it getting pounced on by a hundred other, bigger dogs. Dressed in jeans and a faded grey T-shirt, her hair uncombed and without a scrap of make-up on, she'd left the house to clear her head, after rebooking her flights for 17th August, in a week and a half's time. She hadn't expected to see anyone she knew.

Down by the water's edge, with a group of students, was Finn. He was showing them how to pop up to standing on their surfboards, just as he'd shown her the other day. He demonstrated the move ably, and then the rest of the class floundered around trying to replicate it. He caught sight of her before she could turn away.

'Imogen,' he shouted out, turning his back on the class.

She smiled back and gave a wave, but instinctively picked up her pace. They hadn't spoken since their date at the weekend, and she didn't know what to say to him.

Before she had taken more than a few steps, though, Finn was by her side on the pebbly beach, his hand gently touching her arm.

'Hey,' he said.

'Hi,' Imogen replied, trying to sound relaxed and cool. Hepburn was looking at her with his huge, round brown eyes, questioning. *I like this man*, he seemed to be thinking. *Why are you trying to get away from him?*

'Looks like you're in the middle of a class,' Imogen managed at last.

'Oh, don't worry about that,' Finn said. 'I think they could do with a bit of time to practise.'

Imogen looked over his shoulder and saw the men and women still struggling on their surfboards, emitting loud bursts of giggles as they fell to the ground yet again.

'You might be right,' she said, smiling in spite of her nerves.

'Is everything OK?' Finn asked. 'It's been kind of quiet.'

'Sorry,' she said, thinking of the texts and calls she had been ignoring. 'It's just been a busy week.'

'Look, I'm probably going to regret this,' Finn said, looking her right in the eye. 'But I'm going to lay my cards on the table anyway. I really like you, Imogen, and I've had an incredible time with you over the last few weeks. So that's why I haven't given up. I don't know what's going on with you, but I'm still not giving up.'

'So,' he continued, 'if I was less deluded I'd definitely have accepted that you're not interested. But the truth is I'd really like to see you again.'

Imogen stood in silence on the pebbled beach. Waves crashed, laughter continued to drift over from the surf group, and a gang with a ghetto blaster walked by – but the words she wanted to say escaped her.

'Thanks,' she mumbled finally.

'Thanks?' Finn echoed, a smile of surprise on his lips. 'Not quite the response I was hoping for, but it could have been worse.

'I'd better get back to the group,' he finished, glancing over his shoulder as a cheer went up from the students. One of them had mastered the pop-up move and the others were applauding him. 'Looks like they've been making progress without me.'

'Listen . . . ' Imogen started. She couldn't let him walk away when she was due to fly off in less than a fortnight. 'Tonight. Come by the house? I'll cook you dinner and we can talk.'

The light returned to his eyes. 'I'll see you at eight,' he said, then turned and jogged back towards the water.

Imogen brought the shopping bags into the hallway and closed the door of Vivien's house behind her. It was strange preparing things for her dinner with Finn, as if this were the start of something rather than the end.

She sat down in the armchair next to the fireplace, dark-green velvet, with springs that you could feel through the fabric in places. Next to it was a framed photo of her grandmother holding hands with Imogen and Anna when they were little. As she looked at Vivien's face, her gentle features and neatly styled hair swept back into a loose bun, she thought for a moment she could feel her presence in the room. She looked at the photo, and asked in a low whisper. 'I'm doing the right thing, aren't I, Granny V?'

Imogen wondered, for the first time in her life, whether she might have too much worth keeping to risk walking away.

Imogen poured Finn another glass of wine. It wasn't a night for skimping on the units, she thought to herself as she watched the red liquid flow out.

'So you've already booked your ticket?' he said.

'Yes, well, I already had a return flight booked, but I only fixed the date yesterday.'

'And it's one-way?'

'Yes,' Imogen said, pouring herself a glass and then sitting down at the table. 'I'm sorry. I know it must seem sudden, but it's been on my mind for a while that I want to get back and finish the set of photos I showed you. If it hadn't been for what happened with Granny V, I wouldn't be here at all.'

He shook his head. 'Wow, I really made an idiot out of myself this morning then, didn't I?'

'No,' Imogen replied. 'You were honest. Maybe we could

all do with being a bit more honest. I've really enjoyed spending time with you, Finn.'

'I just didn't expect . . . ' He took a sip of wine, then set the glass back down on the table. 'I don't know what I expected to happen tonight – but it wasn't this.'

'I know,' Imogen said. 'I really like you, and it wasn't an easy decision. Anyway, I didn't want to leave without saying a proper goodbye.'

'Goodbye,' Finn said, with a wry smile. 'Right.'

After dinner, they moved into the living room, each holding a plate laden with apple crumble and ice cream. Since they'd changed the subject from Imogen's future plans the atmosphere had lightened.

'I didn't make the ice cream,' Imogen said, 'so there's nothing for you to worry about. It's courtesy of Sainsbury's, that one.'

'Thanks,' Finn said. 'Although I'm sure you're an expert by now.'

'I don't know about that,' Imogen said. 'I leave the cooking to Anna nowadays.'

'Listen. Obviously I'm trying to be really cool about this whole you-going-away thing, but actually I'm gutted.'

'You want to know something?' Imogen replied, Finn's frankness allowing her to speak her own mind. 'I am too. But you seem really settled and I can't stay here, knowing I'll always have what if's. That wouldn't be fair on either of us.'

'There is one possibility we haven't talked about.'

'OK, go ahead,' Imogen said, her curiosity piqued.

'I'm thinking out loud here, and you may hate the idea. But I've wanted to take a break for a while. For six years, I've been working flat out with no holidays getting the business off the ground. Andy's always saying he wants more responsibility, and I'm sure he could handle running it on his own for a while.'

Imogen began to piece together what he was saying and a smile crept onto her lips.

'How would you feel about some company?' Finn said. 'A few months on a beach – I can't think of anything better than that – or anyone I'd rather spend the time with.'

Imogen let the words sink in and become real. *Finn – Finn and her – in Thailand. Together.*

'It would give us a chance, wouldn't it?' Imogen said.

'Yes,' he said. 'Plus it would be fun. And if it doesn't work out – fine – we go our separate ways. But something tells me, I don't know, a sneaky suspicion . . . I have a feeling it just might.'

'You know what, Finn,' Imogen said, a huge smile on her face now, 'I think it's a brilliant idea.'

Chapter Thirty-Four

On the specials board: Champagne Sorbet

'A double waffle cone with hazelnut and pistachio, please,' said Julie, a woman in her fifties who was fast becoming a regular a Vivien's.

Since sending Matteo her recipe, Anna had heard nothing back from him. With Imogen and Finn's leaving party that evening, and the prospect of running the shop on her own fast becoming a reality, she had plenty of more important things to focus on.

But it had been over a week. Ten whole days since she'd written. And for some reason it was all she could think about. That, and what Matteo had said in his earlier message.

'Right, yes,' Anna said, drifting out of her reverie. 'Coming up.'

'What's going on, love?' Julie asked. 'Only you look like you're in another world this morning.'

'I am a bit,' Anna admitted. 'I'll snap out of it. A few things on my mind, that's all.'

'Well, you're not alone there,' Julie laughed kindly. 'Maybe you should treat yourself to a little of your own medicine.' She pointed at the ice creams in the glass cabinet. 'Certainly helps me.'

Julie took her cone with a smile, and left. *Perhaps she's right,* Anna thought. She didn't normally eat on duty, apart from the odd experimental taster. But today, when she needed some comfort she could count on, seemed like the day to make an exception. She took a cone and scooped out a generous serving of chocolate macadamia, then settled on a stool to eat it. The alternating chunks of chocolate and nut gave it the most addictive texture. As she absorbed the flavours, savouring them, any thoughts of Matteo or the potentially challenging months to come at the shop, faded away.

'Eating your way through the profits?' a familiar male voice said. It was one she knew as well as her own. She looked up and saw her father's welcoming smile. He had a few new lines around his eyes, but other than that, looked just as he'd always been.

'Dad. You're here!'

'Of course I'm here. Wouldn't miss Imogen's leaving party. Me and your mum have been wanting to come and visit for a while, but I haven't felt well enough. I'm sorry,' he said. Anna reached out and took his hand in hers, giving it a little squeeze.

'You look better, Dad,' Anna said. 'Do you feel it?'

'Getting there,' he said, with a smile. 'With no small thanks due to your mum. She's my rock. Anyway, she's been so excited about the party, especially seeing as we haven't met this new man of Imo's yet.'

'It's lovely to see you. And where's Mum now?' She glanced towards the door.

'She's just doing her hair at the hotel. We're staying at the Grand. Thought it would be easier, all round, than staying at the house, with all the memories. Anyway, I couldn't resist popping down right away to say hello.'

Anna reached out her arms and her dad hugged her. In an instant, her twenty-eight years dissolved into eight. She felt protected in his strong arms.

'You got ice cream on my jumper,' her dad laughed, and brushed off a chunk she'd accidentally smeared on the sleeve of his woolly sweater.

'Oops, sorry. Occupational hazard,' Anna laughed. 'But talking of ice cream – what do you think of this place?' she said, opening her arms wide to show off all of the changes the shop had undergone.

'It's just incredible,' he said. 'You've worked so hard, both of you. It looks even better than in the photos you sent.'

'Not bad, eh?' Anna said, feeling a rush of pride.

'Your grandmother would be really proud,' Dad said. His lips were tight, holding in the emotion, and Anna touched his arm gently, knowing that if he cried, it would be certain to set her off too.

'You've done what she dreamed of, haven't you?' he went on. 'It still looks like her place, but you've brought it right up to date.'

'I'm glad you think so,' Anna said. 'I have to admit, there were days when I wondered if we could do it.'

'We always had faith in you,' he said. 'And there was no way in hell I was going to let Françoise trip you up.'

'I loved it when you gave her what for,' Anna said.

Tom smiled. 'That woman had no place bullying any of us.'

'What did Martin make of it all?'

'You won't believe it, but he's finally shown Françoise the door.'

'He hasn't,' Anna said, her hand going to her mouth.

'Yes, he has. Martin said that when he saw how upset and angry I was, it was the confirmation he needed that she wasn't the woman for him any more. You know how the two of us are, Anna. We'd never argued before. Anyway, he said he should have done it a long time ago.'

'Good for him,' Anna said. 'And good for you, Dad,' she smiled. 'How's he coping?'

'He's having a grand old time, considering,' Tom laughed. 'Barely off the golf course, and not without his fair share of admirers. Not that he really notices that.'

'And there's another thing,' her dad said. 'With Françoise gone, he seems to have gone right off the idea of selling Mum's house.'

'He doesn't want to sell it at all? To anyone? That's terrific news, Dad.'

'Oh, it's even better than that, darling,' he said. 'Martin is moving in. But I'll let him tell you about that when you see him.'

'See him?'

'Yes. Before Imogen's party tonight, there's something Martin and I wanted to do. And I'm hoping you and your sister will be able to join us.'

Martin and Tom were standing facing the sea, the urn containing their mother's ashes held tightly in Martin's hands.

Jan stood between her daughters nearby. Sunlight glistened on the quiet stretch of sea in front of them. Anna held Hepburn's lead while he lay calmly on the pebbled beach, as if he had some sense of why they were there and was showing his respect.

'She'll be part of the sea she always loved,' Martin said, looking over at his brother. 'And this is where we can all come to visit and think of her.'

'She used to talk about it,' Tom added. 'How she'd be free, but able to keep one eye on the shop too,' he said, smiling in his daughters' direction.

Martin carefully lifted off the lid of the urn and took a couple of steps towards the water. Tom walked out beside him. Martin scattered some of Vivien's ashes into the sea, and then passed the urn to his brother. 'Goodbye, Mum,' Tom said. Gently, he tipped the urn and let the remainder of the ashes be carried out by the tide.

They walked back silently to Vivien's house. The ceremony seemed to have given them all a chance to let go. It was Imogen who spoke first.

'So, what's all this Dad says, Uncle Martin?' she asked him. 'About you moving into Granny V's house?'

'It won't be right away,' Martin said, 'but now that Françoise has gone . . . ' He paused, and looked sadder than he had all afternoon. 'It feels like time to come home. I don't know what I was thinking, letting her talk me into selling to those awful developers. Mum's house is going to stay right where it's always been. But there are going to be a few changes.'

'Changes?' Anna said.

'Yes. You know how Mum always loved company – how her door was never shut, at the shop or the house.'

'Yes,' Imogen said.

'I'm going to convert the place into a B&B. Even with me in there, there'll be four spare bedrooms, and you know how spacious they are. Plus I could do with a bit of company myself, now that I'm a single man again.'

'What a nice idea,' Anna said. 'You'll be sure to tell them where they can find the best ice creams in town, won't you?'

'Bon voyage!' Imogen's family and friends all raised a toast. They were packed into Finn's front room, drinking champagne and eating canapés, the floor-to-ceiling sea view providing a dramatic backdrop.

Anna looked over at her sister kissing Finn with abandon, oblivious to the other people in the room.

For once it was Imogen who knew where she was going, and who with. It was Anna's life that was the blank canvas.

'So what do you think of him, then?' Anna's mum whispered to her.

'Finn? He's a gem,' she replied.

'He'll take good care of her, won't he?'

'Of course he will, Mum. He's a really kind, straightforward guy,' Anna said. 'He's good for her.'

'That's nice,' Jan said. 'I know she can't see it, but I do admire her. I just wish sometimes that she could be a bit more like you, sweetheart, less inclined to put her life in danger. But perhaps one day that will come.'

'Don't rush it,' Anna said, taking another sip of champagne. 'Come on, Mum, who wants two of me? And I think we'd all miss the entertainment.'

'Perhaps you're right,' Mum said, considering it. 'And you, darling,' she continued. 'I was so sorry to hear about what happened with Jon.'

'Oh, don't be,' Anna said. 'It was for the best. Better now than dragging it out. And I can't begrudge Alfie the chance to have his real parents back together. I know how much it meant to me to grow up with you two.'

Jan smiled, and touched Anna's arm.

'On that note,' Anna said, 'it sounds like things are a bit better between you?'

'Yes. Together by the skin of our teeth, but still somehow together,' she laughed. 'I know I didn't do anything right when he was ill. I'm not the best listener, and I just wanted him to be back to normal. But it was hard to see him so down, distant. Then when he told Françoise to back off over the shop, it was like a flash of the Tom I loved came back, and he's been getting steadily better since then. I've never loved him more, Anna.'

After the party, Anna drove Imogen and Finn to Gatwick Airport, with Tom and Jan travelling with them.

'So, what will you do for money when you're over there?' Jan asked Finn from her position squashed into the back seat of the car. Anna was driving, but her mum had been directing from the back seat since they set off. Anna was relieved that she'd now turned her attention to extracting as much information as she possibly could from Imogen's new boyfriend.

'I've got some savings to tide us over,' Finn said. 'The business has been solid for a while now, and when you work the hours me and Andy do you don't always get the chance to spend the money you make. But now –' Finn glanced over at Imogen with a smile – 'I have the perfect excuse.'

Anna's dad caught her eye. They both knew that it was only a matter of time before Jan was bowled over by Finn's easy charm. It wasn't just his personality that was winning everyone round, it was his effect on Imogen, the way he seemed to bring about a sense of contentment in her none of them had ever seen before.

'Well,' Mum said, clearly holding back on giving her full approval before the car journey was over, 'if you do run out of money, you'll just have to come back home, won't you?'

'Mum,' Imogen protested, 'give it a rest, will you? Finn'll probably change his mind before we get there at this rate.'

They neared Gatwick Airport with a gentle buzz of chatter about Thailand from Imogen and Finn, what they were looking forward to doing first. But as they reached the junction for Gatwick, there was another peep out of Jan.

'What about Christmas?' she said. 'Are you going to be away for another one?'

'We'll Skype you from the beach,' Imogen said. 'We'll find a way to be there.'

They parked up in the airport car park and made their way towards the check-in desks together.

'See you in six months, sis,' Anna whispered into Imogen's ear as they hugged. 'Have fun.'

Imogen smiled back. The sunshine had come back into her eyes already, even there in the air-conditioned airport terminal with nothing but grey clouds visible through the windows.

'We will,' Imogen replied. 'And this summer – well, it's been . . . ' She shrugged, unable to find the words.

'Quite something, hasn't it?' Anna said.

'Emotional,' Imogen said with a smile.

Anna thought back over the time they'd shared, setting up the business. As they'd overcome each obstacle they'd learned more about what they were truly capable of, and what mattered. They were both strong, and their whole family was too. Yes, it would always be missing a piece, but through the shop, and the B&B, they'd found ways to keep Vivien's memory alive.

'I'll miss you,' Anna said, taking her sister's hand in hers. 'Please don't let Mum put you off ever coming home.'

'We'll be back,' Imogen said, laughing and glancing over at Finn, who was hugging their mum and dad goodbye as if he'd known them all his life.

'You've got a good one there,' Anna said, nodding towards Finn.

'Yes,' Imogen replied. 'And it turns out that might not be such a bad thing after all.'

'Of course it's not. Now be nice to him, and take some brilliant photos out there to give us something to smile about when it's cold and rainy over here.'

'I'll get busy,' Imogen said. 'I can't wait to get back to it,' she added, patting her camera bag.

'I look forward to seeing them,' Anna said. She caught sight of Finn trying to disentangle himself from their mum's hearty embrace.

'And you'll be OK, won't you?' Imogen said.

'Why does everyone keep asking me that?' Anna laughed. 'Yes, I'll be fine, and no – because I know this is what you're really thinking – I have no intention of getting back together with Jon.'

'Promise me? No matter what he says?'

'There's nothing he could say,' Anna assured her, feeling bolder now than she had in weeks. 'It wasn't right and if I'm honest, I think I was kidding myself for quite a while.'

An announcement blared over the tannoy.

'British Airways flight 304 to Bangkok is now boarding. Passengers for flight 304 please proceed to Gate 14.'

Imogen reached for her bag, and then for Finn's hand. 'Time to go,' she said.

As her sister walked away through the departure gate, tears came to Anna's eyes. Imogen said she'd be back in six months, and maybe this time she really meant it. But then again – with Imogen, you never really knew.

Back in Brighton, Anna and her mum and dad were in the reception area of the Grand Hotel.

'Let's say goodbye to Anna, and then you can get your glad rags on, Jan.'

'It's like that, is it?' Anna laughed. 'You haven't seen your daughter in ages and then once you're here you can't wait to get away from me?'

'You know it's not that, love,' Jan said. 'But it's not often we get to go out in the city. And your dad's promised me a meal. We missed out anniversary this year,' she said, taking her husband's hand. 'Well, we weren't really up for it then, were we, Tom?'

'It wasn't the right time.'

'So we're going to have our celebration tonight instead.'

'Great. I'm only joking. Don't let me stand in your way,' Anna said. 'Happy Anniversary, and have a wonderful night. I know you will.'

Anna kissed her mum goodbye. When she hugged her dad he held on to her a moment longer than usual.

Nothing beats an Indian summer, Anna thought a fortnight later, as she looked out of her window on a cloudless September sky. Everyone's given in, put away their summer clothes, taken in the garden furniture, thrown away the nearly finished bottles of suncream and uploaded their holiday photos, left only with a bittersweet sense of loss.

And then – out of nowhere – it's back. Anna had opened the curtains expecting to look out on another drizzly September day, and instead had felt the heat almost immediately. The sun was a golden yellow, and even at 8 a.m. the beach was starting to fill up.

Anna put on a gingham teadress and wedges, winding her hair up in kirby grips. She added a slick of lipgloss and a pair of small silver earrings. She was really doing it. Running the business on her own. And it was going well.

She checked the freezer for the ice cream and granitas she'd made the previous night: a rich, comforting praline and a summery fruit granita. She must have sensed somehow that the sun was going to come out. Loading the trays carefully into her freezer bag, she checked her appearance one final time and then left the flat.

At eleven o'clock Vivien's had a queue snaking right out the door. She was working on her own, and it was hot – a trickle of sweat traced its way down her spine.

'Two lemon sorbets, please,' said a teenage couple.

Anna loaded the scoops into cones she'd placed in the stand and took the money in her other hand with a smile. The till was close to overflowing. Parents had been passing ten-pound notes to her left, right and centre in a hurry to appease their hot, excited, squabbling children with the sweet treats.

The next orders were for two chocolate cones, then a Vivien's Super Sundae – the special that day, praline drizzled with a salted caramel sauce.

Anna focused on drizzling the sauce into a heart shape on the sundae, her pride and joy. While she got it perfect, the queue could wait.

'How about a . . . '

The male voice broke her concentration.

' . . . raspberry and mango granita?'

The left-hand side of the heart shape went wobbly as Anna's hand trembled on hearing the new order. It was written up large on the blackboard, but no one had ordered a granita all day.

She looked up from the sundae she was decorating and saw, standing in front of her, the man who'd hardly left her thoughts that summer.

Matteo took the sundae and cones from her and with a warm smile, handed them over to the children who were waiting for them before turning back to face her.

'I've come all this way to try one,' Matteo said, a cheeky glint in his eye. 'You're not going to leave me here to starve, are you?'

Epilogue

July, the following year: New York

'Come right in,' Imogen said to a stylish young couple. 'Here's a catalogue with details of all the works.'

She was at an upmarket gallery in Chelsea, New York, with Finn, at a mid-week private view. On the wall were framed prints and sophisticated guests were sipping cocktails and milling around discussing the artwork.

But this isn't just any exhibition, she thought proudly. *It's mine.*

Each underwater photo told a story, unveiled a hidden corner of a world that, with an oxygen tank and goggles, she'd briefly been part of. Clownfish, manta rays and – the largest print of all – a close-up of a whale shark, brought a riot of colour to the sober white gallery walls.

'Reckon you've got a buyer over there,' Finn whispered in Imogen's ear, pointing to a sharp-suited gentleman who was staring intently at the page of the catalogue where the prices were listed.

'He looks interested, doesn't he?' she said hopefully. There were already a few red spots dotted around on some of her photos, and it wasn't even ten o'clock yet.

For eight months she and Finn had been living on Koh Tao. For the first two weeks it had been a blur of sunshine and kisses, long swims in the sea and evenings in the beach bars. But then Imogen had started to focus on her photography again, diving most days and building up her collection.

Finn had been at a loose end for a while, and found it difficult to let go completely of running the surf school – he'd been checking in with Andy almost daily at one point. But eventually he'd relaxed, and found a job at a local smoothie bar, mixing fruit and coconut drinks for thirsty sunbathers. He and Imogen had worked through the day-to-day business of running a home together. To Finn's initial surprise, even in a beach hut with a hammock there was still recycling to do and groceries to buy.

They hadn't lived in each other's pockets, they had found new friends and separate interests. But they both savoured the time alone together in the evening, enjoying a cool beer or fresh barbecued fish on their veranda.

After six months in Thailand, Imogen had finished compiling her photographs and had set up her website with Finn's help. Then over the next few months had come the nerve-wracking task of approaching agents and gallery owners, pitching her work and hoping that someone would take an interest. Emails went unanswered and phone calls left her downhearted. Until Nikki arrived. A New York gallery owner, dedicated to discovering new talent and with an equally keen passion for diving, she and Imogen had clicked the moment they'd met at Davy's dive shop. Nine months had taken her and Finn a long way.

Imogen rang her sister the morning after the private view, as she and Finn finished up brunch at their apartment in Brooklyn. Nikki's friends were away so she'd arranged for them to house-sit for the run of the exhibition, and the warehouse-style loft was the perfect base for them to explore the city.

'Anna!' Imogen said, as soon as her sister picked up. Finn smiled at her indulgently and took his mug of coffee over to the futon, knowing the conversation was likely to go on for a while. 'You won't *believe* how well it went last night.'

'The exhibition? People liked the photos?' Anna said. Her voice sounded close in spite of the ocean between them.

'They went down a storm, Anna. Get this – I sold twelve of them. Nikki said it was one of the most successful private views she's had.'

'That's terrific, Imo,' Anna said. 'I knew you had it in you. Maybe we should have a little exhibition here at Vivien's? I mean, I know it's hardly New York, but . . . '

'I'd love that,' Imogen said, imagining some of the smaller prints up on the walls of the ice cream shop.

'Now, sorry to sound like Mum – but when exactly are you and Finn coming back?'

'Next week,' Imogen said gleefully. 'He and I have a flight

booked for Thursday. So we'll be back in plenty of time to get the van fired up and ready for its summer festival tour.'

'Next week?' Anna squealed.

'Yes. I can't wait to see you. Oh, and talking of the van – Finn's got this obsession with making smoothies now, so we'll be able to expand our range a bit.'

Finn's ears pricked up at the sound of his name, and he peered cheekily at Imogen over the edge of the sofa. They hadn't really thought much beyond the summer – apart from one thing. Imogen would be moving in with Finn, and she had barely stopped smiling since they'd decided it.

'Well, we'll be here,' Anna said, 'waiting with open arms.'

'I've missed you, sis,' Imogen said. 'Dad too, even Mum, would you believe it?'

'We've all missed you too. Now make sure you don't miss your flight, or I'll have Mum and Dad's broken hearts to deal with.'

'See you in a week. Bye.' Imogen put down the phone.

She walked back across the sunlit loft apartment and dived into Finn's open arms. 'We're going home,' she said with a smile.

July, the following year: Vivien's Heavenly Ice Cream Shop, Hove

Anna hung up the shop phone, and returned to the counter.

'Your sister?' Matteo asked.

'Yes,' she said, unable to keep the smile from her face. 'Guess what? She's coming back next week.'

'That's fantastic,' he said, giving her a hug. 'I'll get to meet the famous Imogen at last.'

'Oh, yes,' Anna said, laughing. 'Prepare yourself.'

He smiled. 'That's what your mum said too. Now I'm starting to get nervous.'

'You'll get on really well,' Anna reassured him. 'She's going to love meeting you.'

'And did you tell her?' Matteo asked, his arms slipping around Anna's waist and coming to rest on her baby bump. Five months in, it was starting to show a little even under her apron.

'Not yet,' Anna said. 'It'll be a surprise.'

Matteo kissed her neck gently, then turned her round to face him. 'I thought you hated surprises, *Signora*. What's changed?'

'Maybe I've had a few good ones lately,' Anna said with a shrug. 'That changed my mind.'

Matteo leaned in to kiss her gently on the lips. After a busy lunchtime, she was grateful that the shop was empty. She kissed him again and her hand drifted on to his bum.

'I think this is getting a little unprofessional,' Matteo joked.

'That's what I like best about it. And we're the bosses, remember?'

It was difficult now to remember a time when she and Matteo hadn't run the shop together. In nine months they'd become a really strong team – devising the menu together, creating the ice creams and serving a loyal base of customers. In spring, a flurry of mentions in food blogs had brought a stream of new visitors, and they'd worked flat out for most of June.

When Imogen got back though, she'd find a shop that looked much the same as the one she'd left. There were just a few minor changes. A photo of their grandma, framed by Evie, was on the wall behind the counter – Vivien had her place, keeping an eye on things. On the opposite wall were photos of the shop through the ages, and the older customers loved looking over them, sharing their own memories of the seafront at that time.

Anna's parents came down from time to time to visit,

staying with Martin at his flourishing B&B when he had a room available, or with Anna, Matteo and Hepburn in their spare room. Matteo had just finished painting the nursery a pale yellow. It was easier for Anna that the room looked different – she didn't imagine Alfie in there each time she passed but she still missed him. She probably always would.

The main change was Matteo. He'd brought a sunshine into Anna's life she'd never known before.

'Are you sure you're still happy to be here?' Anna said, looking at him. 'Promise me you're not longing to get back to Italy?'

'Anna, I thought we'd talked about this,' he said, shaking his head and laughing. 'Italy may have a lot of beautiful things, but there's one thing I'll never find there, and that's the crazy Englishwoman I fell in love with. And the family we're going to have.' He stroked a loose strand of her hair back behind her ear.

'Well, good. I'm glad.'

'But I do have one condition,' Matteo said.

'Oh yes?' Anna furrowed her brow with suspicion.

'When the baby is bigger,' he said, 'we have to go there and educate her, or him, in the ways of gelato. I'm not having them think that a Cornetto from the corner shop is proper Italian ice cream. We need to show our child the real Italian ways.'

'Now that,' Anna said, recalling the delicious flavours that had started her journey in ice cream making, 'I'm more than happy to agree to.'

*

Hi,

I hope you've enjoyed reading about Imogen and Anna's adventures in ice cream. If the story's set your tastebuds tingling, here are five exclusive recipes for you to try out for yourselves!

Love, Abby x

p.s. Mine's a scoop of the Salted Caramel - thanks.

CLASSIC VANILLA

*The perfect place to start, and a great base
for the tasty Supermix over the page.*

INGREDIENTS

90g sugar
2 eggs
a pinch of salt

360ml milk
240ml cream
2 teaspoons vanilla extract

PREPARATION

★ Combine sugar and eggs and beat with a whisk until mixture is frothy. Add salt and mix.

★ In a saucepan, heat the milk until it starts to simmer, then remove from heat. Slowly add milk to egg mixture, and whisk until all of the milk has been added.

★ Pour the egg-milk mixture back into the pan and cook over medium-low heat, stirring until the mixture thickens enough to coat the back of a spoon.

★ Remove from heat, strain the mixture into a bowl. Cool slightly.

★ Stir in cream and vanilla, leave mixture to cool.

★ Freeze in an ice cream maker according to manufacturer's directions.

* * *

SUPERMIX

Make as the vanilla ice cream above, but just before removing from the ice cream maker, add chopped marshmallows, Maltesers, nuts, broken toffee pieces and dried cranberries, or any other goodies you have in your store cupboard. Delicious!

MARSALA WINE TIRAMISU ICE CREAM

For an authentic taste of Italy, try out this decadent flavour.

INGREDIENTS

90g sugar
2 eggs
a pinch of salt
120ml milk
200g cream cheese

240ml cream
1 teaspoon coffee granules
200g chocolate sponge
100ml Marsala wine

PREPARATION

★ Prepare as vanilla ice cream adding the coffee granules to the hot milk.

★ Add cream cheese at the end with the cream.

★ Soak your chocolate sponge in the Marsala wine.

★ Ripple the Marsala-wine soaked sponge into the ice cream as you remove it from the ice cream maker, then pop it into freezer for 20 minutes before serving.

SALTED CARAMEL

Seriously addictive . . .

INGREDIENTS

480ml whole milk	1 tbsp flour
260g sugar	240ml cream
1 tablespoon salted butter	1 teaspoon vanilla extract
4 egg yolks	1 teaspoon sea salt

PREPARATION

★ Heat the milk over medium-low heat until it's just about to simmer and turn off.

★ Heat the sugar over medium heat, stirring until the sugar melts and turns golden brown. Continue cooking until the sugar is completely melted and turned into syrup. Add the butter to the sugar and stir.

★ Slowly add the warm milk to the caramel, stirring until the caramel dissolves into the milk. The caramel will sizzle at first, but over medium-low heat it will gradually melt into the milk.

★ Whisk the egg yolks, flour and salt. When the caramel-milk mixture is smooth, gradually whisk the caramel-milk mixture into the egg mixture. Put the ingredients back into the saucepan. Over medium-low heat, heat the mixture until it's thick enough to coat the back of a spoon, stirring constantly with a whisk.

★ Strain.

★ Stir in the cream and the vanilla and leave mixture to cool.

★ Freeze in an ice cream maker according to the manufacturer's instructions.

BLUEBERRY ICE CREAM

Fresh and tasty, and a superfood to boot...

INGREDIENTS

90g sugar
350g fresh or frozen blueberries

1/4 tsp. vanilla extract
Pinch of salt
1 tbsp. lemon juice

PREPARATION

★ Dissolve sugar in 2 tbsp water in a saucepan over low heat.

★ Once dissolved, add the blueberries, lemon juice, vanilla extract and salt.

★ Cook over a low heat, stirring occasionally, until the blueberries are soft.

★ Remove from heat and mash.

★ Leave mixture to cool

★ Freeze in an ice cream maker according to the manufacturer's instructions.

* * *

Thanks to Tracey and Paul Kindred at Heavenly! - a charming and unique chocolate and ice cream shop based in Wales - for their kind permission to use these recipes.

Find them at www.heavenlychoc.co.uk for a full run-down of flavours, history, opening times and contact details, or give them a wave at https://www.facebook.com/HeavenlyChoc

Acknowledgements

Thanks to my editor, Jo Dickinson, for her support and insights at every stage, and to my agent, Caroline Hardman, for the same.

To the brilliant team at Quercus: Jenny Richards, for the delicious cover, Kathryn Taussig, Georgina Difford, Caroline Butler, David North and everyone else who has worked so hard to make this book happen.

On the ice cream front, a huge thank you to Tracy and Paul Kindred of Heavenly! in Wales for their ice cream expertise, and for letting us reproduce their delicious ice cream recipes here. I'm also grateful to the inspirational Kitty Travers of La Grotta Ices, who taught me how to make ice cream at the Artisan Cookery School, and whose delicious seasonal ices you can find at Bermondsey Market. Her tales of espresso granitas and the quince ice cream we made feature here, but any errors, and anything Imogen did along the way, are entirely down to me!

I've been lucky enough to meet some fantastic book lovers online: a big thanks to Kirsty of I Heart Books (@Kinks26) for the champagne-sorbet and pretzel-ice-cream ideas! And to my nephew Jake and niece Eloise for their help with research, and to my friends for so many things.

Thanks finally to James, for an unforgettable trip to Florence.